A CARTOON NETWORK ORIGINAL

VOLUME

③

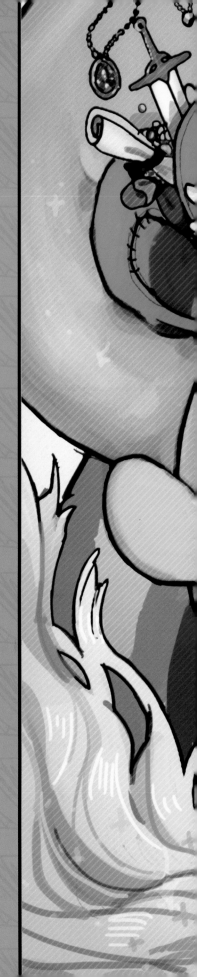

ADVENTURE TIME COMICS Volume Three, November 2017.
Published by KaBOOM!, a division of Boom Entertainment, Inc.
ADVENTURE TIME, CARTOON NETWORK, the logos, and all related
characters and elements are trademarks of and © Cartoon Network.
(S17) Originally published in single magazine form as ADVENTURE
TIME COMICS No. 9-12. © Cartoon Network. (S17) All rights reserved.
KaBOOM!™ and the KaBOOM! logo are trademarks of Boom
Entertainment, Inc., registered in various countries and categories.
All characters, events, and institutions depicted herein are fictional.
Any similarity between any of the names, characters, persons, events,
and/or institutions in this publication to actual names, characters,
and persons, whether living or dead, events, and/or institutions is
unintended and purely coincidental. KaBOOM! does not read or
accept unsolicited submissions of ideas, stories, or artwork.

BOOM! Studios, 5670 Wilshire Boulevard, Suite 450, Los Angeles, CA
90036-5679. Printed in China. First Printing.

ISBN: 978-1-68415-041-0, eISBN: 978-1-61398-718-6

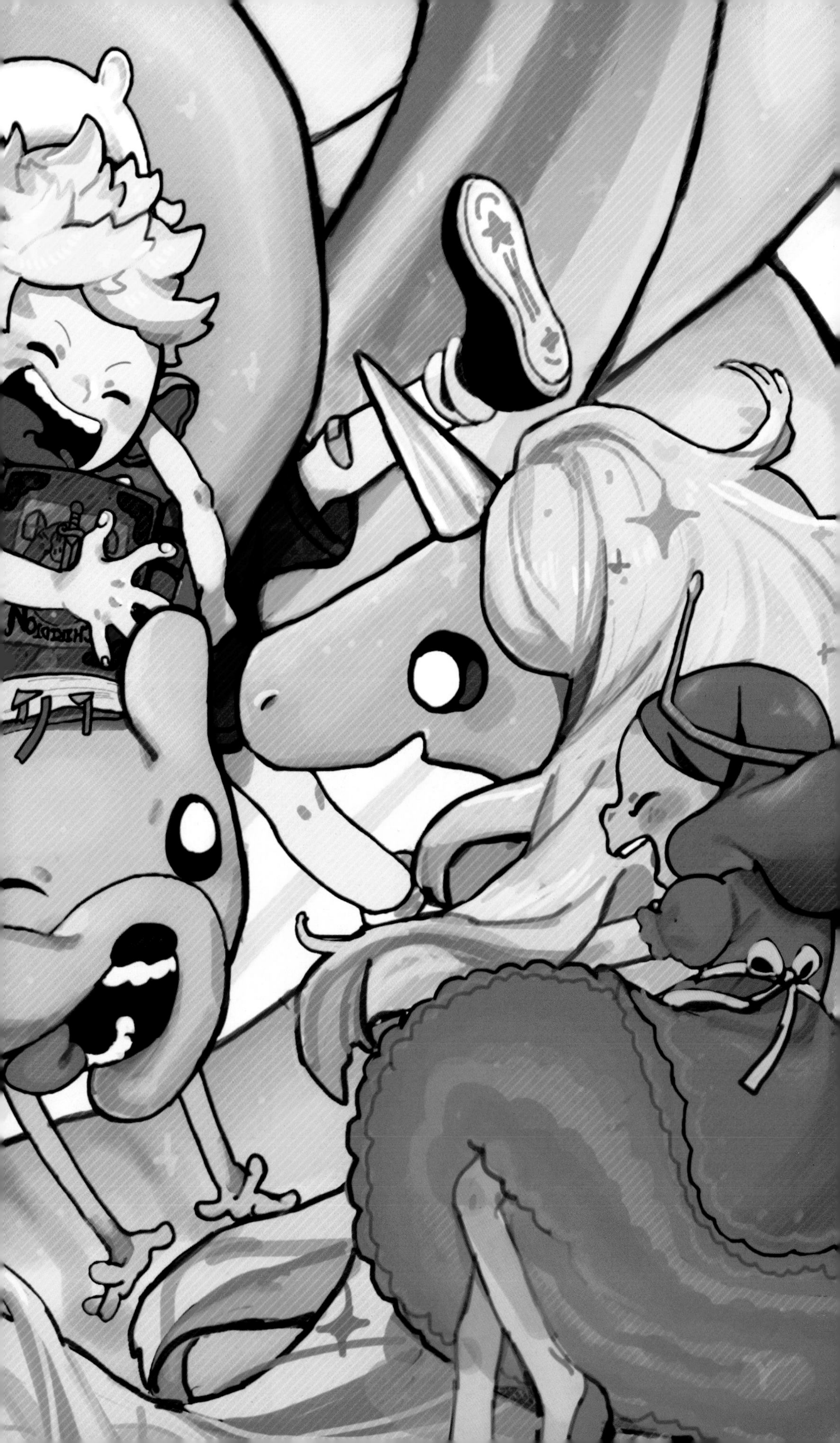

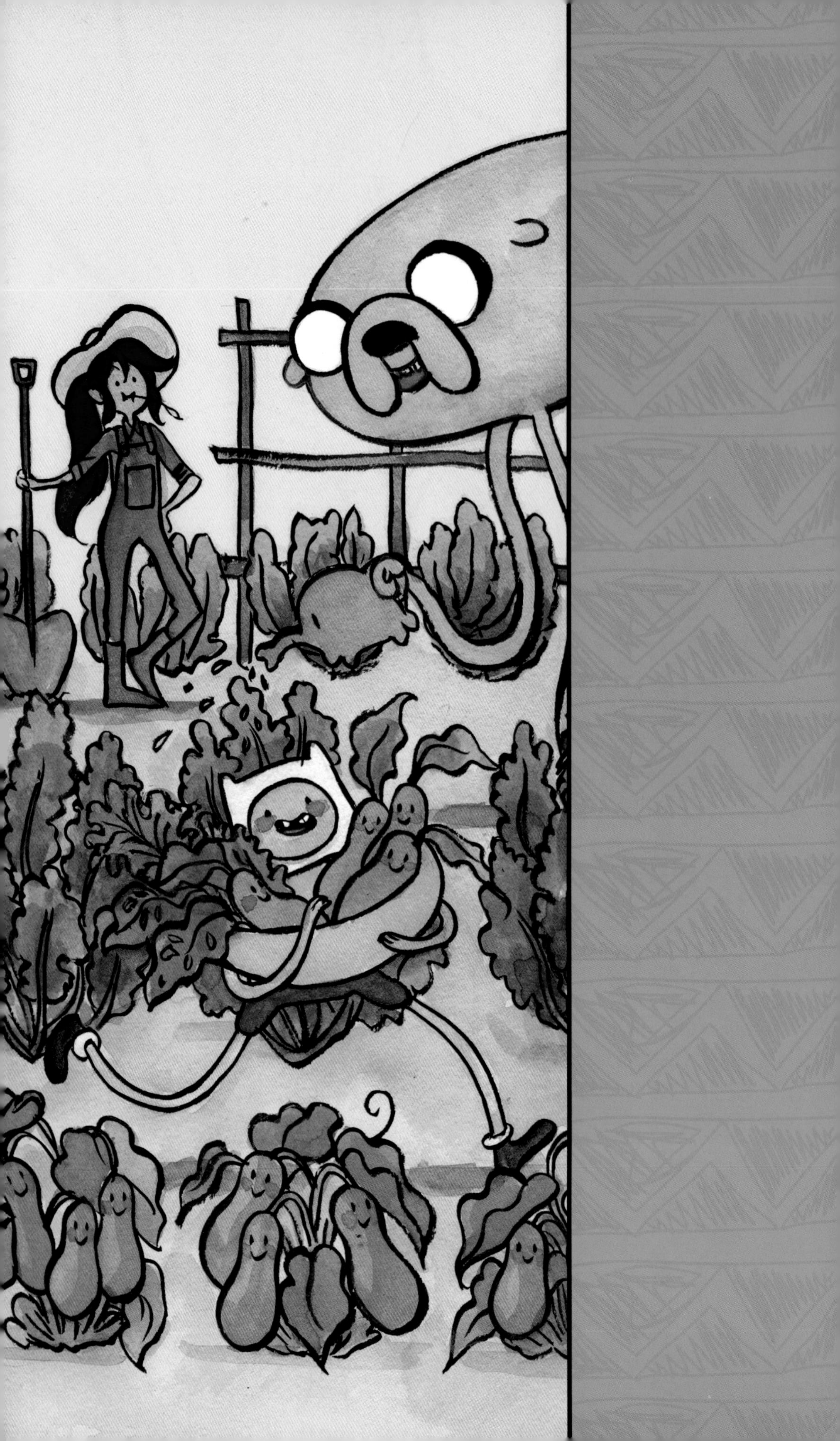

ADVENTURE TIME™
Created by **PENDLETON WARD**

"BAD RADISHES"
Written & Illustrated by
RII ABREGO

"THE LAN PARTY"
Written by
ZACHARY CLEMENTE
Illustrated by
COLE OTT

"THE FORGETTING TREE"
Written by
CAT SEATON
Illustrated by
KIT SEATON

"JUST PEACHY"
Written & Illustrated by
JENNA AYOUB

"WINNING AT WINNING"
Written & Illustrated by
JORGE CORONA
Colors by
JEREMY LAWSON

"DIAMOND MONSTER"
Written & Illustrated by
NICKY SOH

"SUNDAY MORNING"
Written & Illustrated by
K.L. RICKS

"THIRD EYE"
Written & Illustrated by
CHRISTINE LARSEN

"PRINCESS RAP BATTLE"
Written & Illustrated by
JARRETT WILLIAMS
Colors by
JENNA AYOUB

"CHEF BMO"
Written & Illustrated by
GRACE KRAFT

"LAUGH CRY LAUGH"
Written & Illustrated by
PATSY CHEN

"FEELING PEACHY"
Written & Illustrated by
LUCIE EBREY

"FUTURE'S FUTURE"
Written & Illustrated by
DIIGII DAGUNA
Letters by
WARREN MONTGOMERY

"SUNDAE MORNING"
Written by
NICOLE ANDELFINGER
Illustrated by
IRENE FLORES
Letters by
WARREN MONTGOMERY

"PLAYING WITH GIANTS"
Written & Illustrated by
JOEY MCCORMICK
Letters by
JIM CAMPBELL

Cover by
GREG SMALLWOOD

Designer	Assistant Editor	Associate Editor	Editor
MICHELLE ANKLEY	**MATTHEW LEVINE**	**ALEX GALER**	**WHITNEY LEOPARD**

With Special Thanks to Marisa Marionakis, Janet No, Curtis Lelash,
Conrad Montgomery, Kelly Crews, Scott Malchus, Adam Muto
and the wonderful folks at Cartoon Network.

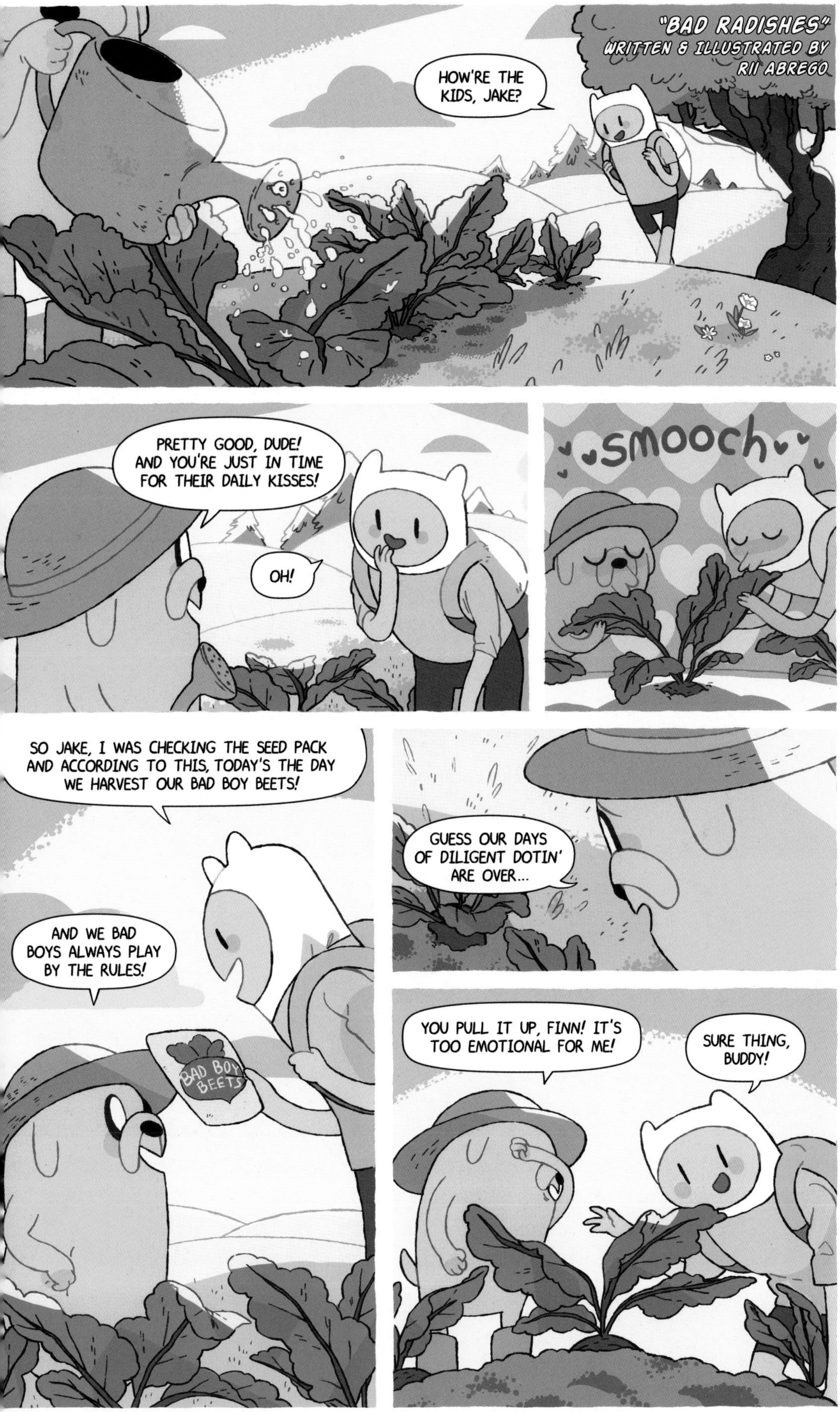
"BAD RADISHES"
WRITTEN & ILLUSTRATED BY
RII ABREGO
HOW'RE THE KIDS, JAKE?
PRETTY GOOD, DUDE! AND YOU'RE JUST IN TIME FOR THEIR DAILY KISSES!
OH!
SMOOCH
SO JAKE, I WAS CHECKING THE SEED PACK AND ACCORDING TO THIS, TODAY'S THE DAY WE HARVEST OUR BAD BOY BEETS!
AND WE BAD BOYS ALWAYS PLAY BY THE RULES!
BAD BOY BEETS
GUESS OUR DAYS OF DILIGENT DOTIN' ARE OVER...
YOU PULL IT UP, FINN! IT'S TOO EMOTIONAL FOR ME!
SURE THING, BUDDY!

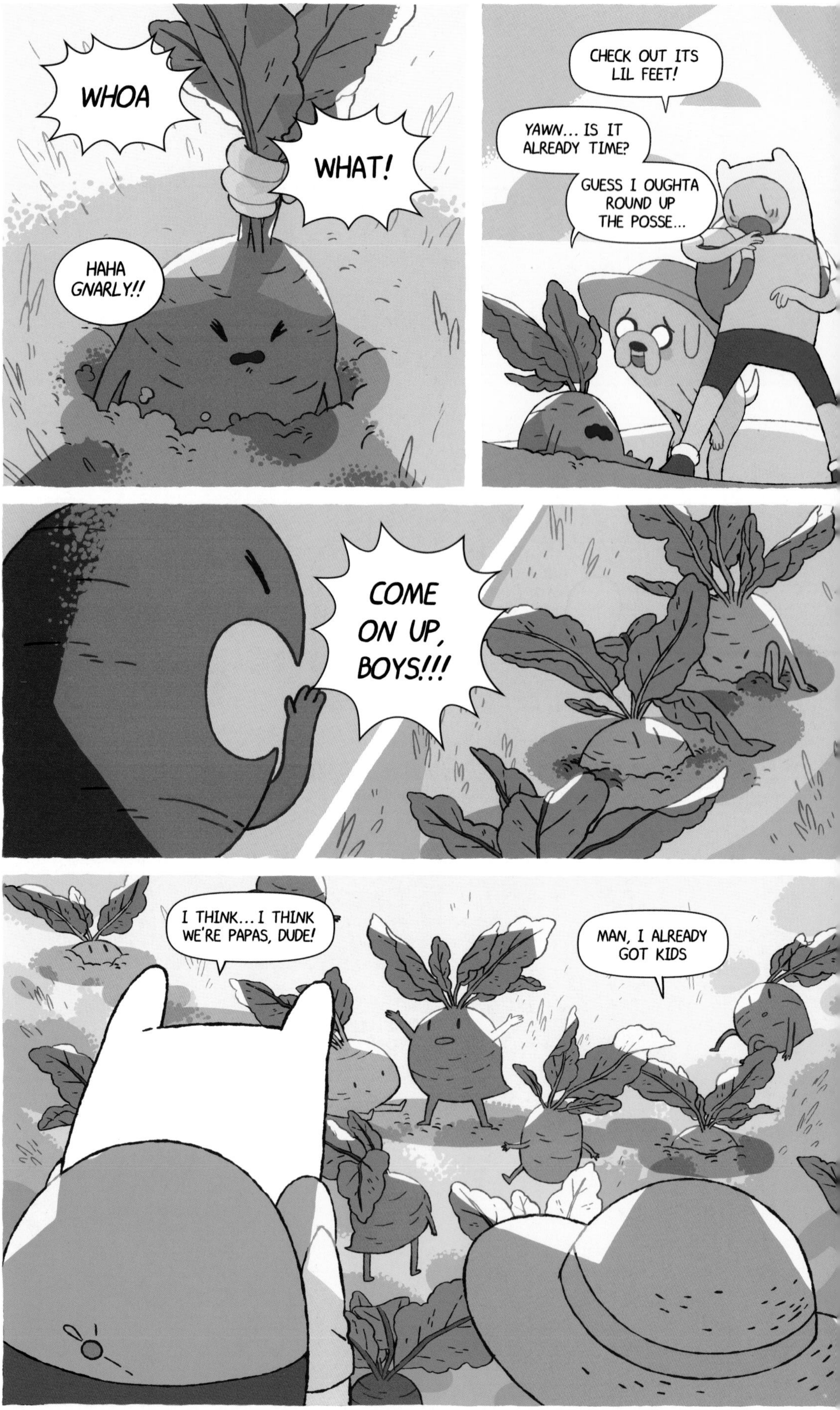
WHOA
WHAT!
HAHA GNARLY!!
CHECK OUT ITS LIL FEET!
YAWN... IS IT ALREADY TIME?
GUESS I OUGHTA ROUND UP THE POSSE...
COME ON UP, BOYS!!!
I THINK... I THINK WE'RE PAPAS, DUDE!
MAN, I ALREADY GOT KIDS

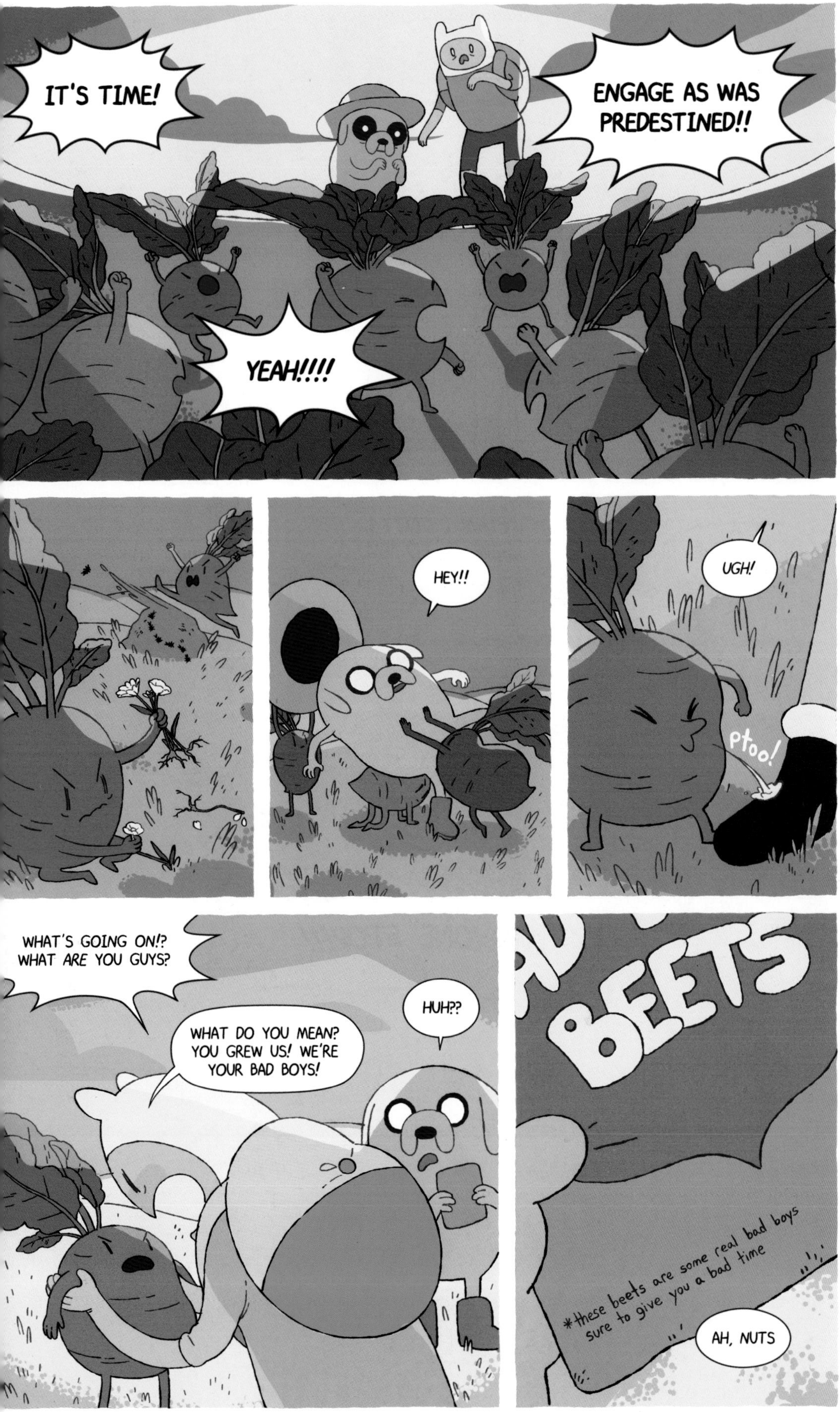
IT'S TIME!
ENGAGE AS WAS PREDESTINED!!
YEAH!!!!
HEY!!
UGH!
ptoo!
WHAT'S GOING ON!? WHAT ARE YOU GUYS?
WHAT DO YOU MEAN? YOU GREW US! WE'RE YOUR BAD BOYS!
HUH??
BEETS
*these beets are some real bad boys sure to give you a bad time
AH, NUTS

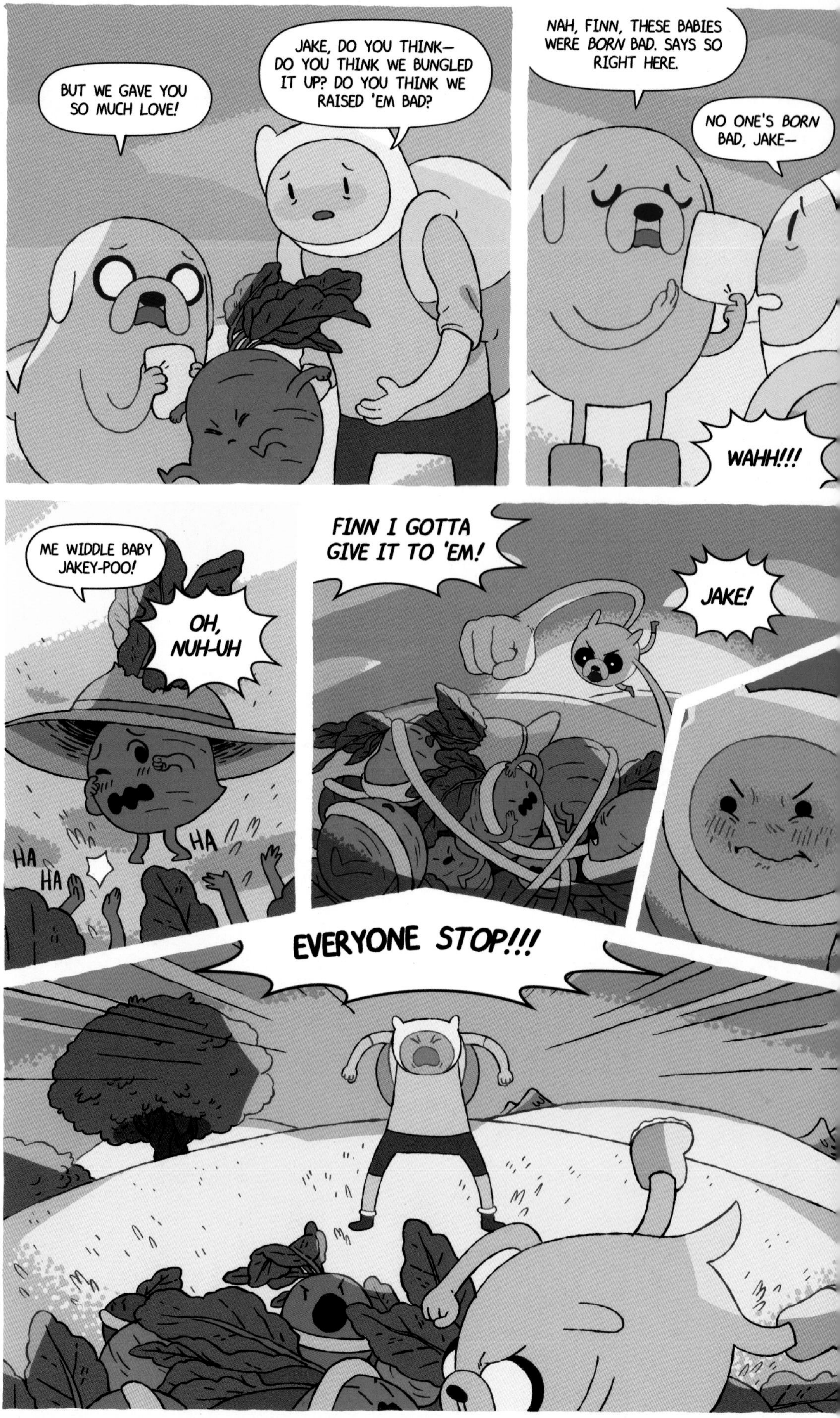
BUT WE GAVE YOU SO MUCH LOVE!
JAKE, DO YOU THINK— DO YOU THINK WE BUNGLED IT UP? DO YOU THINK WE RAISED 'EM BAD?
NAH, FINN, THESE BABIES WERE *BORN* BAD. SAYS SO RIGHT HERE.
NO ONE'S *BORN* BAD, JAKE—
WAHH!!!
ME WIDDLE BABY JAKEY-POO!
OH, NUH-UH
HA
HA
HA
FINN I GOTTA GIVE IT TO 'EM!
JAKE!
EVERYONE STOP!!!

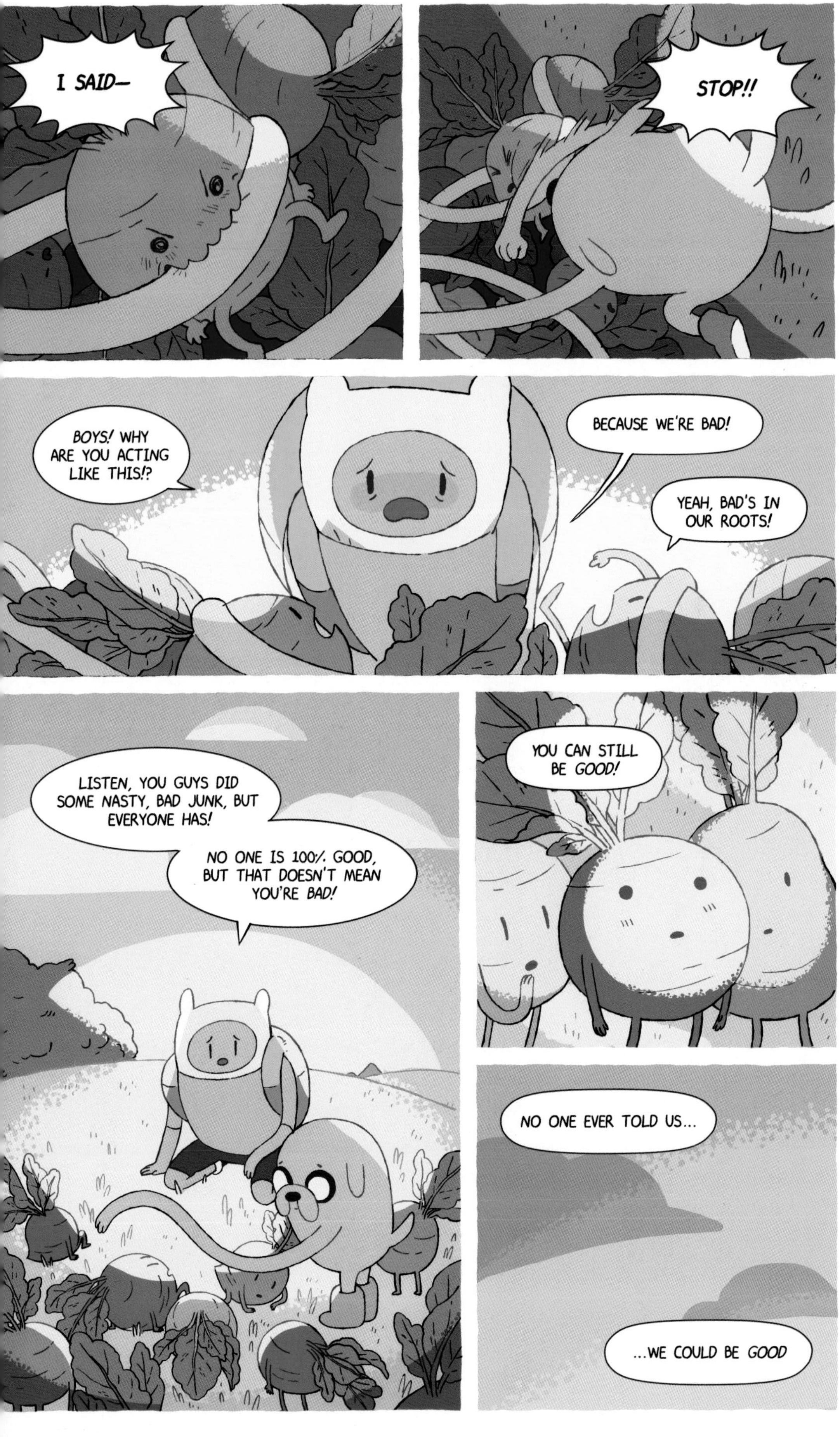
I SAID—
STOP!!
BOYS! WHY ARE YOU ACTING LIKE THIS!?
BECAUSE WE'RE BAD!
YEAH, BAD'S IN OUR ROOTS!
LISTEN, YOU GUYS DID SOME NASTY, BAD JUNK, BUT EVERYONE HAS!
NO ONE IS 100% GOOD, BUT THAT DOESN'T MEAN YOU'RE BAD!
YOU CAN STILL BE GOOD!
NO ONE EVER TOLD US...
...WE COULD BE GOOD

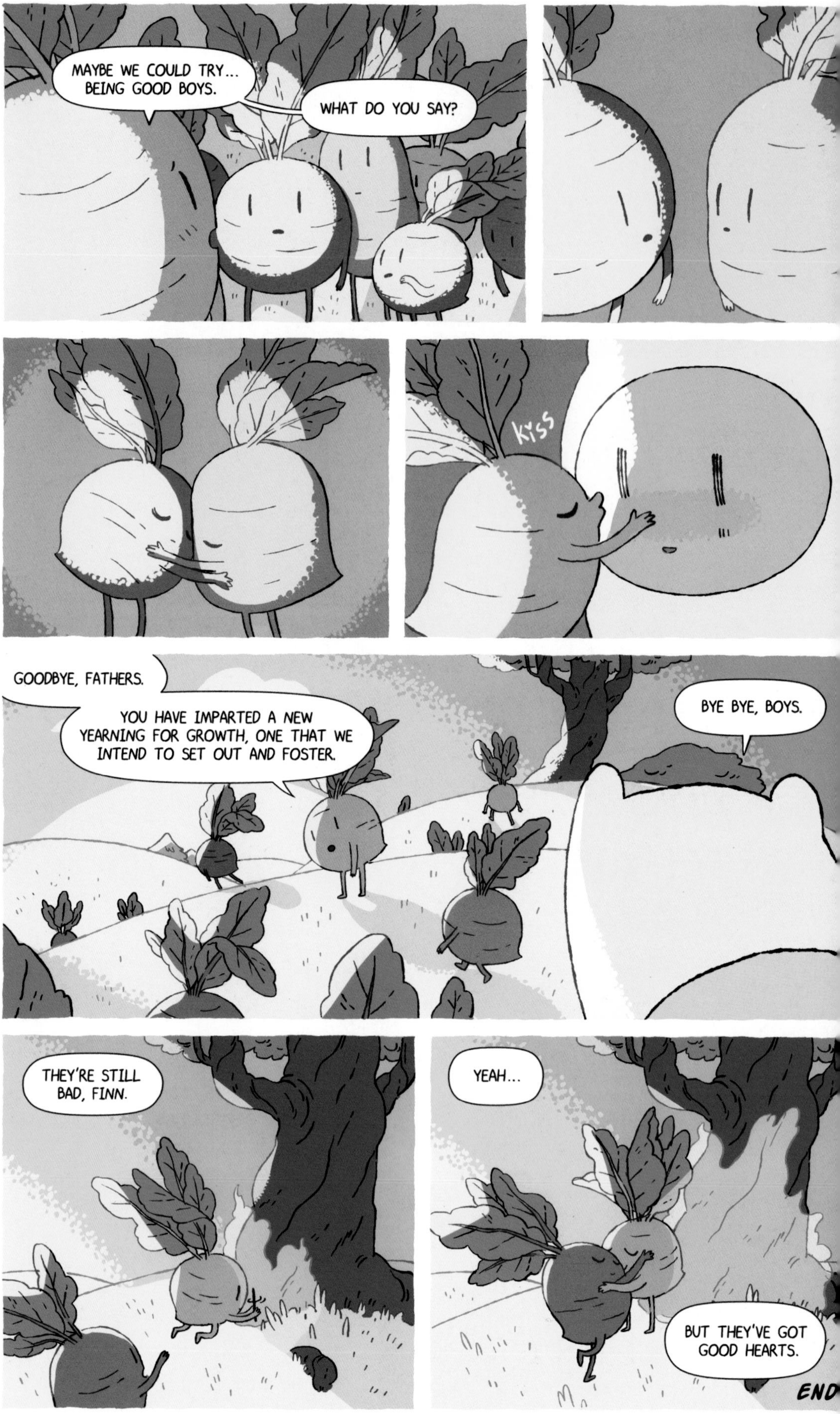
MAYBE WE COULD TRY... BEING GOOD BOYS.
WHAT DO YOU SAY?
KISS
GOODBYE, FATHERS.
YOU HAVE IMPARTED A NEW YEARNING FOR GROWTH, ONE THAT WE INTEND TO SET OUT AND FOSTER.
BYE BYE, BOYS.
THEY'RE STILL BAD, FINN.
YEAH...
BUT THEY'VE GOT GOOD HEARTS.
END

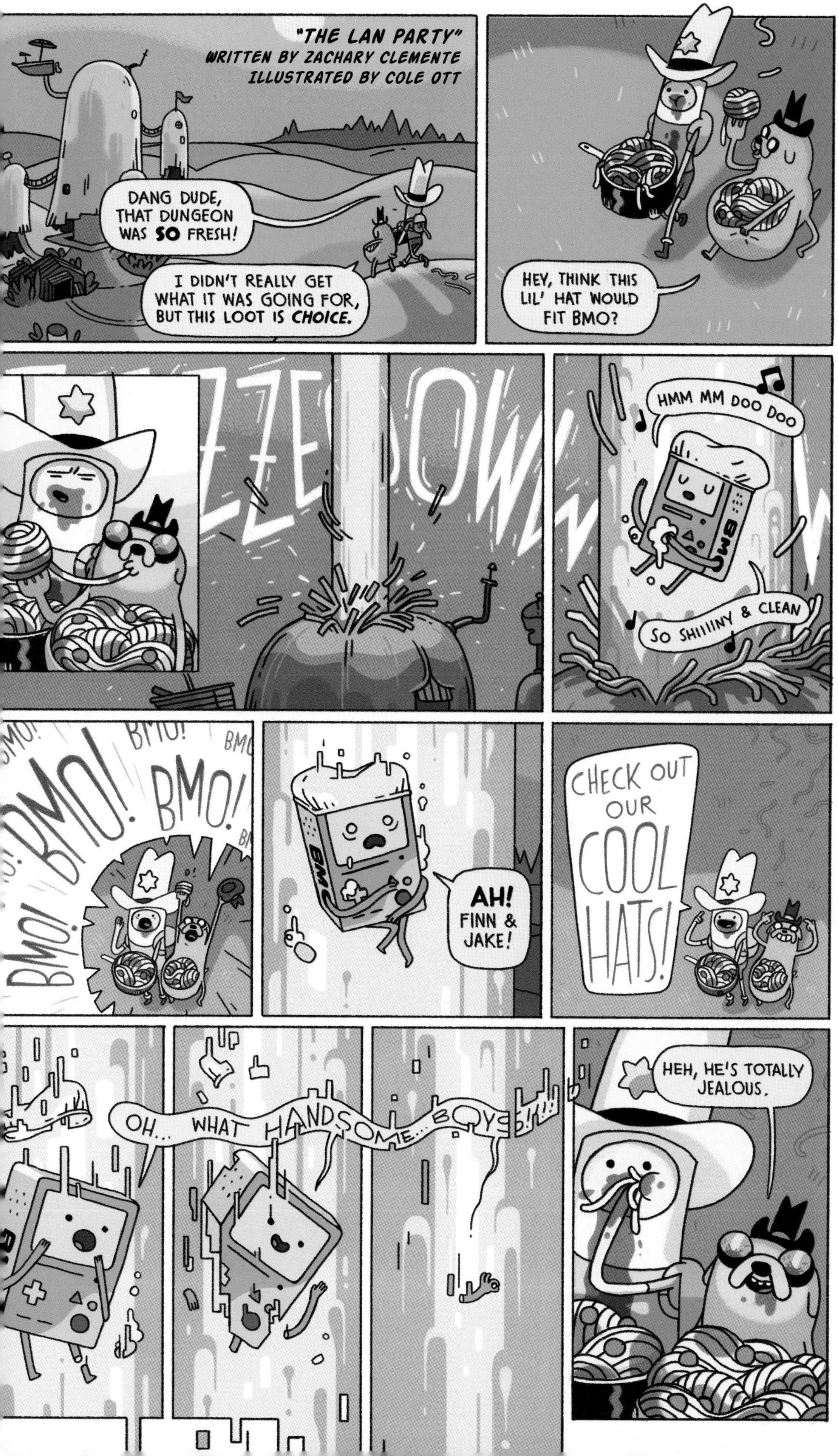
"THE LAN PARTY"
WRITTEN BY ZACHARY CLEMENTE
ILLUSTRATED BY COLE OTT
DANG DUDE, THAT DUNGEON WAS SO FRESH!
I DIDN'T REALLY GET WHAT IT WAS GOING FOR, BUT THIS LOOT IS CHOICE.
HEY, THINK THIS LIL' HAT WOULD FIT BMO?
HMM MM DOO DOO
SO SHIIIINY & CLEAN
BMO! BMO! BMO! BMO!
AH! FINN & JAKE!
CHECK OUT OUR COOL HATS!
OH... WHAT HANDSOME... BOYS!!!
HEH, HE'S TOTALLY JEALOUS.

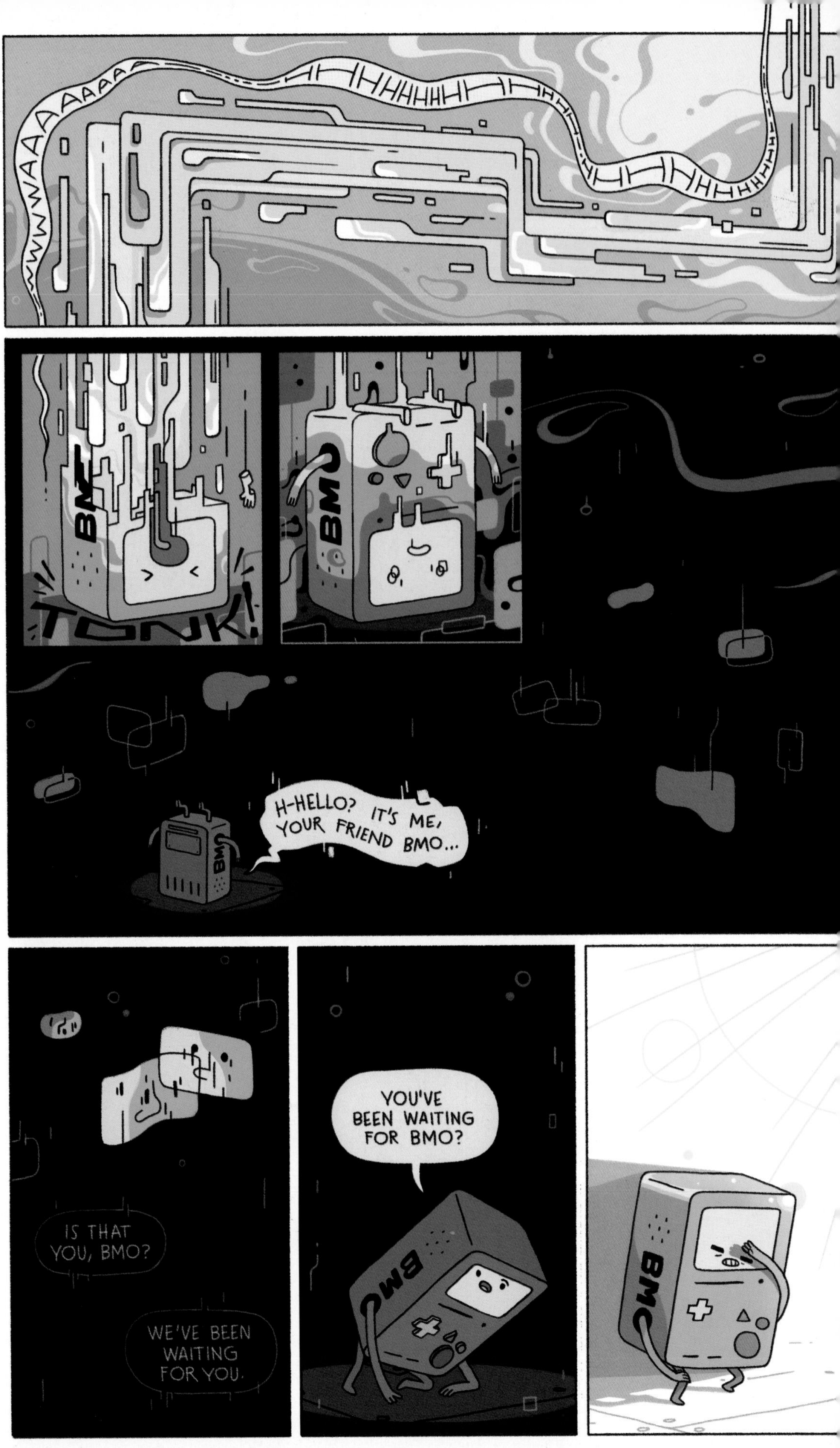
WWWWAAAAAAAA—HHHHHHHHH
TONK!
H-HELLO? IT'S ME, YOUR FRIEND BMO...
IS THAT YOU, BMO?
WE'VE BEEN WAITING FOR YOU.
YOU'VE BEEN WAITING FOR BMO?

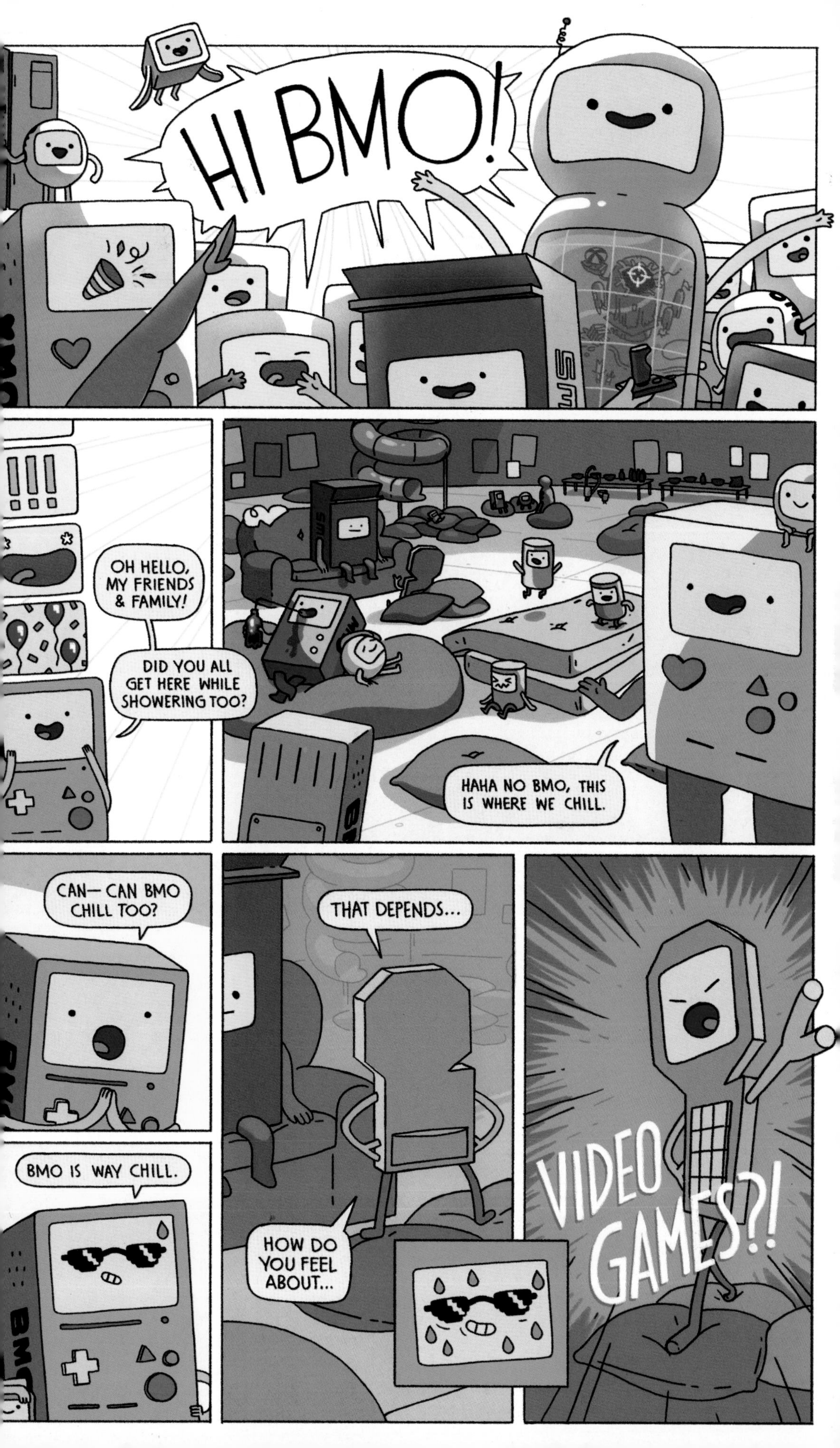
HI BMO!
OH HELLO, MY FRIENDS & FAMILY!
DID YOU ALL GET HERE WHILE SHOWERING TOO?
HAHA NO BMO, THIS IS WHERE WE CHILL.
CAN— CAN BMO CHILL TOO?
BMO IS WAY CHILL.
THAT DEPENDS...
HOW DO YOU FEEL ABOUT...
VIDEO GAMES?!

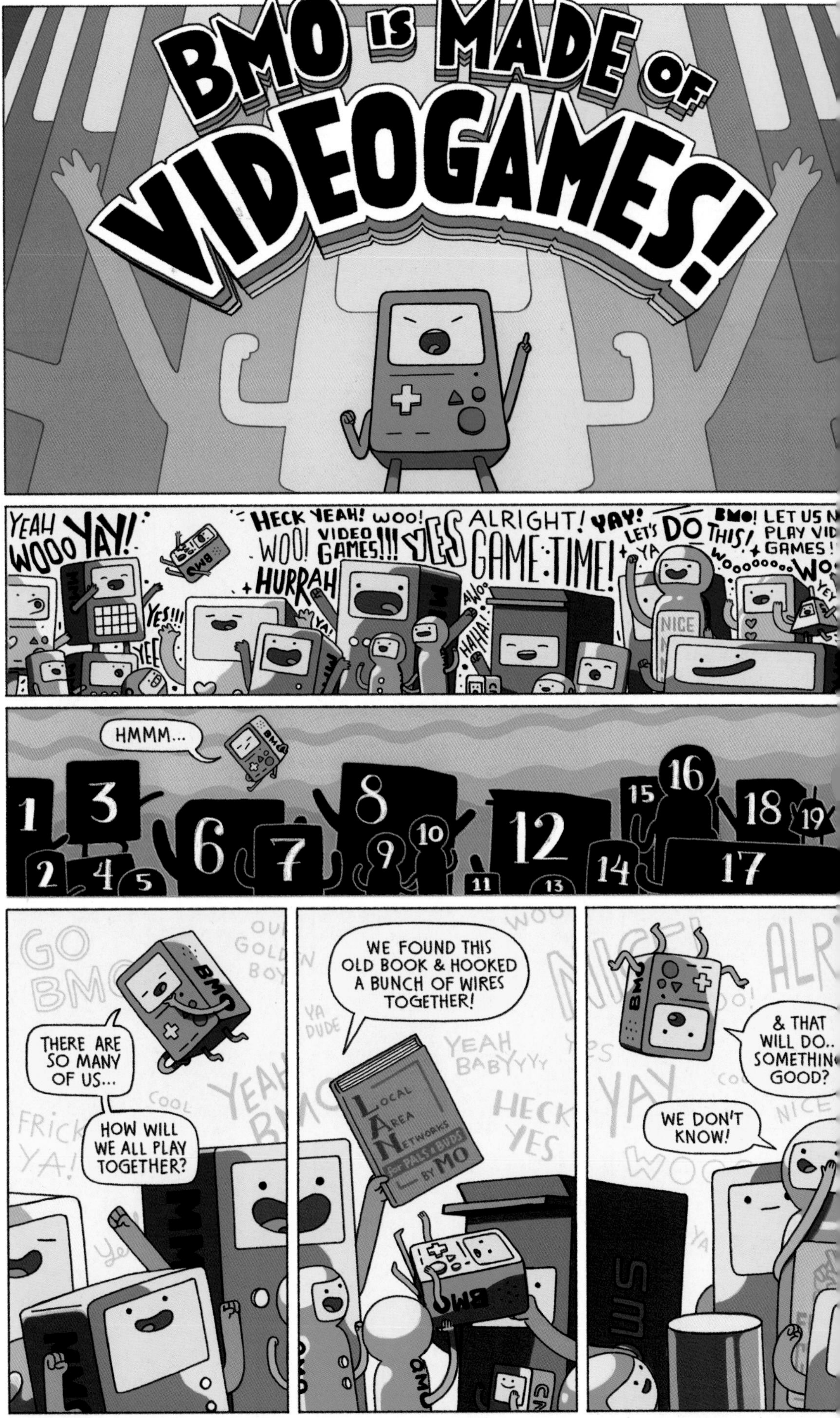
BMO IS MADE OF VIDEOGAMES!
YEAH WOOO YAY!
HECK YEAH! WOO!
WOO!
VIDEO GAMES!!!
YES
HURRAH
ALRIGHT!
YAY!
LET'S DO THIS!
GAME TIME!
YES!!!
YEE
YA!
AWOO
HAHA!
NICE
HMMM...
1 2 3 4 5 6 7 8 9 10 11 12 13 14 15 16 17 18 19
THERE ARE SO MANY OF US...
HOW WILL WE ALL PLAY TOGETHER?
GO BMO
OUR GOLDEN BOY
COOL
FRICK YA!
WE FOUND THIS OLD BOOK & HOOKED A BUNCH OF WIRES TOGETHER!
LOCAL AREA NETWORKS for PALS & BUDS BY MO
YA DUDE
YEAH BABYYYY
HECK YES
& THAT WILL DO.. SOMETHING GOOD?
WE DON'T KNOW!
YAY
NICE

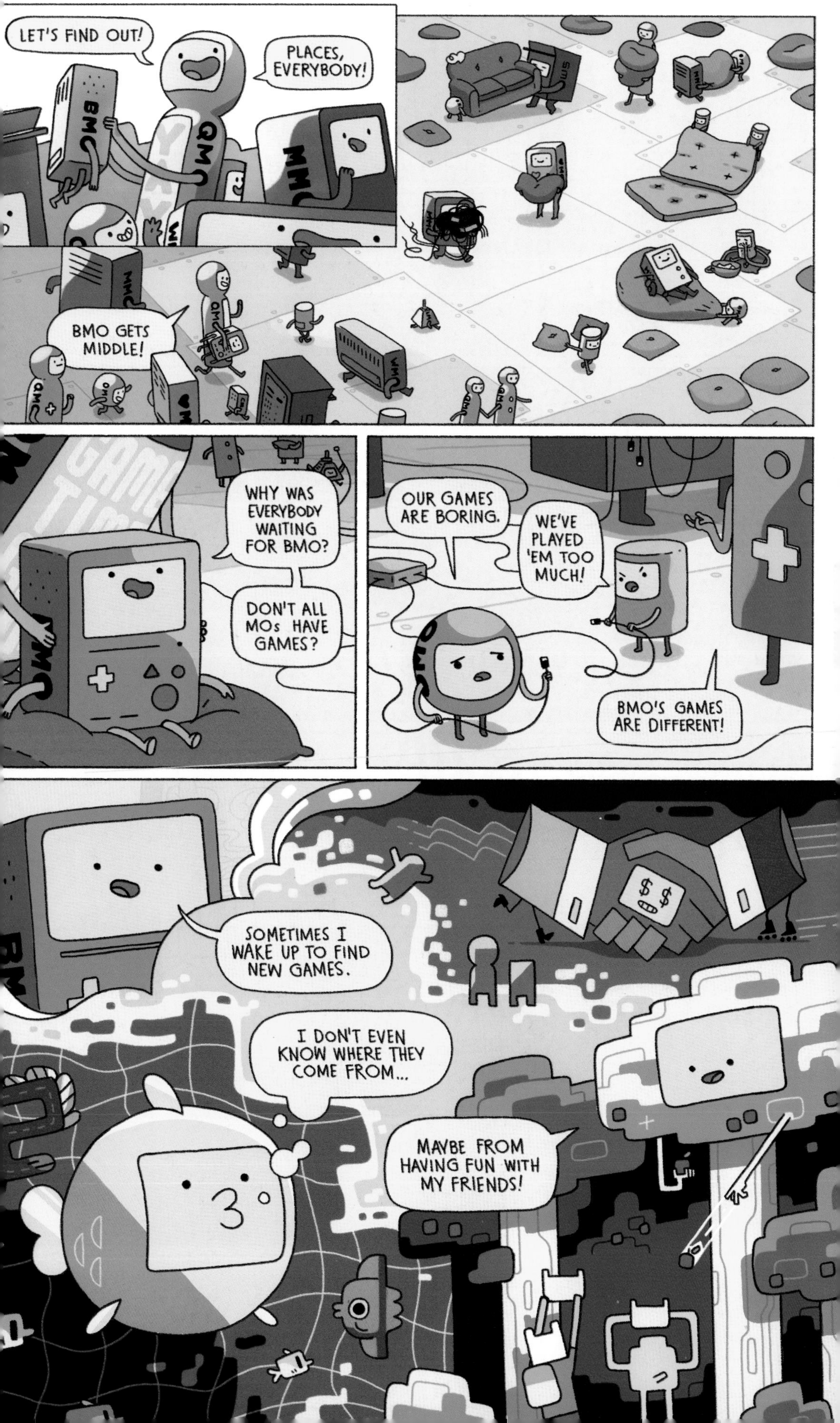
LET'S FIND OUT!
PLACES, EVERYBODY!
BMO GETS MIDDLE!
WHY WAS EVERYBODY WAITING FOR BMO?
DON'T ALL MOs HAVE GAMES?
OUR GAMES ARE BORING.
WE'VE PLAYED 'EM TOO MUCH!
BMO'S GAMES ARE DIFFERENT!
SOMETIMES I WAKE UP TO FIND NEW GAMES.
I DON'T EVEN KNOW WHERE THEY COME FROM...
MAYBE FROM HAVING FUN WITH MY FRIENDS!

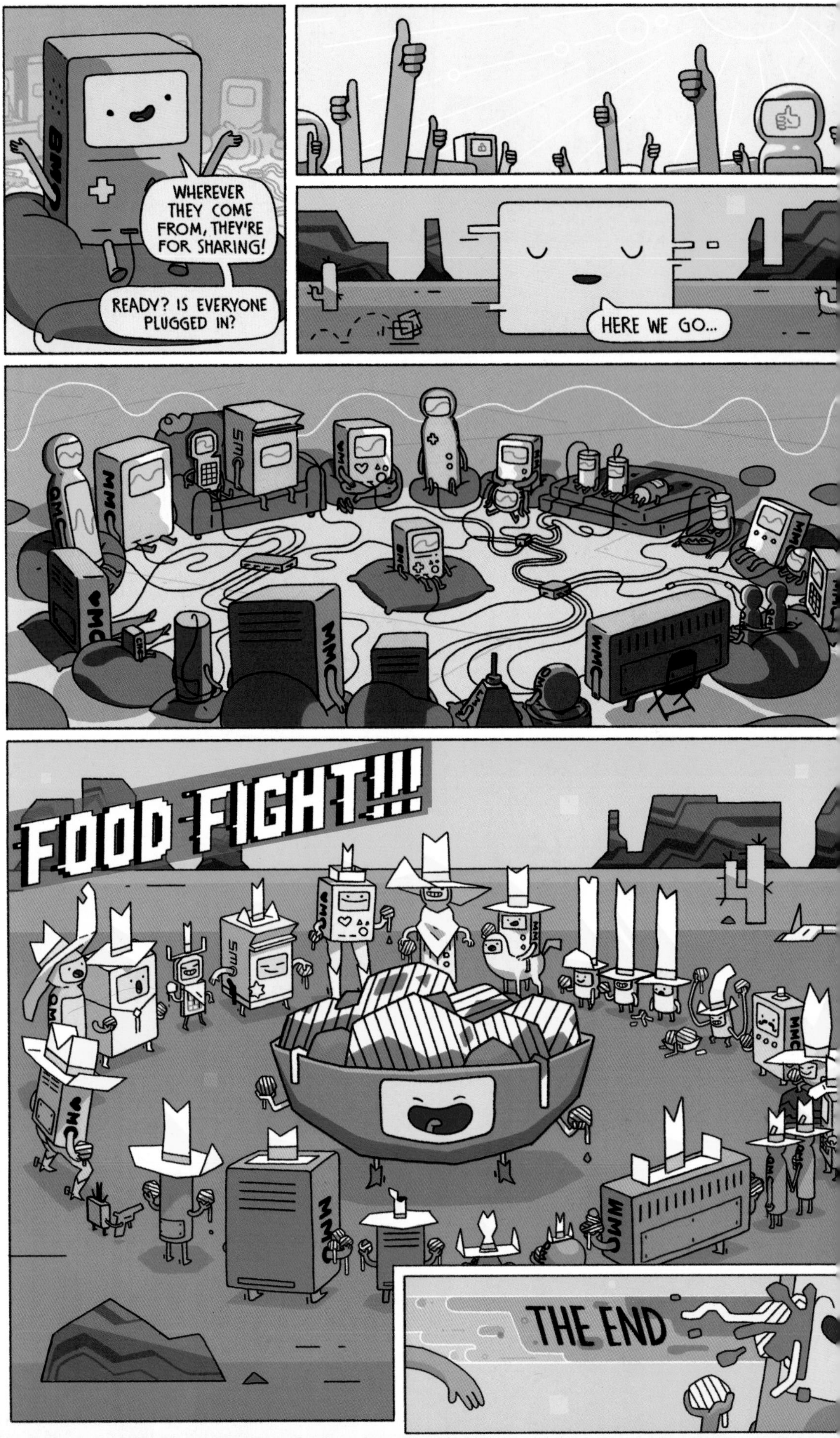

WHEREVER THEY COME FROM, THEY'RE FOR SHARING!
READY? IS EVERYONE PLUGGED IN?
HERE WE GO...
FOOD FIGHT!!!
THE END

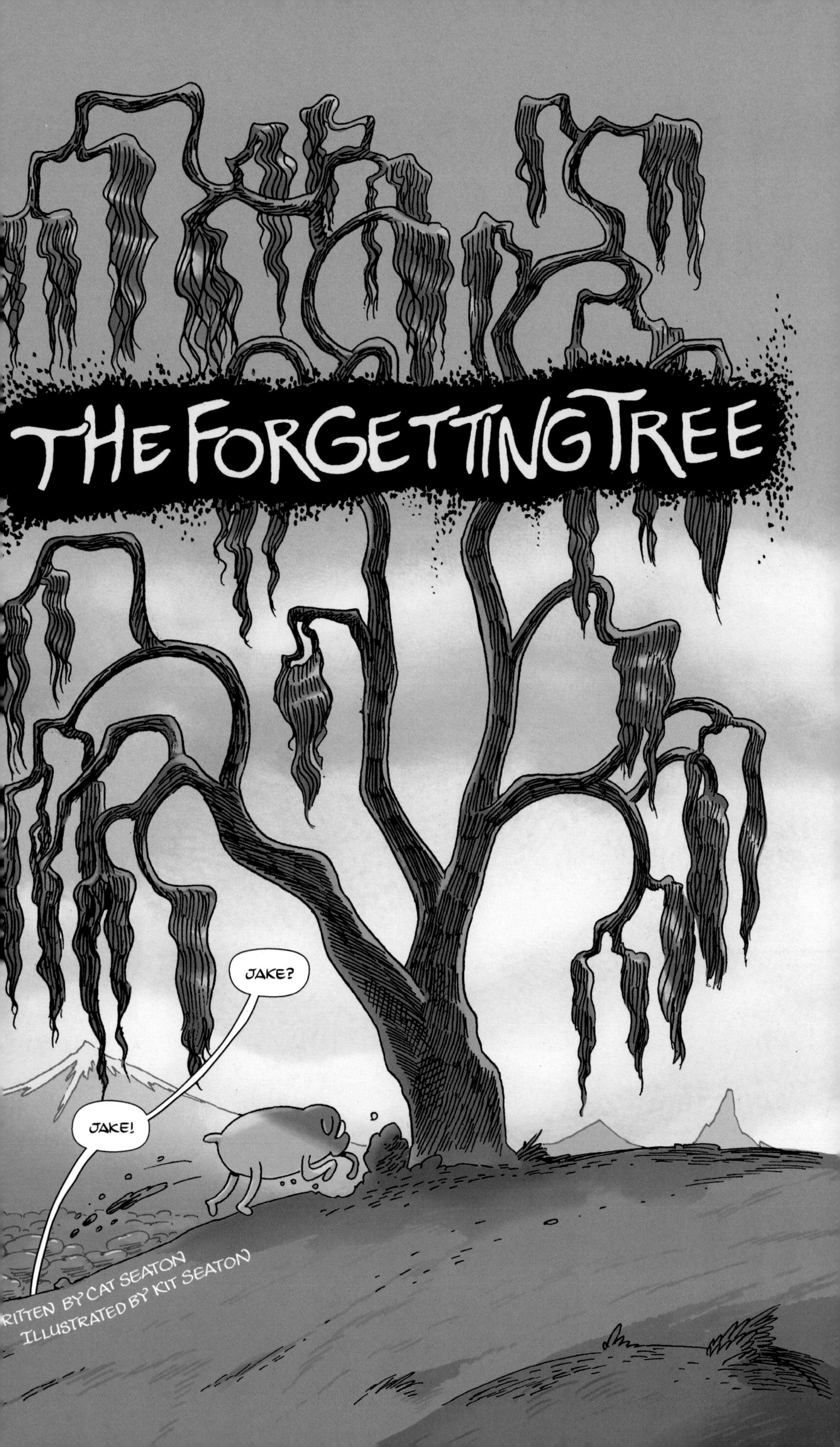
THE FORGETTING TREE
JAKE?
JAKE!
RITTEN BY CAT SEATON
ILLUSTRATED BY KIT SEATON

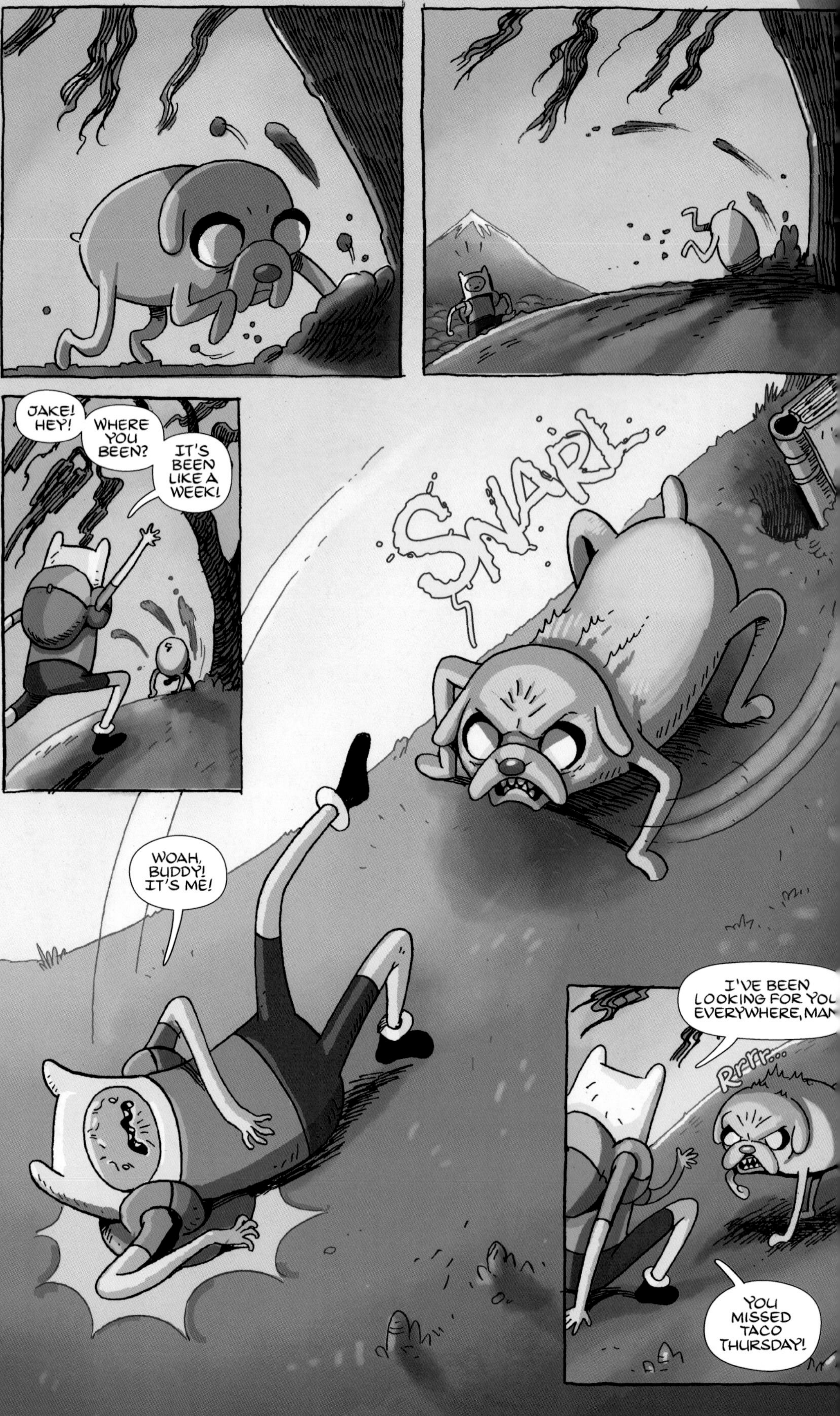
JAKE! HEY!
WHERE YOU BEEN?
IT'S BEEN LIKE A WEEK!
SNARL
WOAH, BUDDY! IT'S ME!
I'VE BEEN LOOKING FOR YOU EVERYWHERE, MAN
Rrrr...
YOU MISSED TACO THURSDAY?!

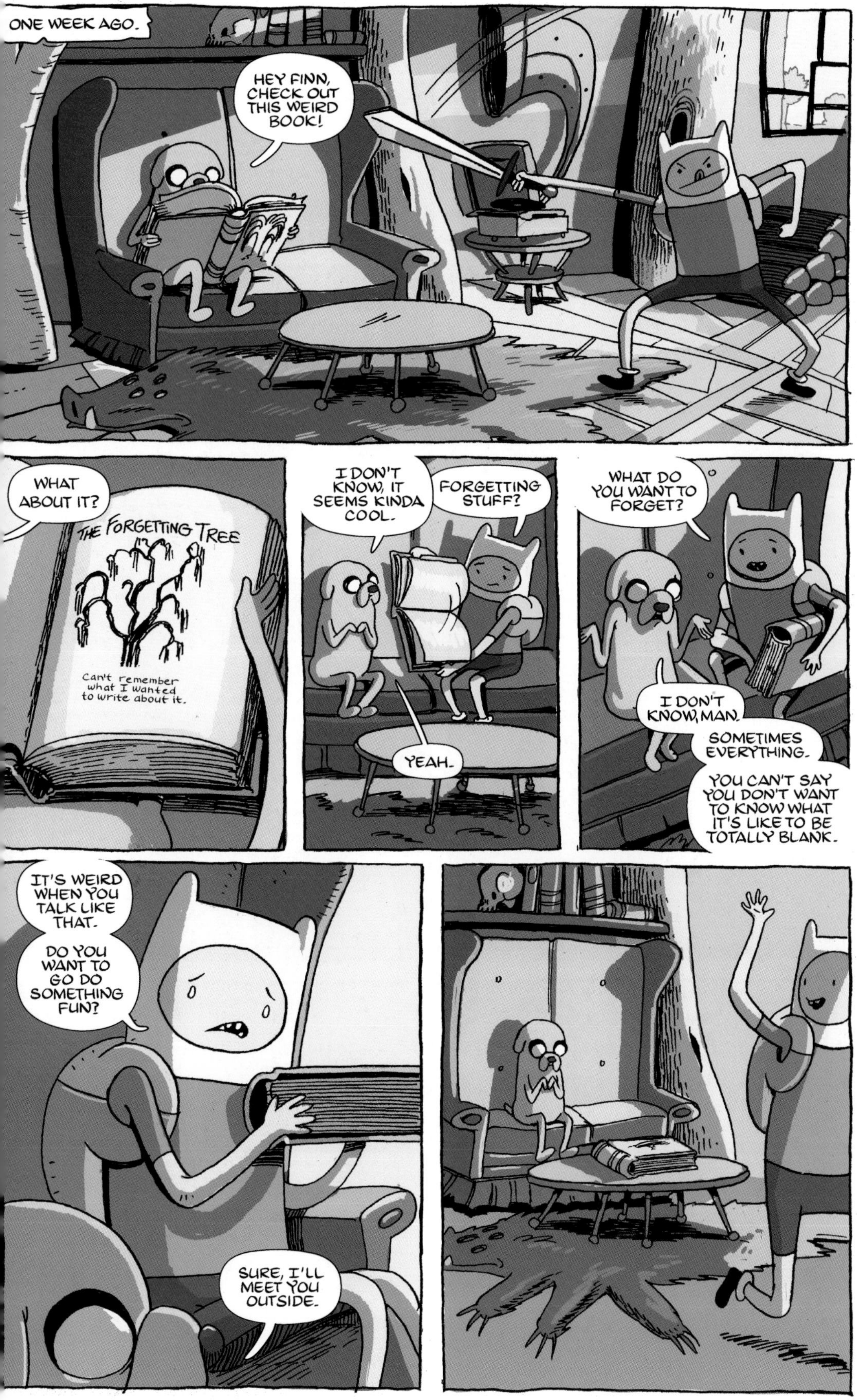

ONE WEEK AGO.
HEY FINN, CHECK OUT THIS WEIRD BOOK!
WHAT ABOUT IT?
THE FORGETTING TREE
Can't remember what I wanted to write about it.
I DON'T KNOW, IT SEEMS KINDA COOL.
FORGETTING STUFF?
YEAH.
WHAT DO YOU WANT TO FORGET?
I DON'T KNOW, MAN.
SOMETIMES EVERYTHING.
YOU CAN'T SAY YOU DON'T WANT TO KNOW WHAT IT'S LIKE TO BE TOTALLY BLANK.
IT'S WEIRD WHEN YOU TALK LIKE THAT.
DO YOU WANT TO GO DO SOMETHING FUN?
SURE, I'LL MEET YOU OUTSIDE.

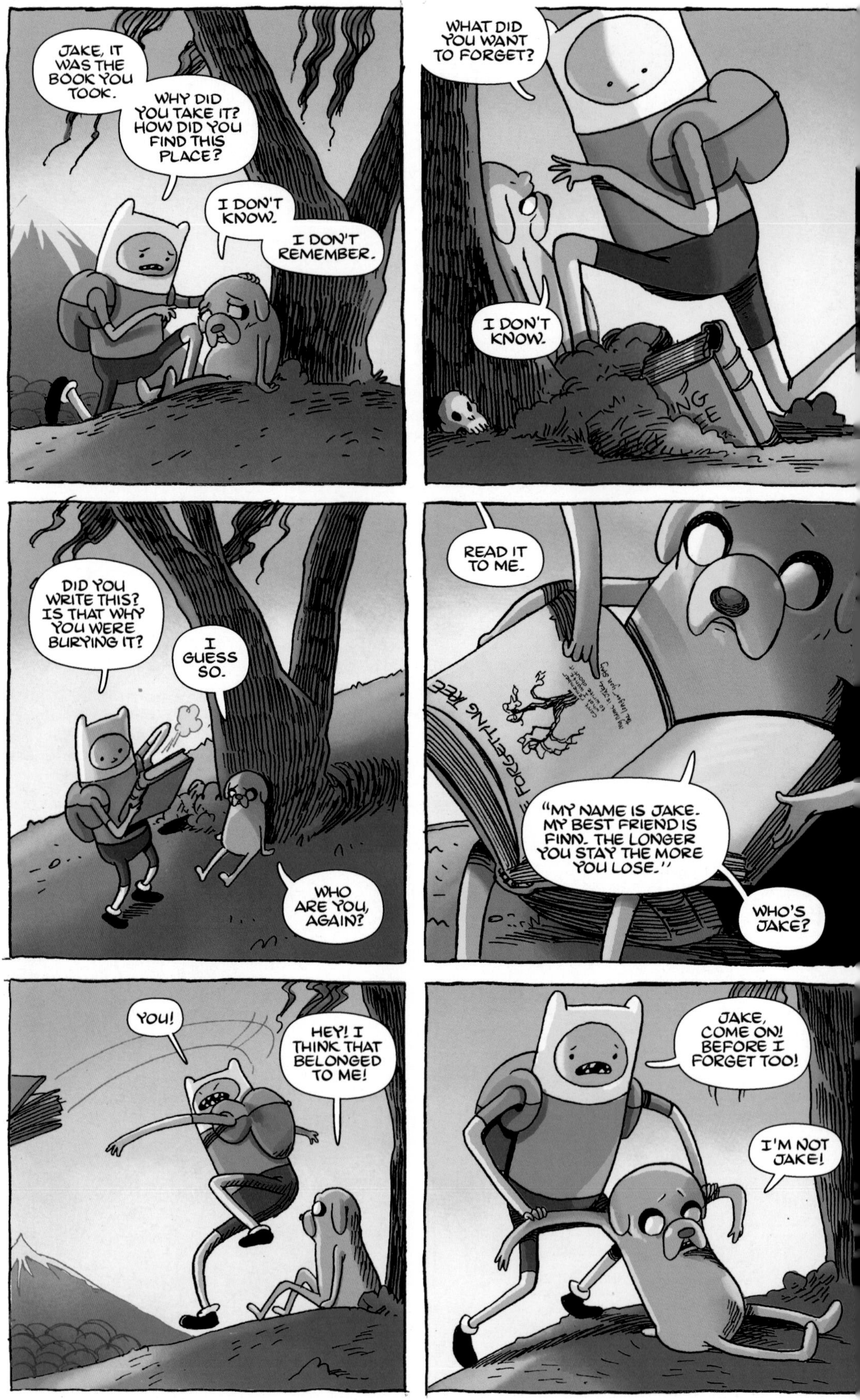
JAKE, IT WAS THE BOOK YOU TOOK.
WHY DID YOU TAKE IT? HOW DID YOU FIND THIS PLACE?
I DON'T KNOW.
I DON'T REMEMBER.
WHAT DID YOU WANT TO FORGET?
I DON'T KNOW.
DID YOU WRITE THIS? IS THAT WHY YOU WERE BURYING IT?
I GUESS SO.
WHO ARE YOU, AGAIN?
READ IT TO ME.
FORGETTING TREE
"MY NAME IS JAKE. MY BEST FRIEND IS FINN. THE LONGER YOU STAY THE MORE YOU LOSE."
WHO'S JAKE?
YOU!
HEY! I THINK THAT BELONGED TO ME!
JAKE, COME ON! BEFORE I FORGET TOO!
I'M NOT JAKE!

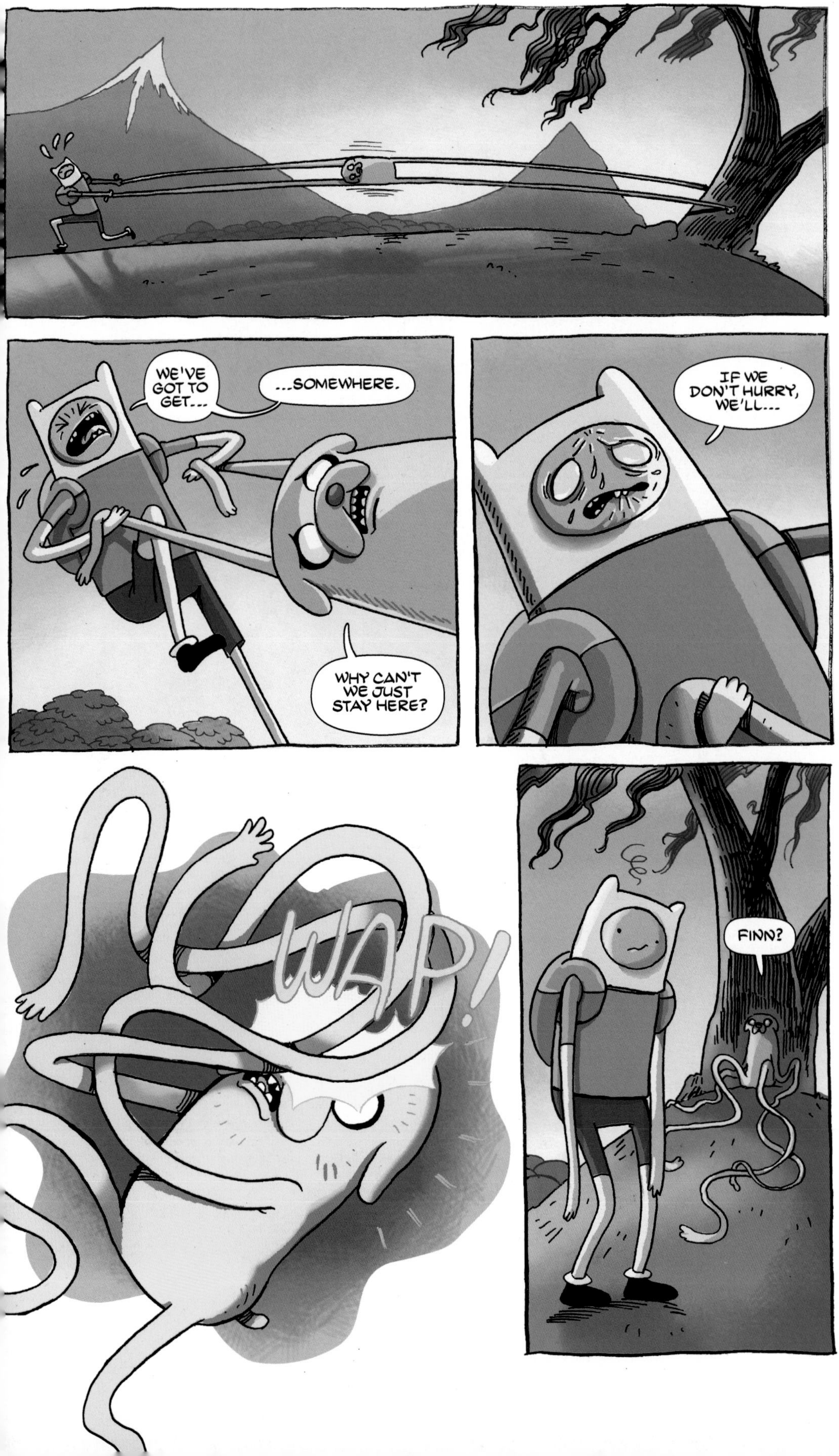
WE'VE GOT TO GET...
...SOMEWHERE.
WHY CAN'T WE JUST STAY HERE?
IF WE DON'T HURRY, WE'LL...
WAP!
FINN?

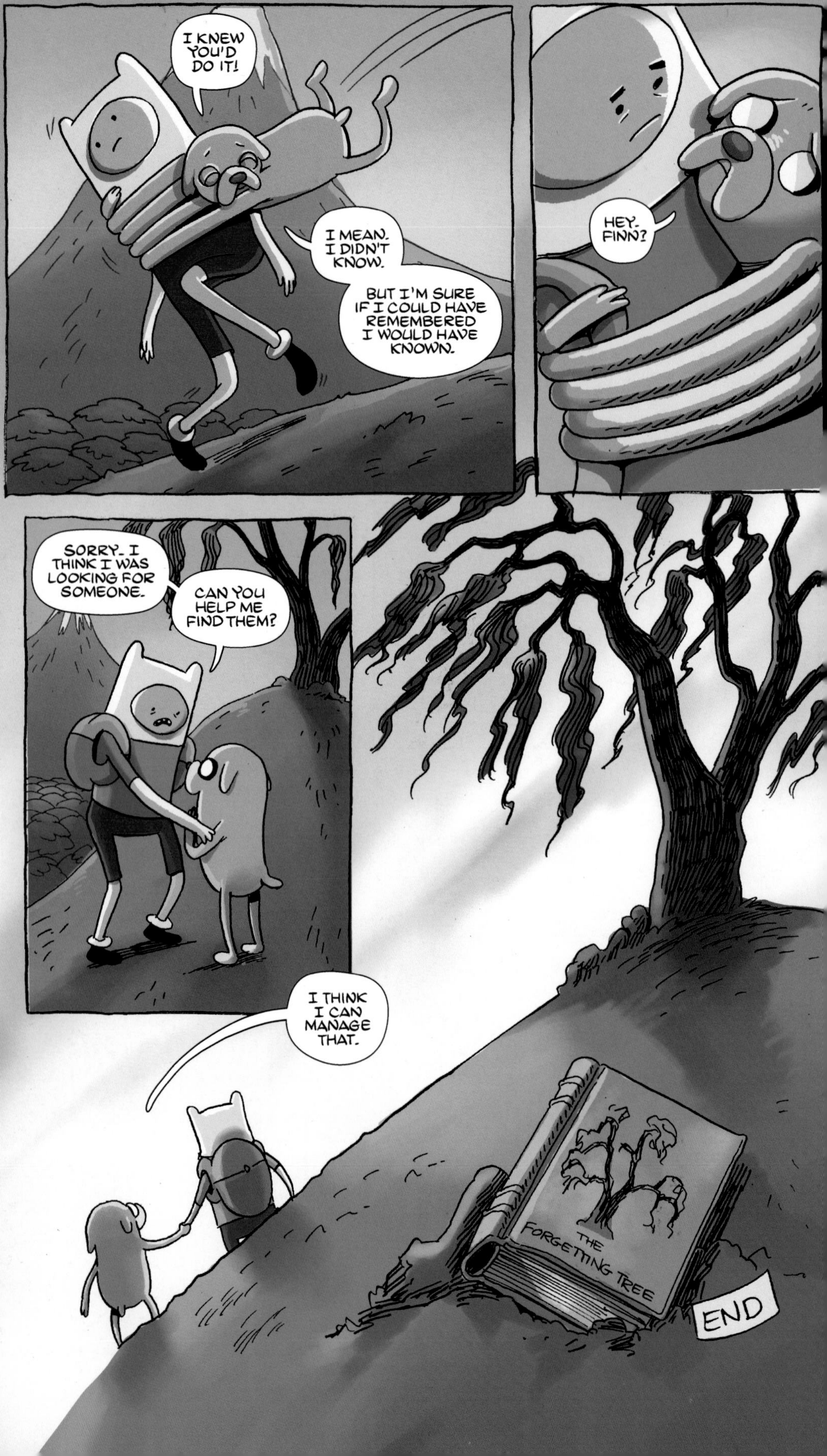
I KNEW YOU'D DO IT!
I MEAN. I DIDN'T KNOW.
BUT I'M SURE IF I COULD HAVE REMEMBERED I WOULD HAVE KNOWN.
HEY. FINN?
SORRY. I THINK I WAS LOOKING FOR SOMEONE.
CAN YOU HELP ME FIND THEM?
I THINK I CAN MANAGE THAT.
THE FORGETTING TREE
END

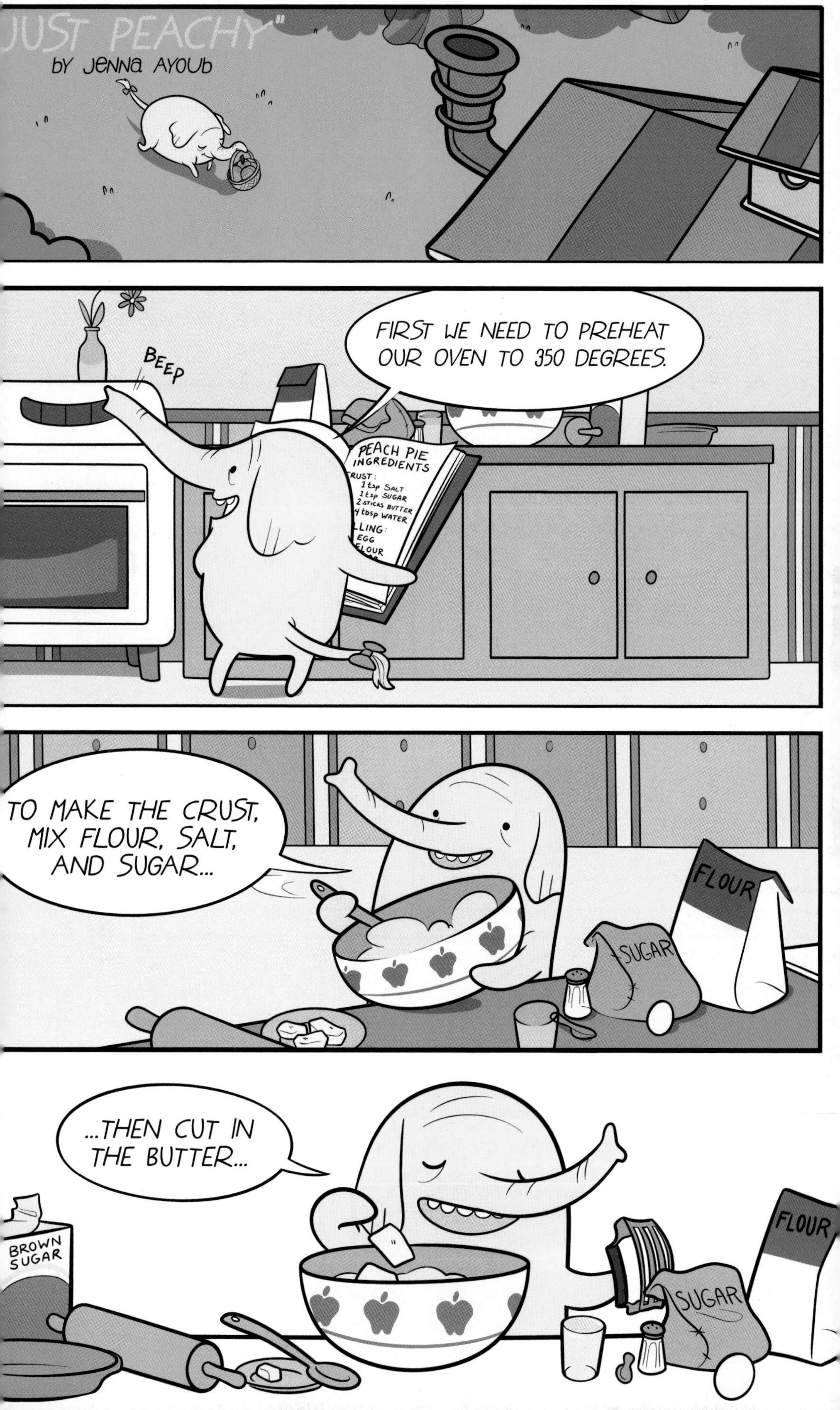
"JUST PEACHY"
by JENNA AYOUB
BEEP
FIRST WE NEED TO PREHEAT OUR OVEN TO 350 DEGREES.
PEACH PIE
INGREDIENTS
1 tsp SALT
1 tsp SUGAR
2 STICKS BUTTER
TO MAKE THE CRUST, MIX FLOUR, SALT, AND SUGAR...
FLOUR
SUGAR
...THEN CUT IN THE BUTTER...
BROWN SUGAR
FLOUR
SUGAR

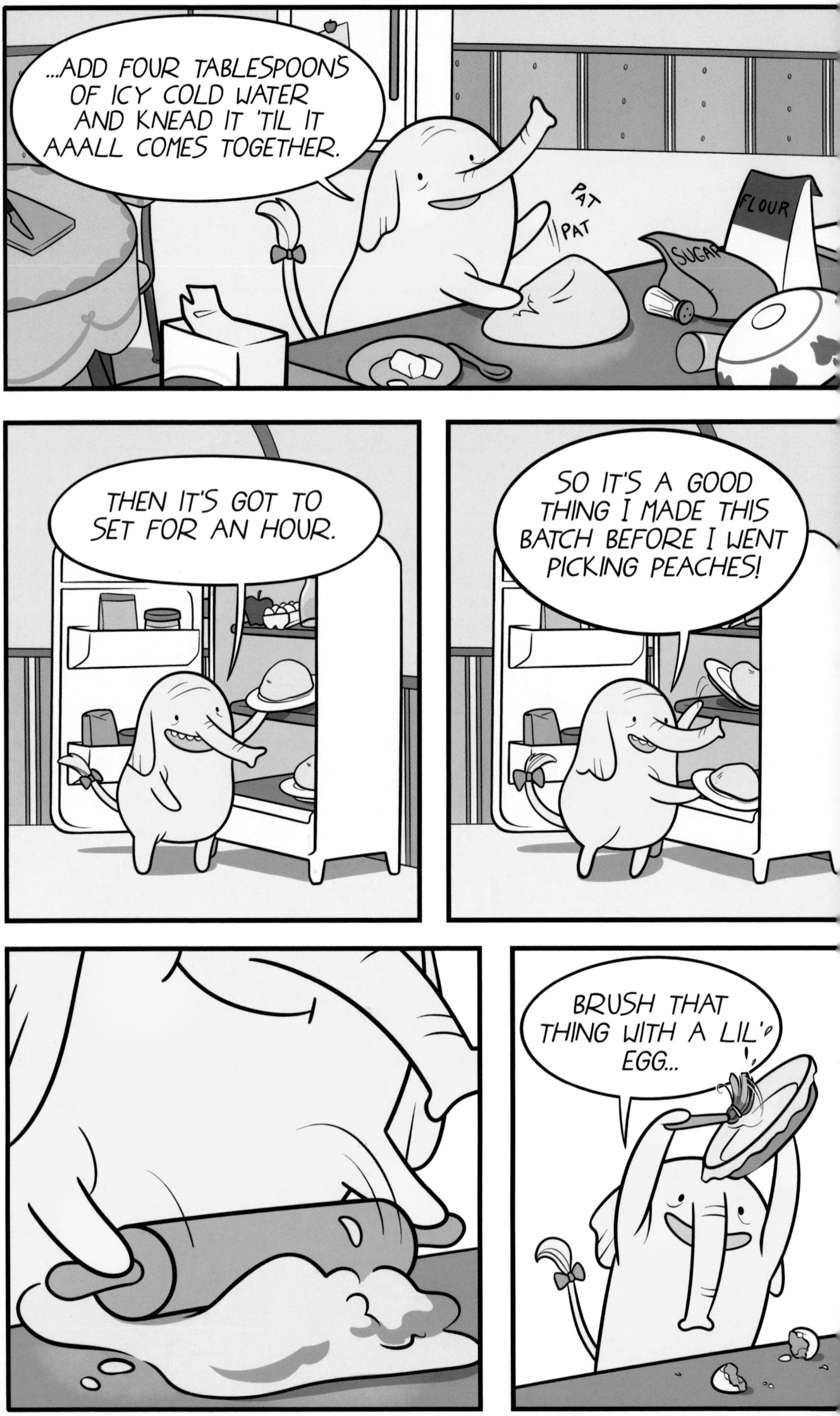
...ADD FOUR TABLESPOONS OF ICY COLD WATER AND KNEAD IT 'TIL IT AAALL COMES TOGETHER.
PAT
PAT
FLOUR
SUGAR
THEN IT'S GOT TO SET FOR AN HOUR.
SO IT'S A GOOD THING I MADE THIS BATCH BEFORE I WENT PICKING PEACHES!
BRUSH THAT THING WITH A LIL' EGG...

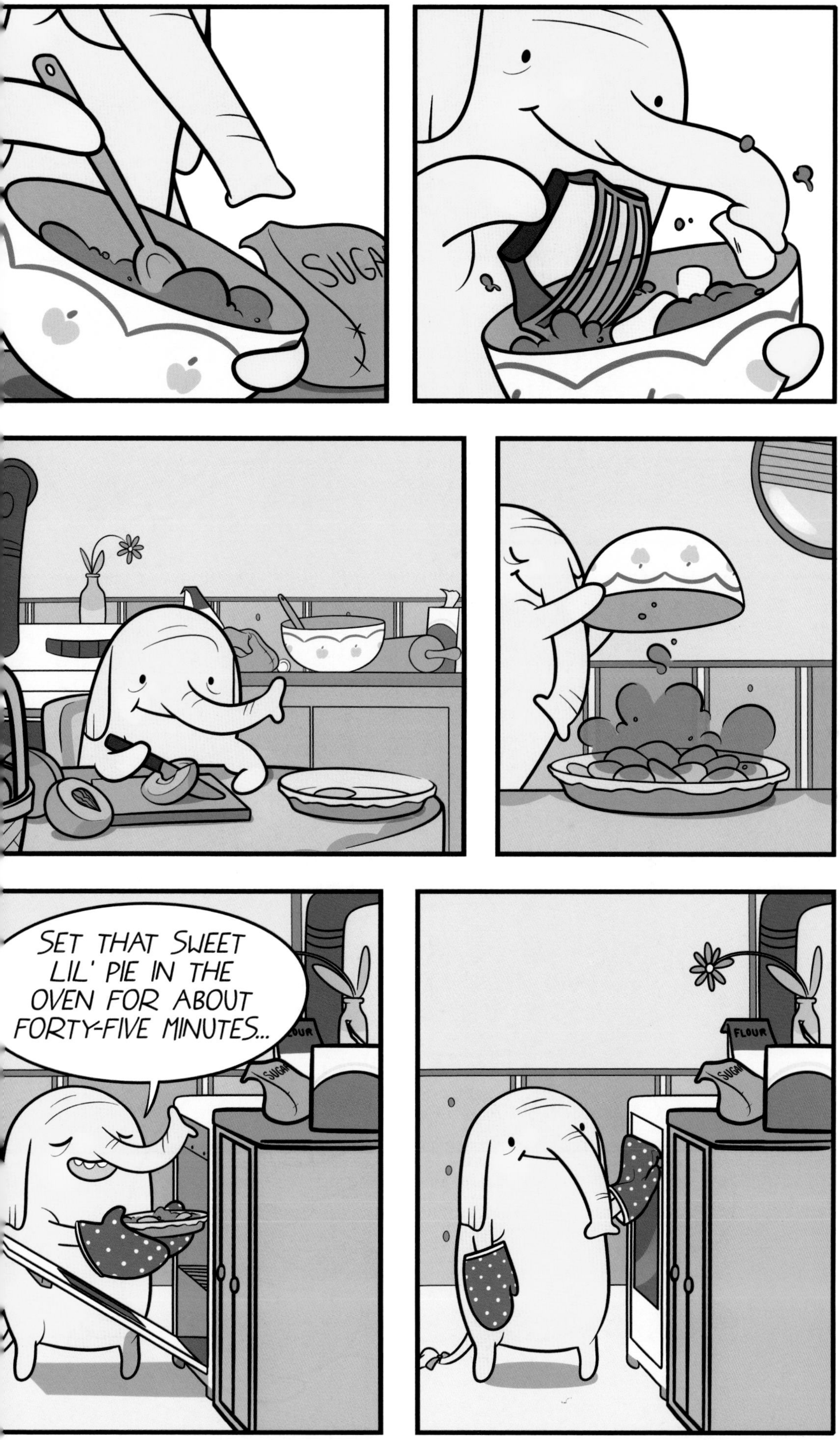
SUGA
SET THAT SWEET LIL' PIE IN THE OVEN FOR ABOUT FORTY-FIVE MINUTES...
SUGAR
FLOUR
SUGAR

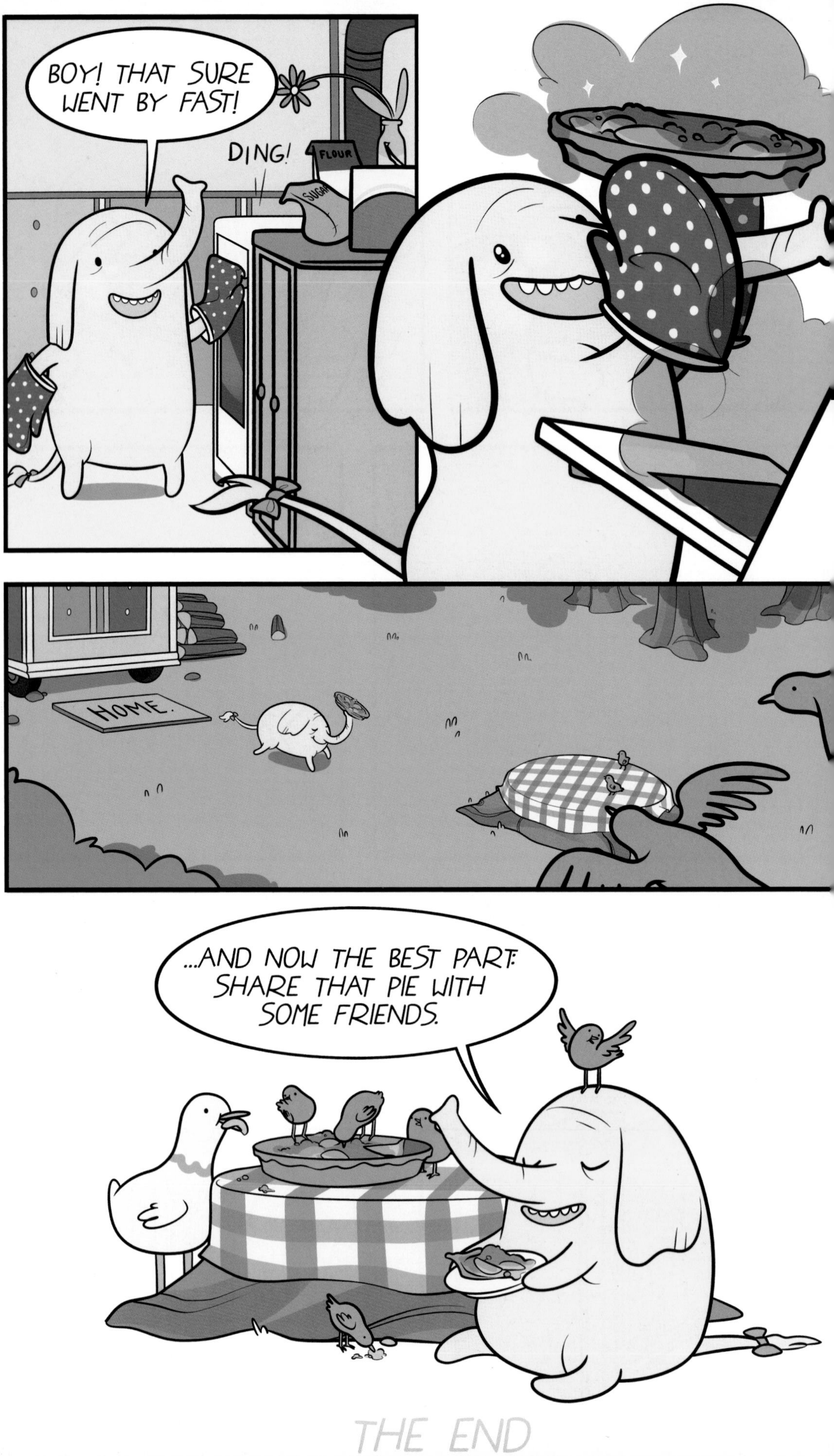
BOY! THAT SURE WENT BY FAST!
DING!
FLOUR
SUGAR
HOME
...AND NOW THE BEST PART: SHARE THAT PIE WITH SOME FRIENDS.
THE END

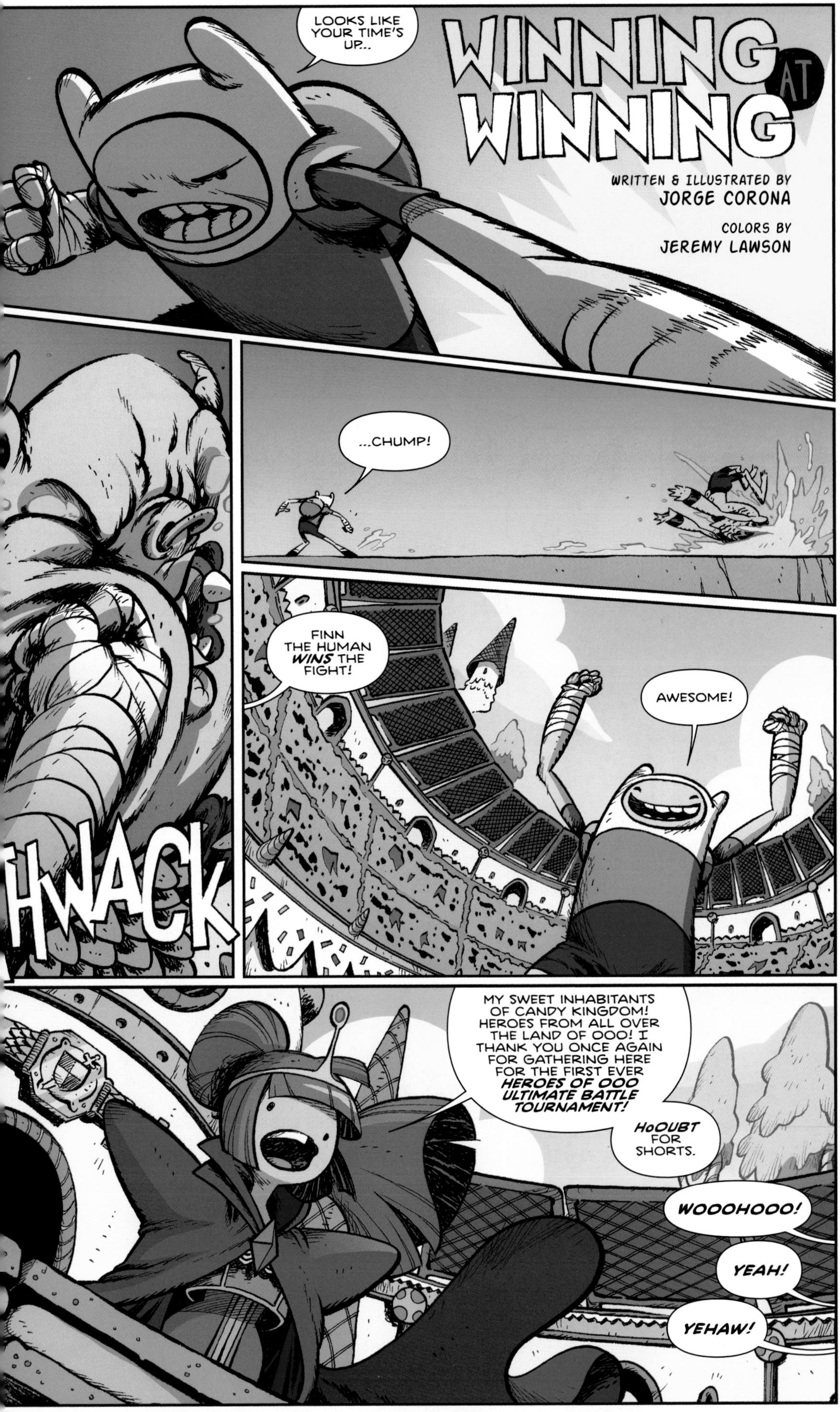
LOOKS LIKE YOUR TIME'S UP...
WINNING AT WINNING
WRITTEN & ILLUSTRATED BY
JORGE CORONA
COLORS BY
JEREMY LAWSON
...CHUMP!
THWACK
FINN THE HUMAN WINS THE FIGHT!
AWESOME!
MY SWEET INHABITANTS OF CANDY KINGDOM! HEROES FROM ALL OVER THE LAND OF OOO! I THANK YOU ONCE AGAIN FOR GATHERING HERE FOR THE FIRST EVER HEROES OF OOO ULTIMATE BATTLE TOURNAMENT!
HoOUBT FOR SHORTS.
WOOOHOOO!
YEAH!
YEHAW!

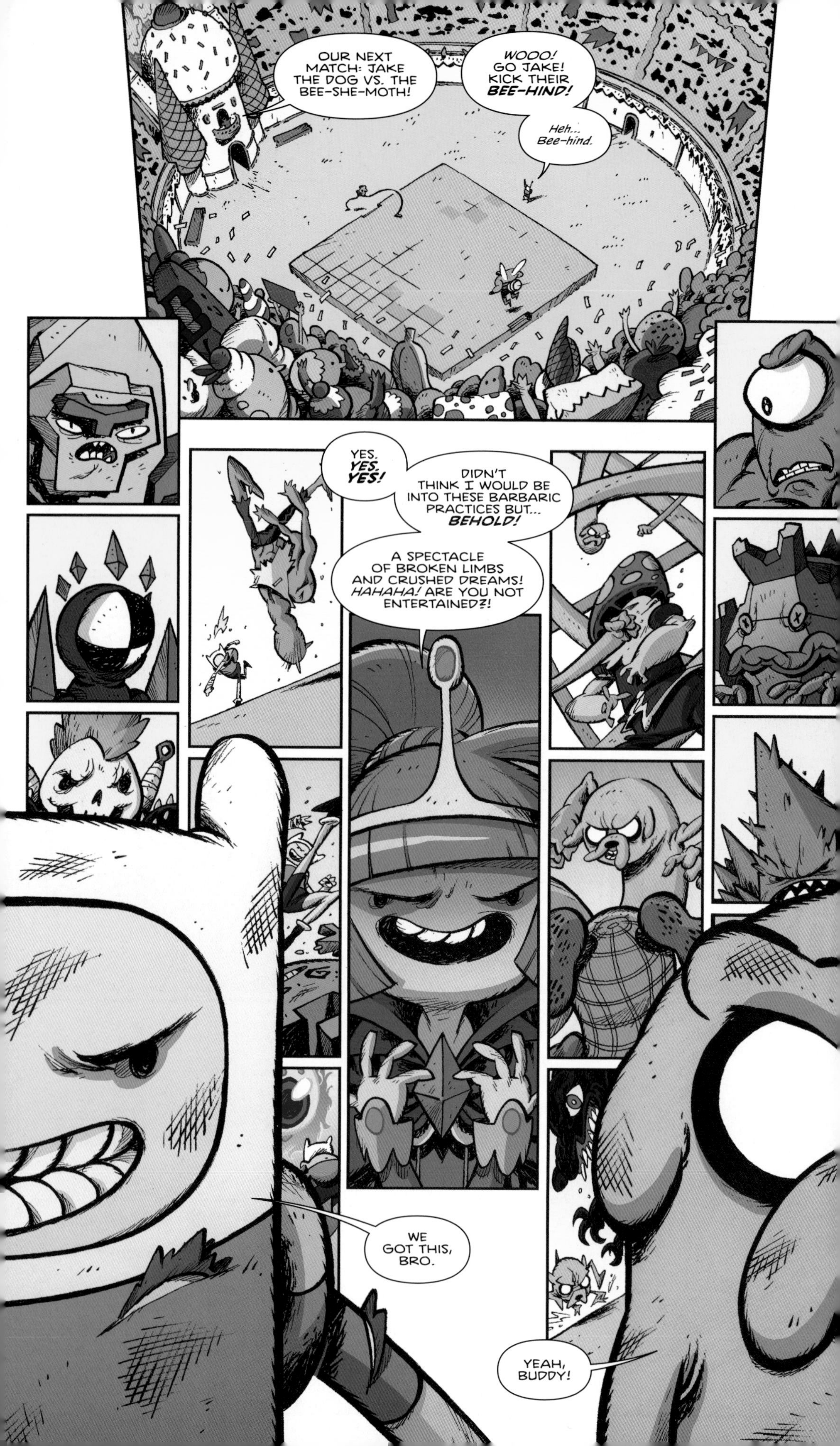
OUR NEXT MATCH: JAKE THE DOG VS. THE BEE-SHE-MOTH!
WOOO! GO JAKE! KICK THEIR BEE-HIND!
Heh... Bee-hind.
YES. YES. YES!
DIDN'T THINK I WOULD BE INTO THESE BARBARIC PRACTICES BUT... BEHOLD!
A SPECTACLE OF BROKEN LIMBS AND CRUSHED DREAMS! HAHAHA! ARE YOU NOT ENTERTAINED?!
WE GOT THIS, BRO.
YEAH, BUDDY!

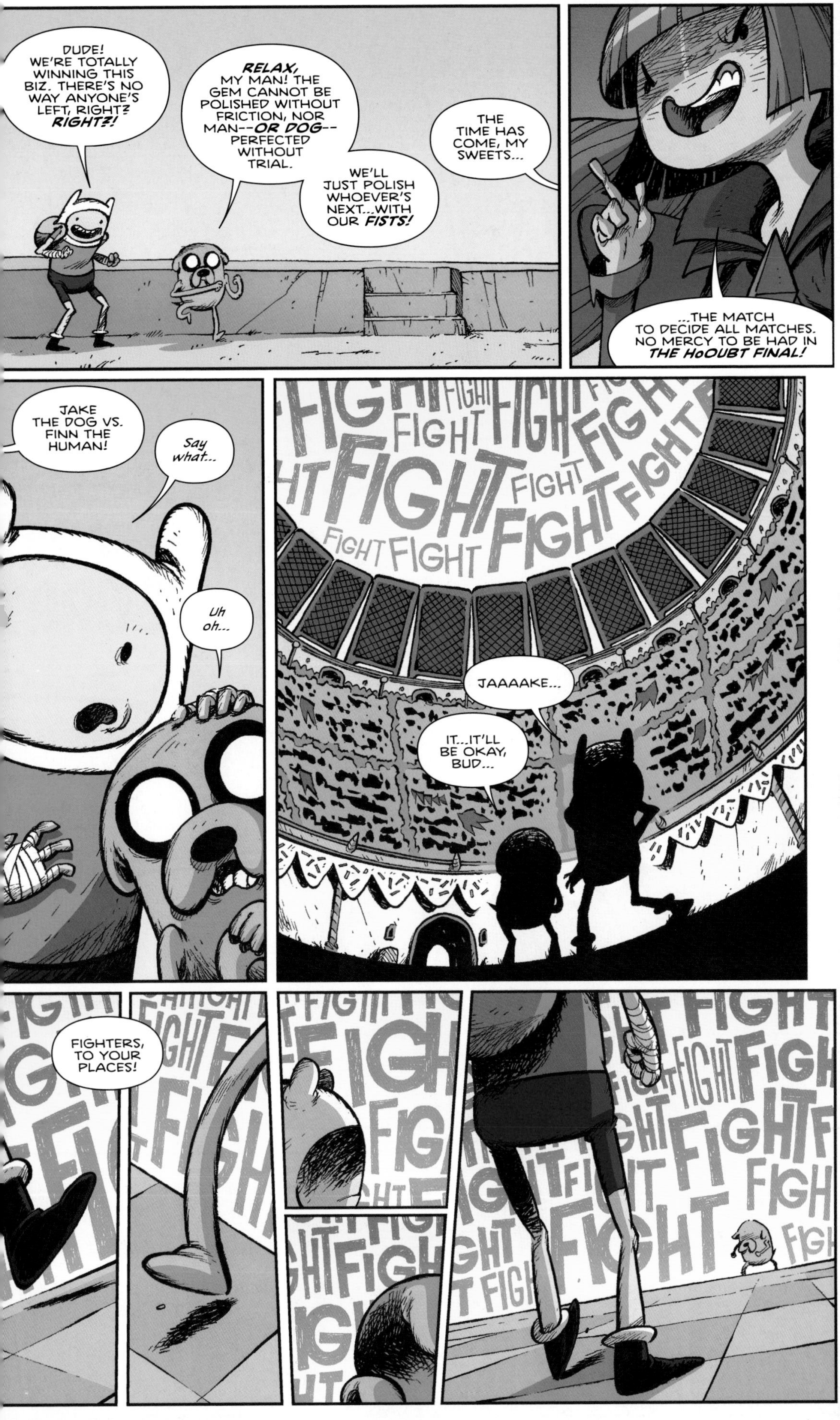

DUDE! WE'RE TOTALLY WINNING THIS BIZ. THERE'S NO WAY ANYONE'S LEFT, RIGHT? RIGHT?!
RELAX, MY MAN! THE GEM CANNOT BE POLISHED WITHOUT FRICTION, NOR MAN--OR DOG-- PERFECTED WITHOUT TRIAL.
WE'LL JUST POLISH WHOEVER'S NEXT...WITH OUR FISTS!
THE TIME HAS COME, MY SWEETS...
...THE MATCH TO DECIDE ALL MATCHES. NO MERCY TO BE HAD IN THE HoOUBT FINAL!
JAKE THE DOG VS. FINN THE HUMAN!
Say what...
Uh oh...
FIGHT FIGHT FIGHT FIGHT FIGHT FIGHT FIGHT FIGHT FIGHT FIGHT FIGHT FIGHT
JAAAAKE...
IT...IT'LL BE OKAY, BUD...
FIGHTERS, TO YOUR PLACES!

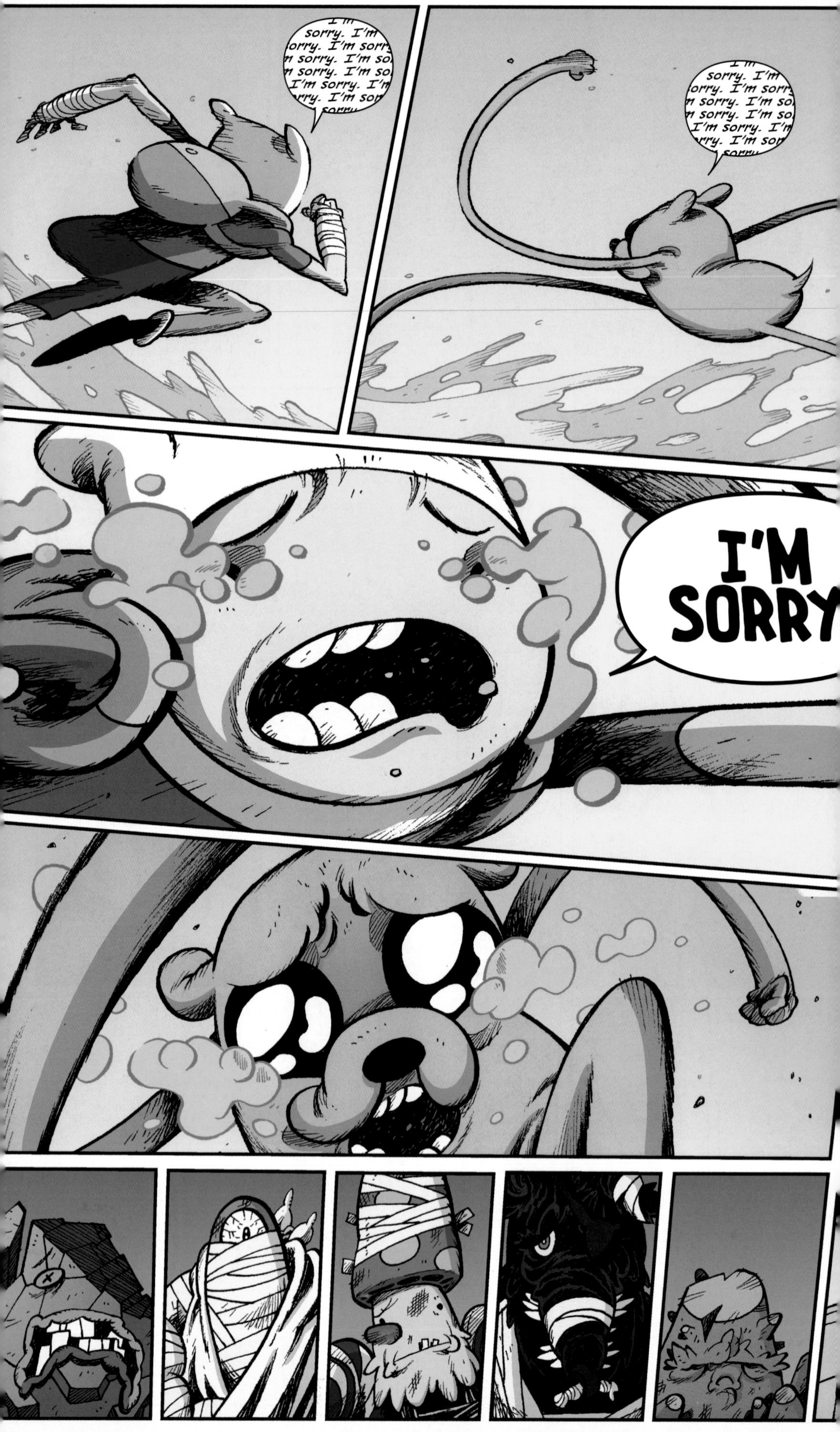
I'M SORRY

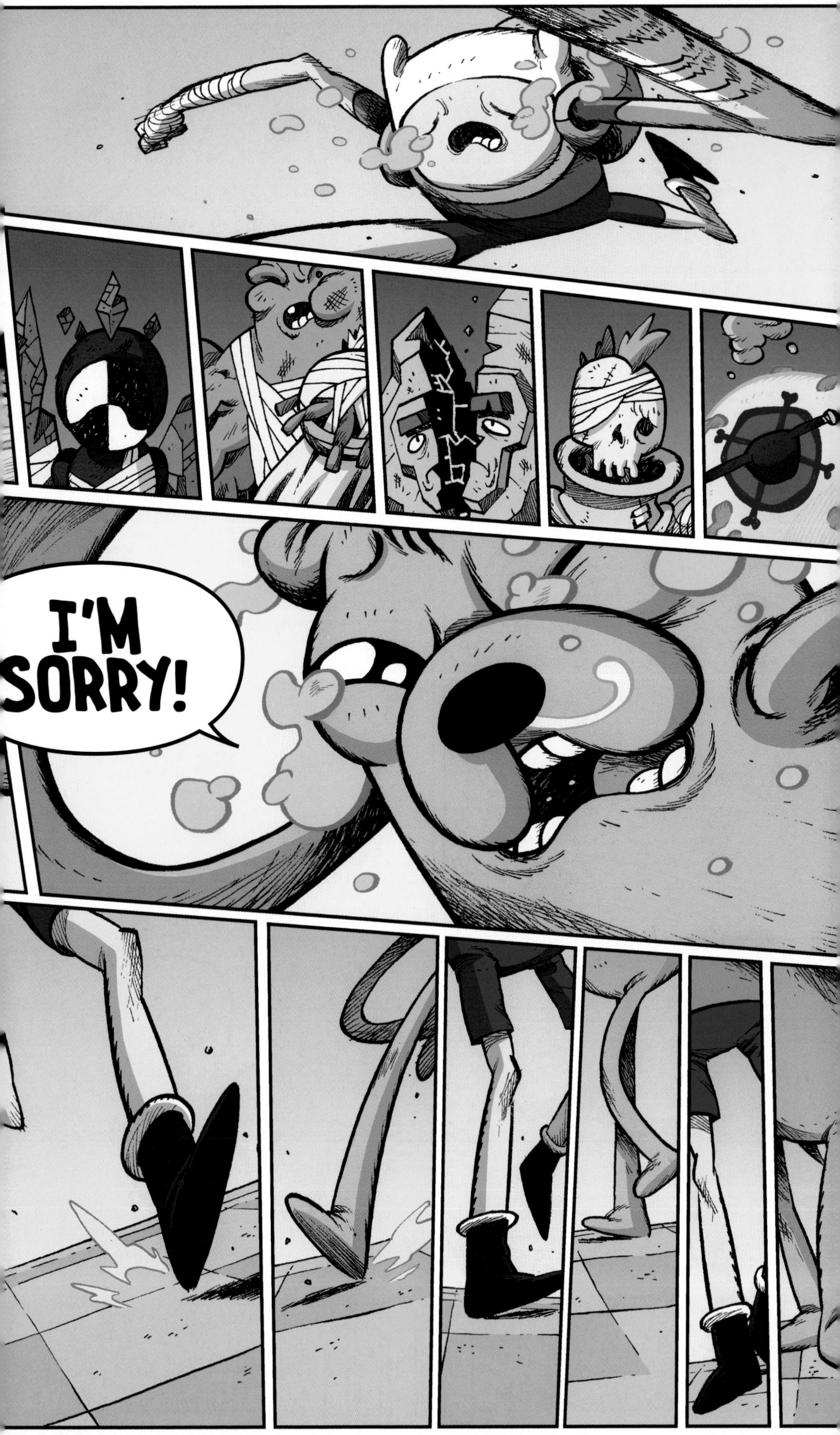
I'M SORRY!

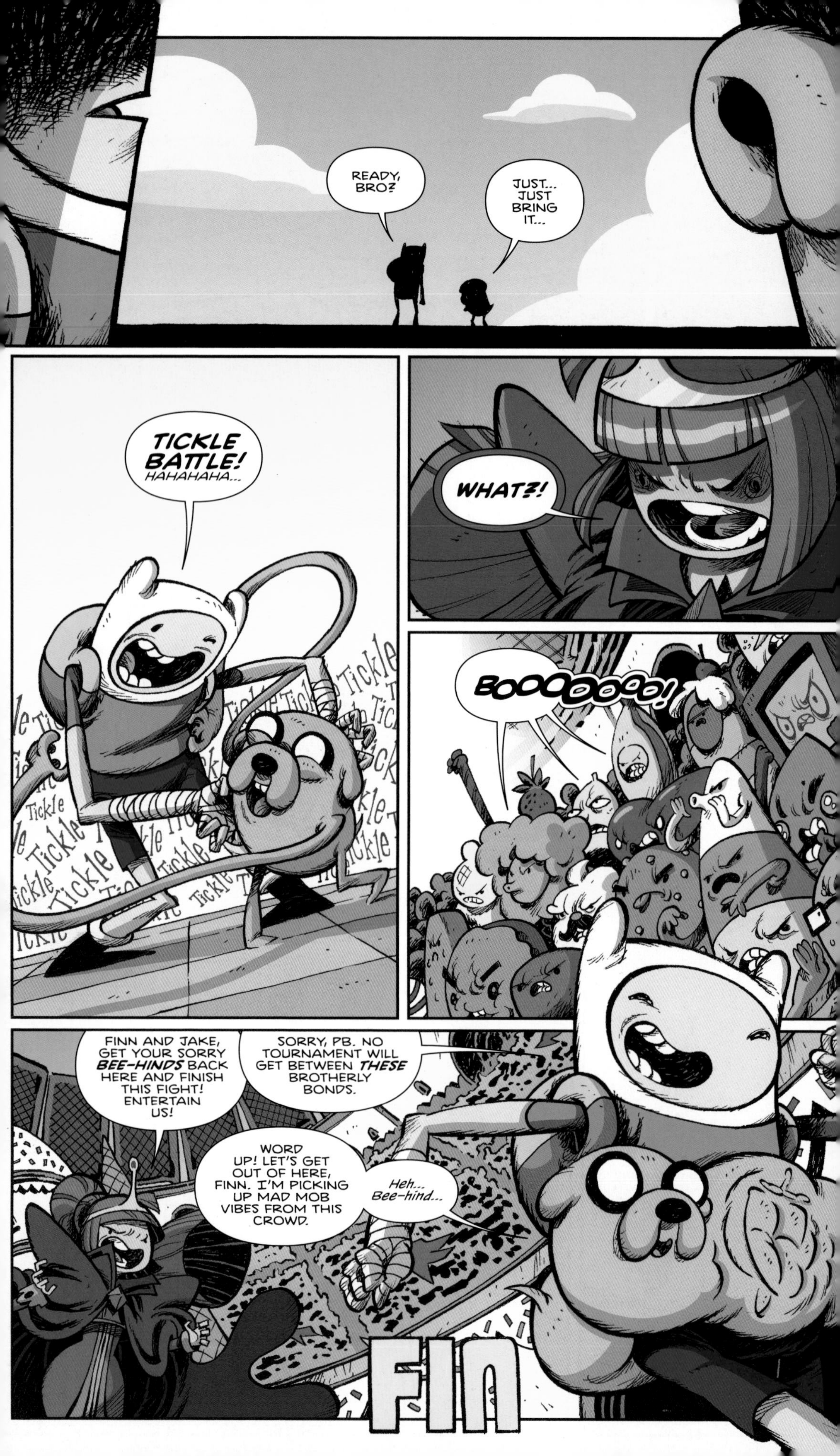
READY, BRO?
JUST... JUST BRING IT...
TICKLE BATTLE! HAHAHAHA...
WHAT?!
BOOOOOOOO!
FINN AND JAKE, GET YOUR SORRY BEE-HINDS BACK HERE AND FINISH THIS FIGHT! ENTERTAIN US!
SORRY, PB. NO TOURNAMENT WILL GET BETWEEN THESE BROTHERLY BONDS.
WORD UP! LET'S GET OUT OF HERE, FINN. I'M PICKING UP MAD MOB VIBES FROM THIS CROWD.
Heh... Bee-hind...
FIN

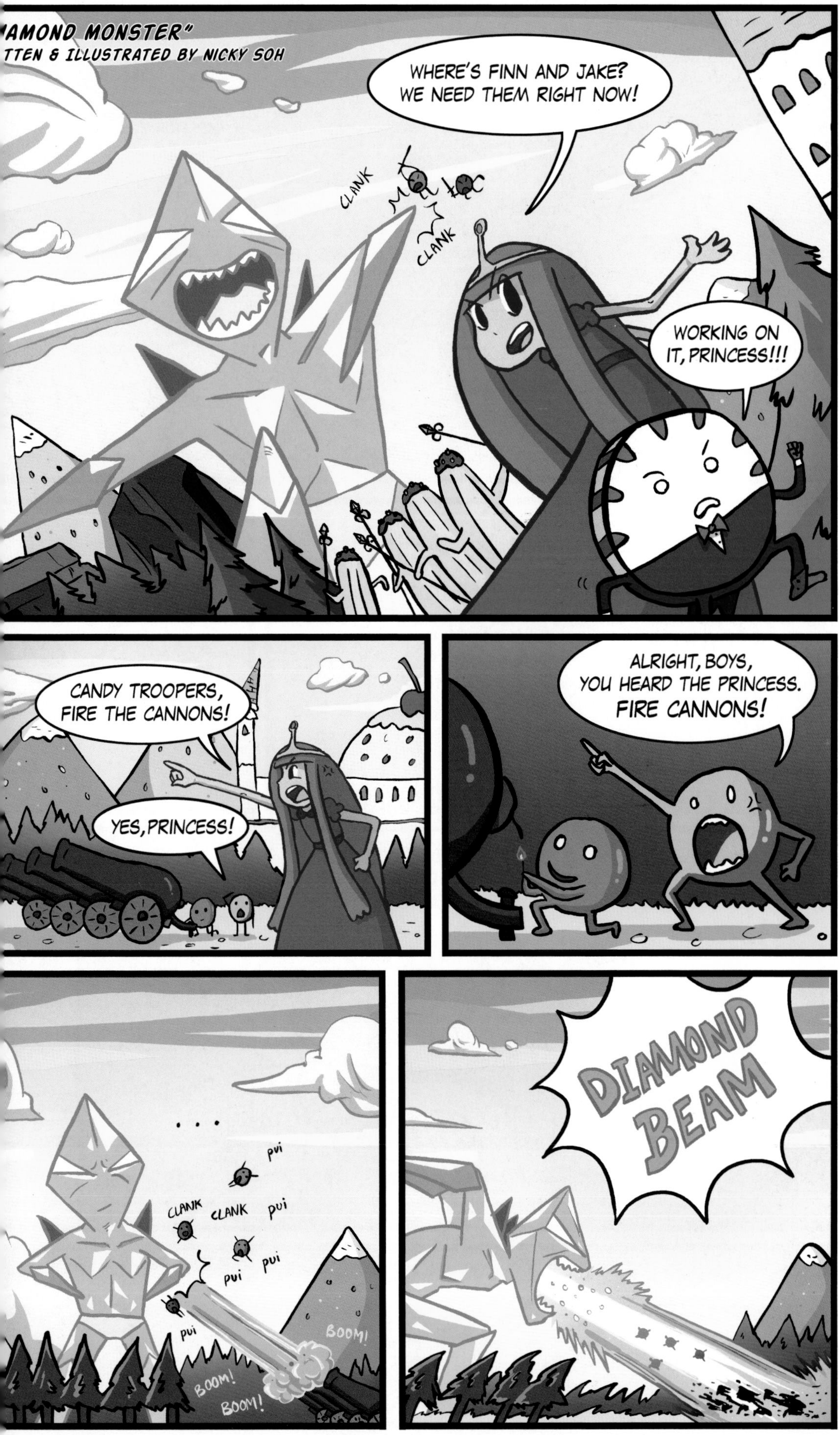

"...AMOND MONSTER"
...TTEN & ILLUSTRATED BY NICKY SOH
WHERE'S FINN AND JAKE? WE NEED THEM RIGHT NOW!
CLANK
CLANK
WORKING ON IT, PRINCESS!!!
CANDY TROOPERS, FIRE THE CANNONS!
YES, PRINCESS!
ALRIGHT, BOYS, YOU HEARD THE PRINCESS. FIRE CANNONS!
. . .
pui
CLANK
CLANK
pui
pui
pui
pui
BOOM!
BOOM!
BOOM!
DIAMOND BEAM

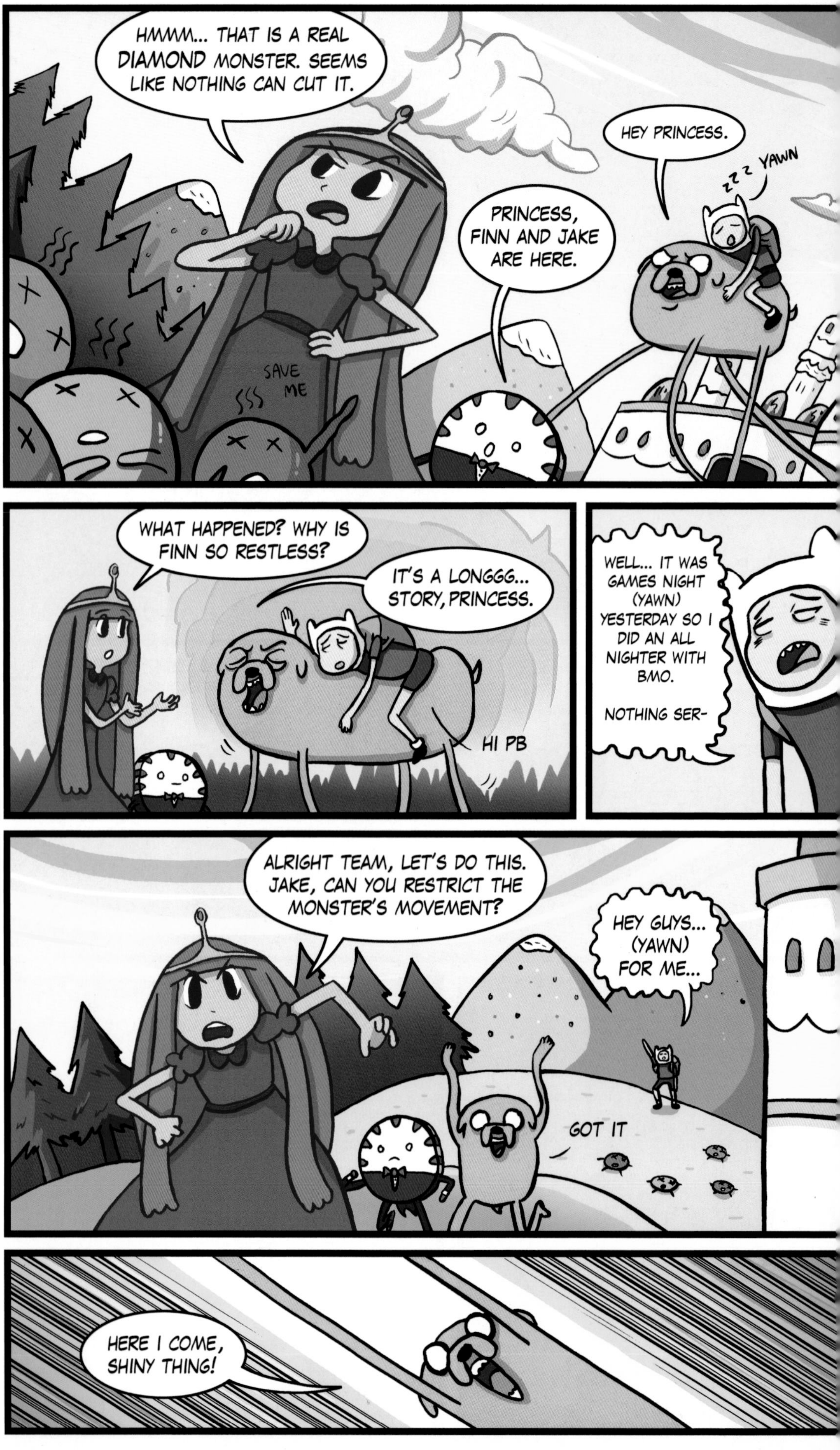
HMMM... THAT IS A REAL DIAMOND MONSTER. SEEMS LIKE NOTHING CAN CUT IT.
SAVE ME
HEY PRINCESS.
ZZZ YAWN
PRINCESS, FINN AND JAKE ARE HERE.
WHAT HAPPENED? WHY IS FINN SO RESTLESS?
IT'S A LONGGG... STORY, PRINCESS.
HI PB
WELL... IT WAS GAMES NIGHT (YAWN) YESTERDAY SO I DID AN ALL NIGHTER WITH BMO.
NOTHING SER-
ALRIGHT TEAM, LET'S DO THIS. JAKE, CAN YOU RESTRICT THE MONSTER'S MOVEMENT?
HEY GUYS... (YAWN) FOR ME...
GOT IT
HERE I COME, SHINY THING!

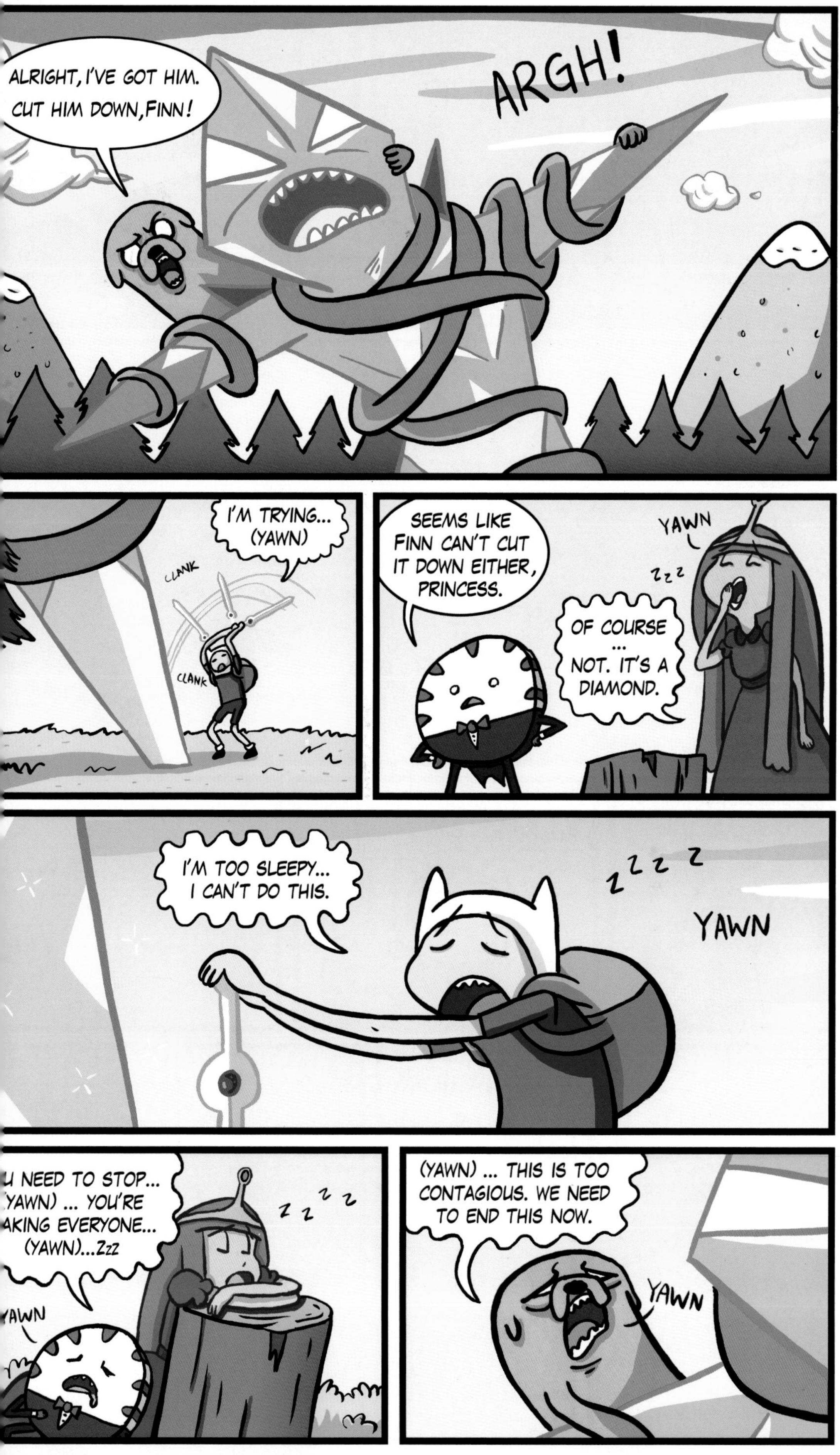
ALRIGHT, I'VE GOT HIM. CUT HIM DOWN, FINN!
ARGH!
I'M TRYING... (YAWN)
CLANK
CLANK
SEEMS LIKE FINN CAN'T CUT IT DOWN EITHER, PRINCESS.
YAWN
Z z z
OF COURSE ... NOT. IT'S A DIAMOND.
I'M TOO SLEEPY... I CAN'T DO THIS.
Z Z z Z
YAWN
U NEED TO STOP... (YAWN) ... YOU'RE AKING EVERYONE... (YAWN)...Zzz
Z z z z
YAWN
(YAWN) ... THIS IS TOO CONTAGIOUS. WE NEED TO END THIS NOW.
YAWN

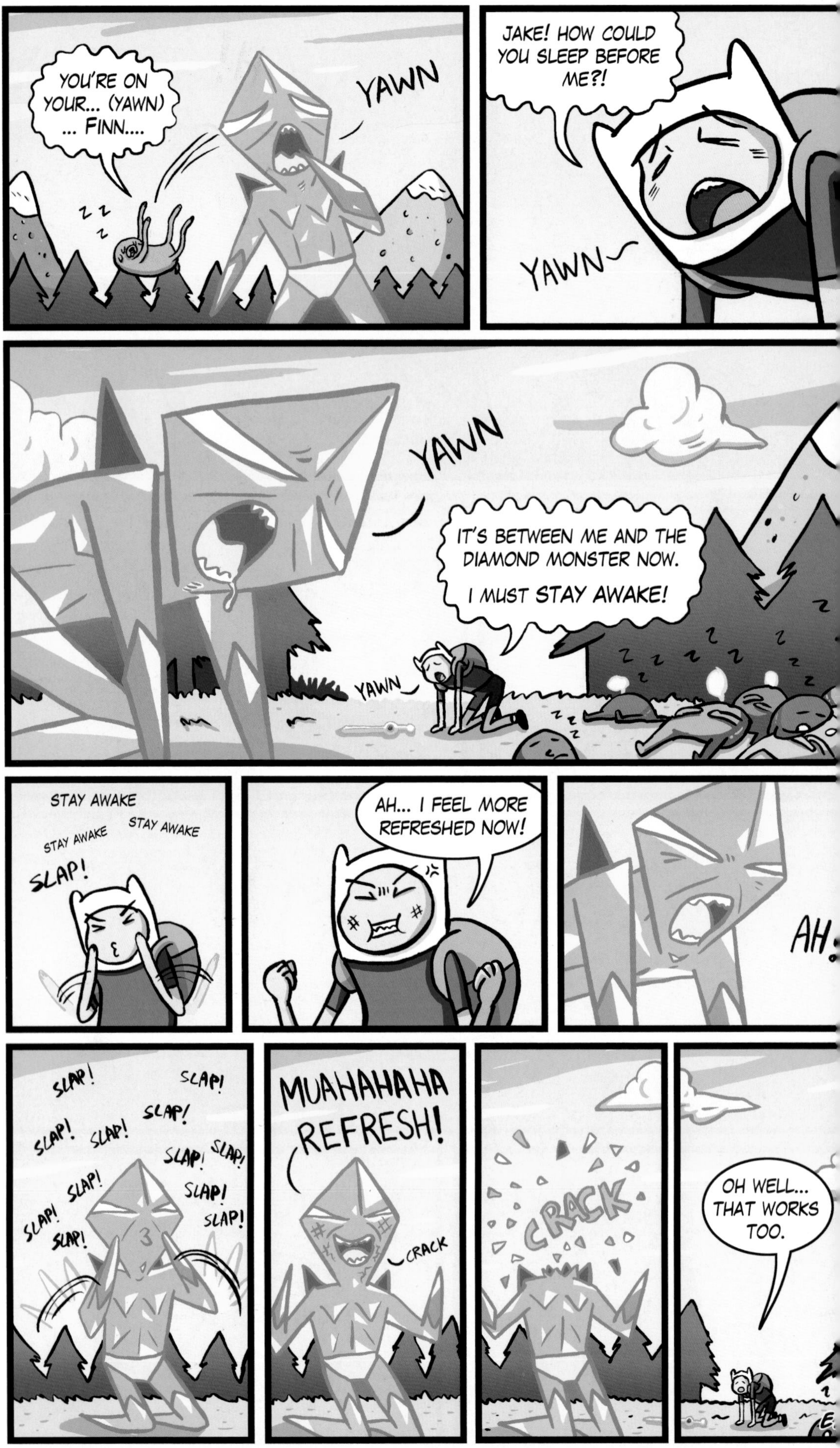
YOU'RE ON YOUR... (YAWN) ... FINN....
YAWN
Z Z Z
JAKE! HOW COULD YOU SLEEP BEFORE ME?!
YAWN
YAWN
IT'S BETWEEN ME AND THE DIAMOND MONSTER NOW.
I MUST STAY AWAKE!
YAWN
STAY AWAKE
STAY AWAKE
STAY AWAKE
SLAP!
AH... I FEEL MORE REFRESHED NOW!
AH
SLAP!
SLAP!
SLAP!
SLAP!
SLAP!
SLAP!
SLAP!
SLAP!
SLAP!
SLAP!
SLAP!
SLAP!
MUAHAHAHA REFRESH!
CRACK
CRACK
OH WELL... THAT WORKS TOO.

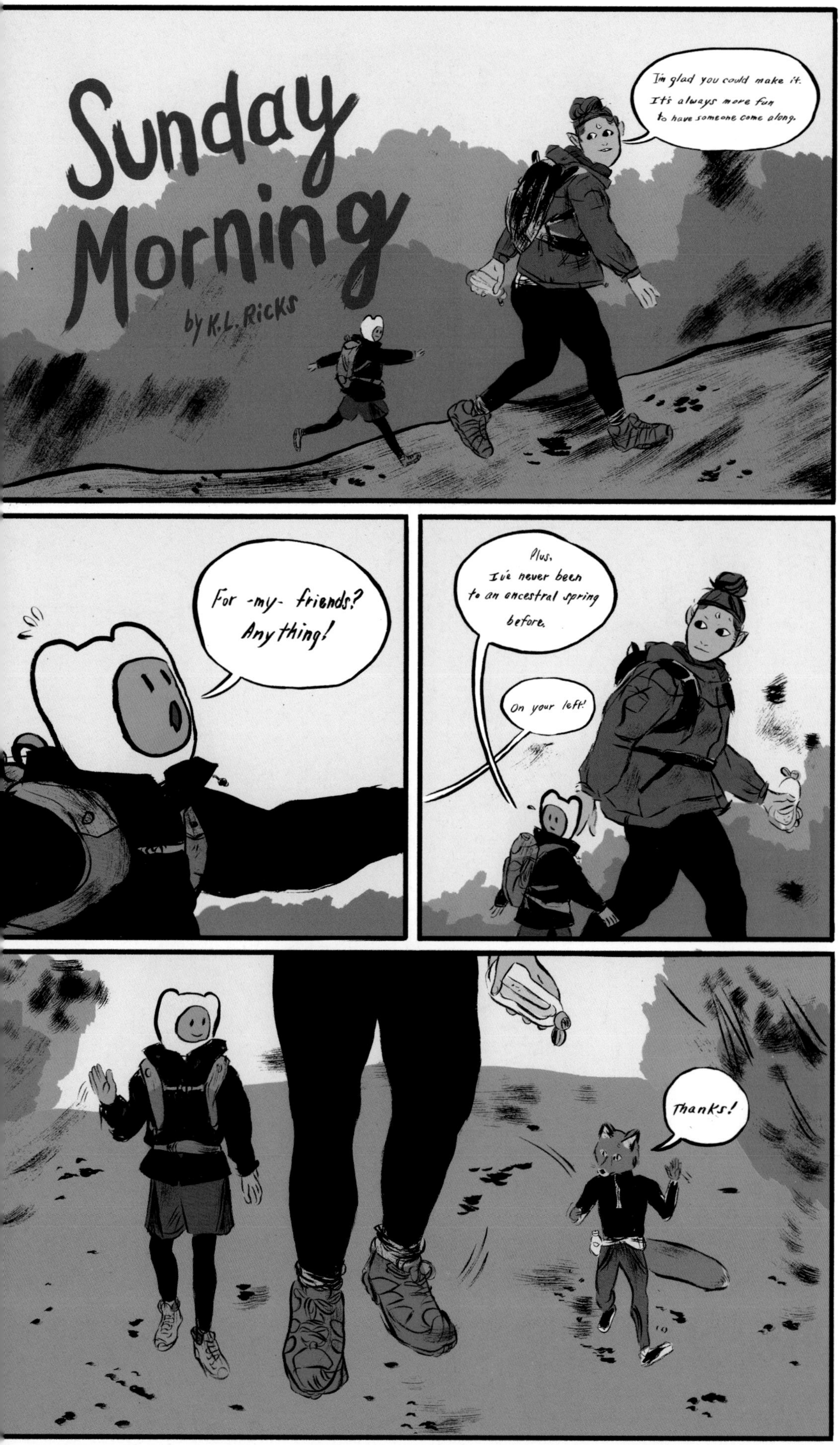
Sunday Morning
by K.L. Ricks
I'm glad you could make it. It's always more fun to have someone come along.
For -my- friends? Anything!
Plus, I've never been to an ancestral spring before.
On your left!
Thanks!

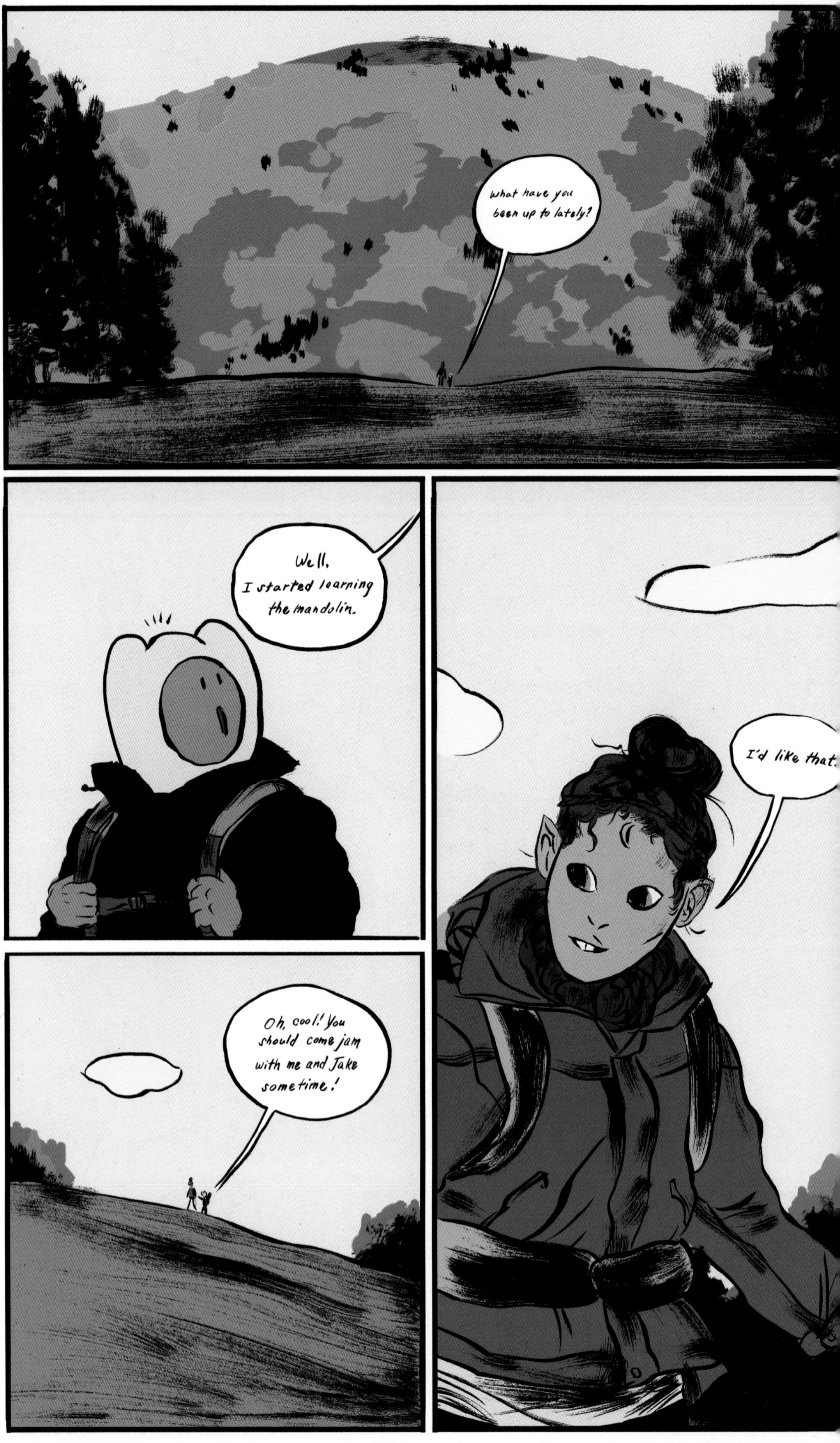
what have you been up to lately?
Well, I started learning the mandolin.
Oh, cool! You should come jam with me and Jake sometime!
I'd like that.

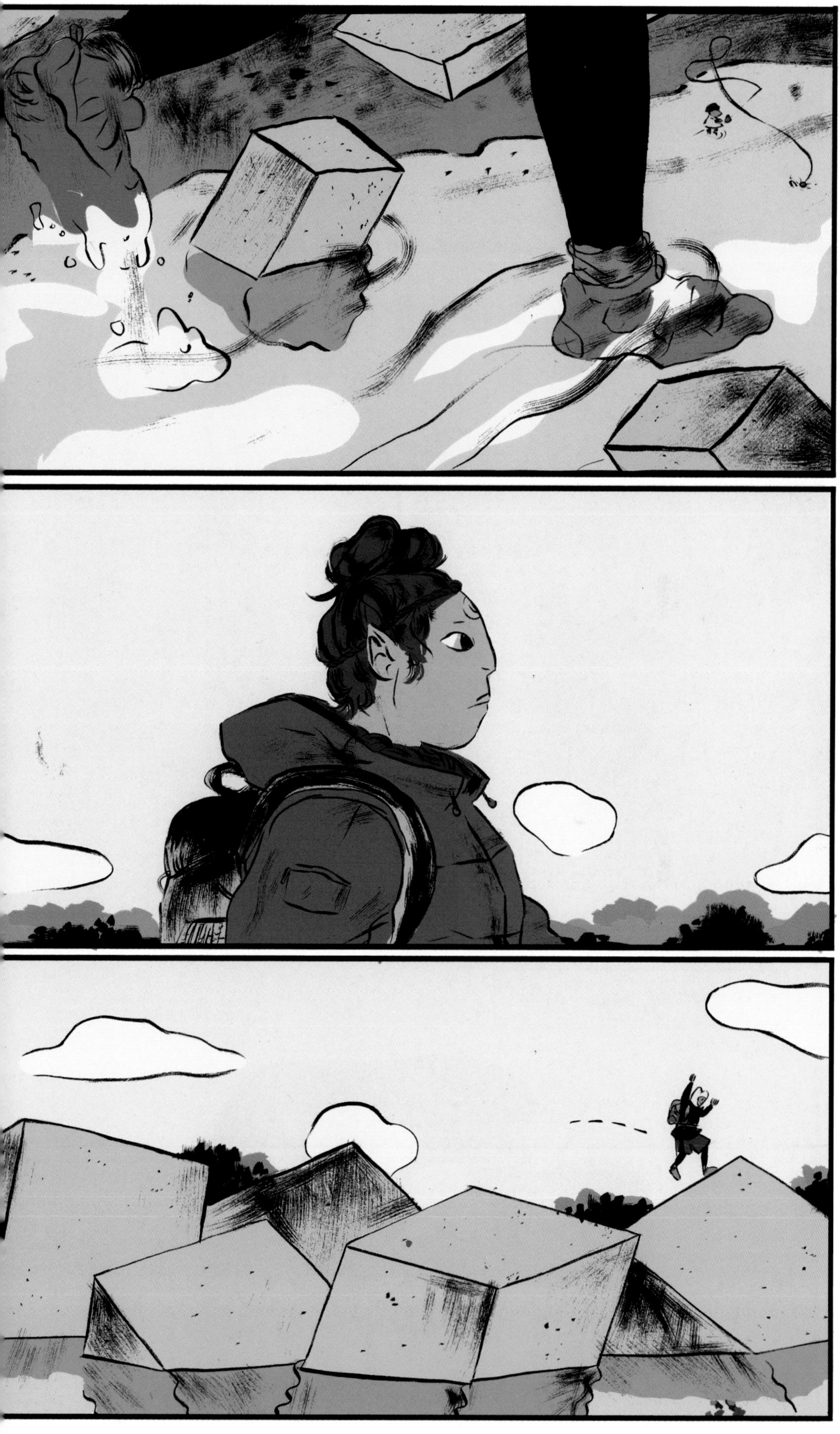

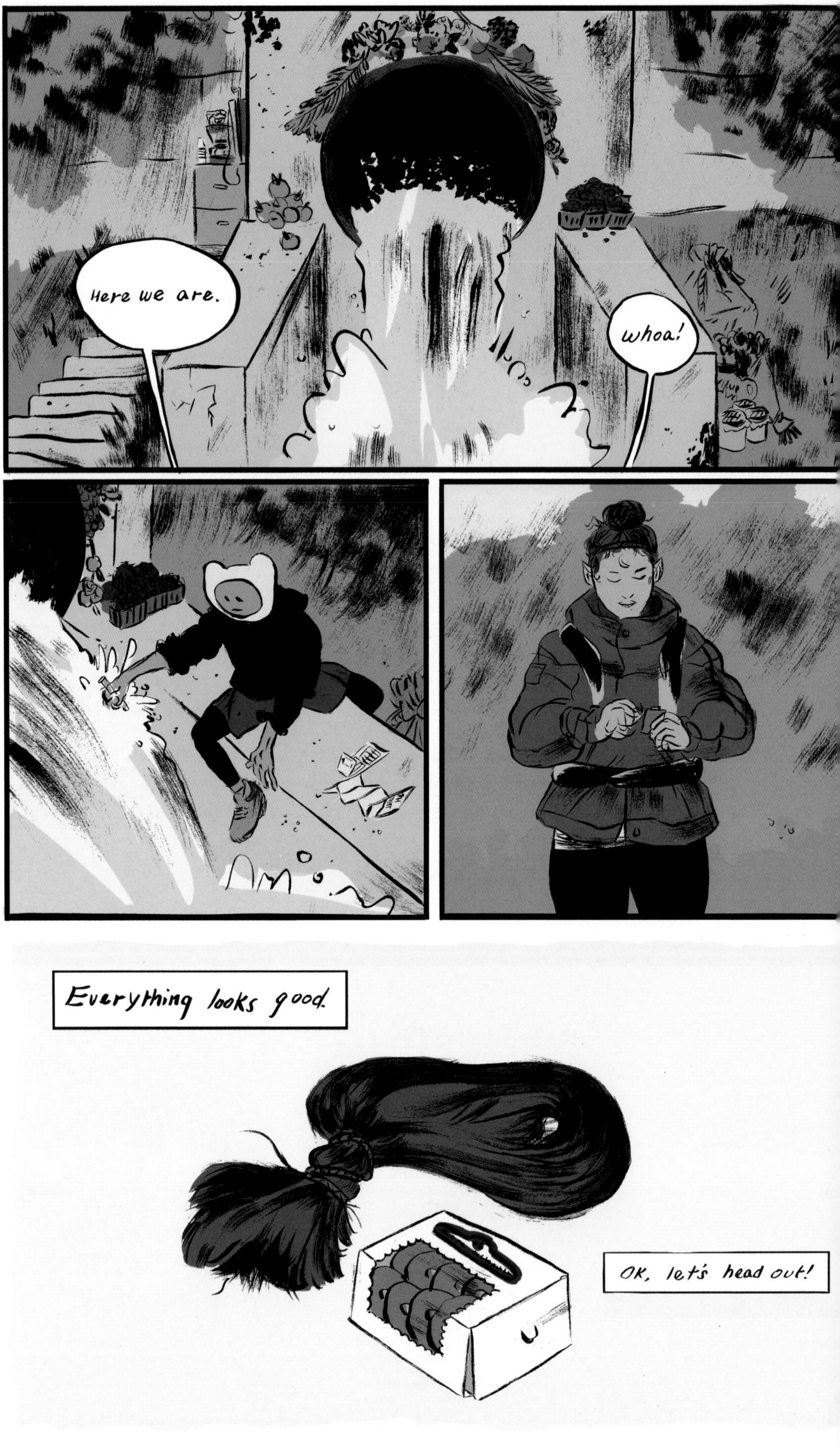
Here we are.
Whoa!
Everything looks good.
OK, let's head out!

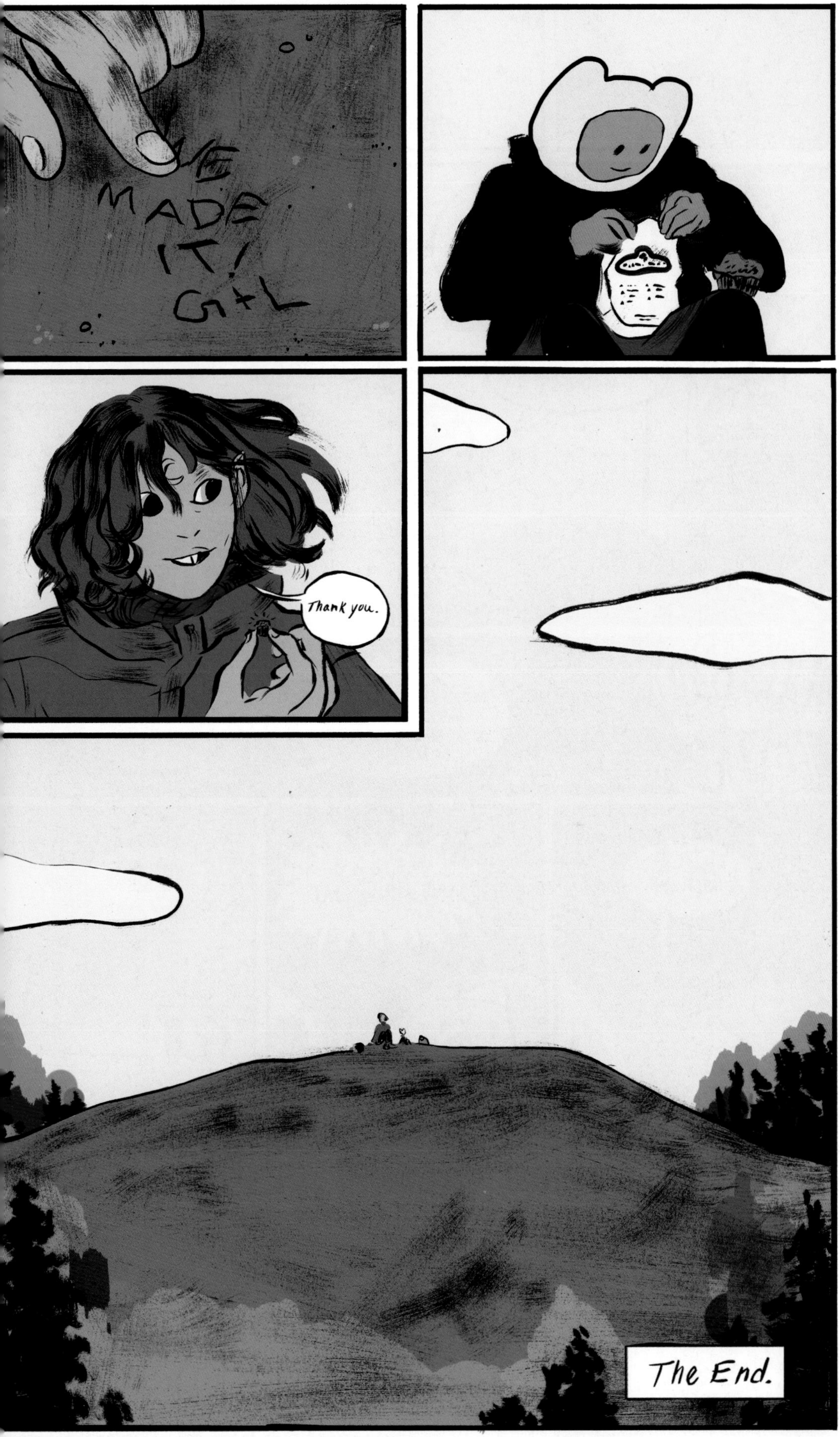

WE MADE IT! G+L
Thank you.
The End.

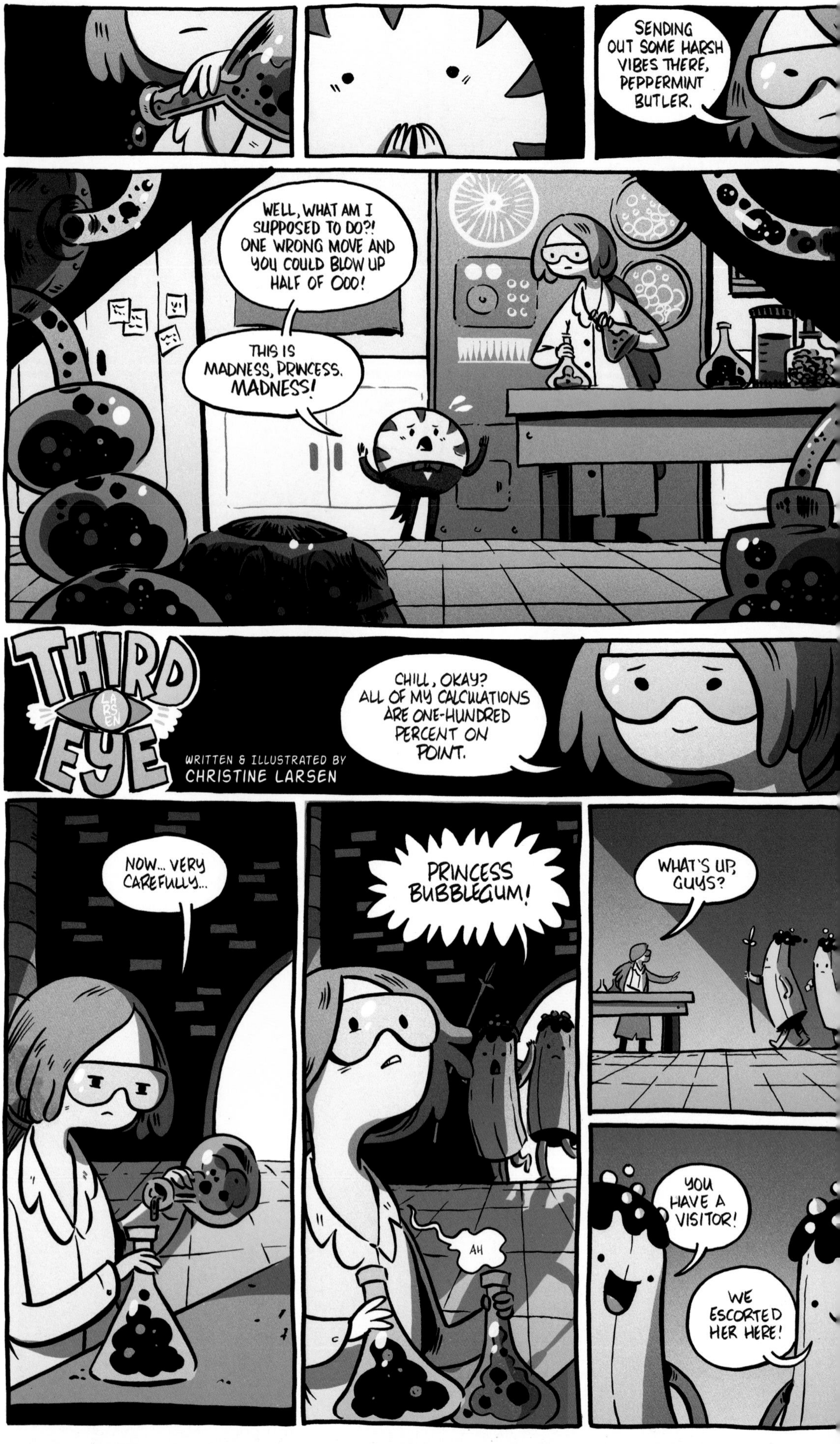
SENDING OUT SOME HARSH VIBES THERE, PEPPERMINT BUTLER.
WELL, WHAT AM I SUPPOSED TO DO?! ONE WRONG MOVE AND YOU COULD BLOW UP HALF OF OOO!
THIS IS MADNESS, PRINCESS. MADNESS!
THIRD EYE
LARSEN
WRITTEN & ILLUSTRATED BY
CHRISTINE LARSEN
CHILL, OKAY? ALL OF MY CALCULATIONS ARE ONE-HUNDRED PERCENT ON POINT.
NOW... VERY CAREFULLY...
PRINCESS BUBBLEGUM!
AH
WHAT'S UP, GUYS?
YOU HAVE A VISITOR!
WE ESCORTED HER HERE!

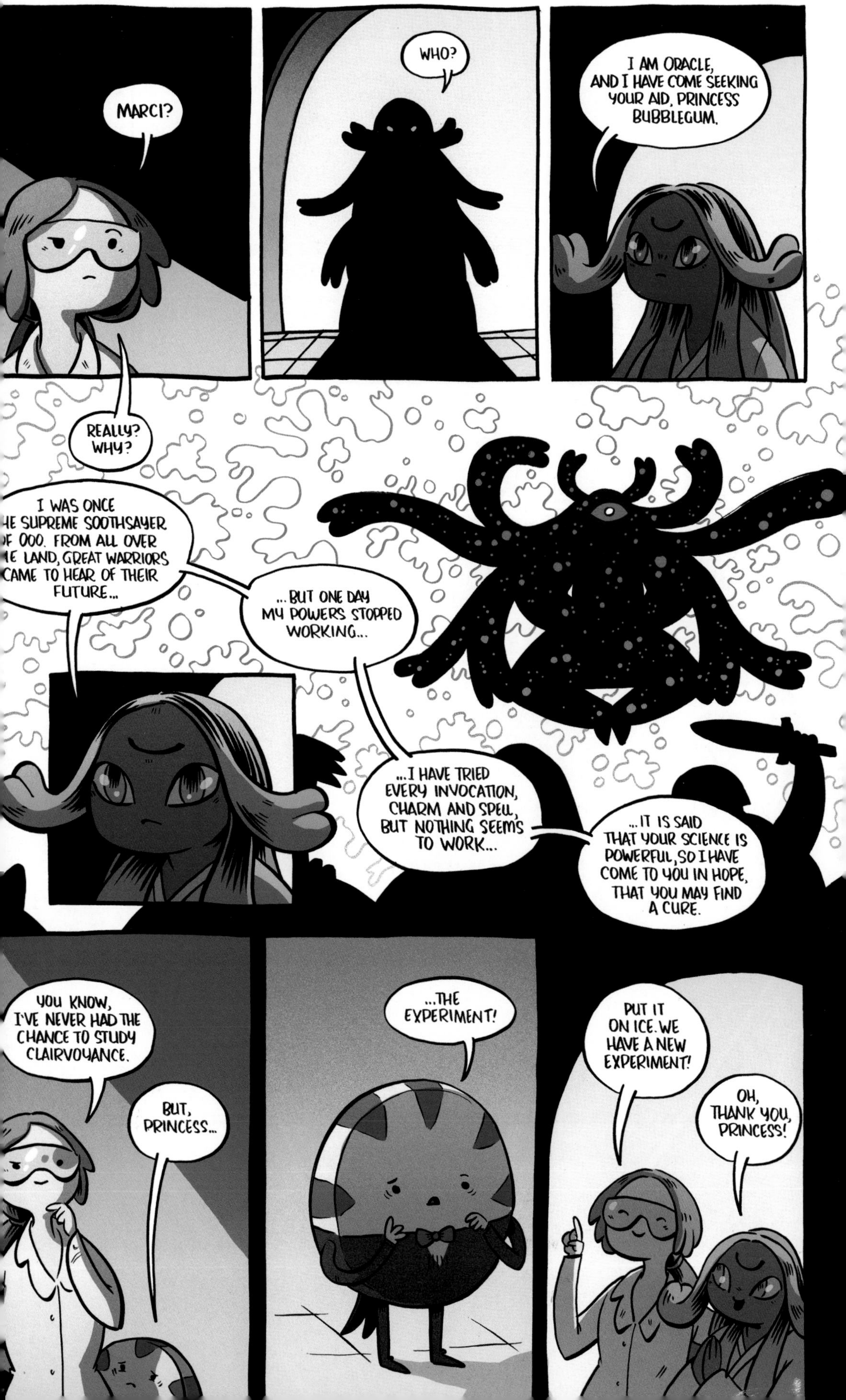
MARCI?
WHO?
I AM ORACLE, AND I HAVE COME SEEKING YOUR AID, PRINCESS BUBBLEGUM.
REALLY? WHY?
I WAS ONCE HE SUPREME SOOTHSAYER F OOO. FROM ALL OVER E LAND, GREAT WARRIORS CAME TO HEAR OF THEIR FUTURE...
...BUT ONE DAY MY POWERS STOPPED WORKING...
...I HAVE TRIED EVERY INVOCATION, CHARM AND SPELL, BUT NOTHING SEEMS TO WORK...
...IT IS SAID THAT YOUR SCIENCE IS POWERFUL, SO I HAVE COME TO YOU IN HOPE, THAT YOU MAY FIND A CURE.
YOU KNOW, I'VE NEVER HAD THE CHANCE TO STUDY CLAIRVOYANCE.
BUT, PRINCESS...
...THE EXPERIMENT!
PUT IT ON ICE. WE HAVE A NEW EXPERIMENT!
OH, THANK YOU, PRINCESS!

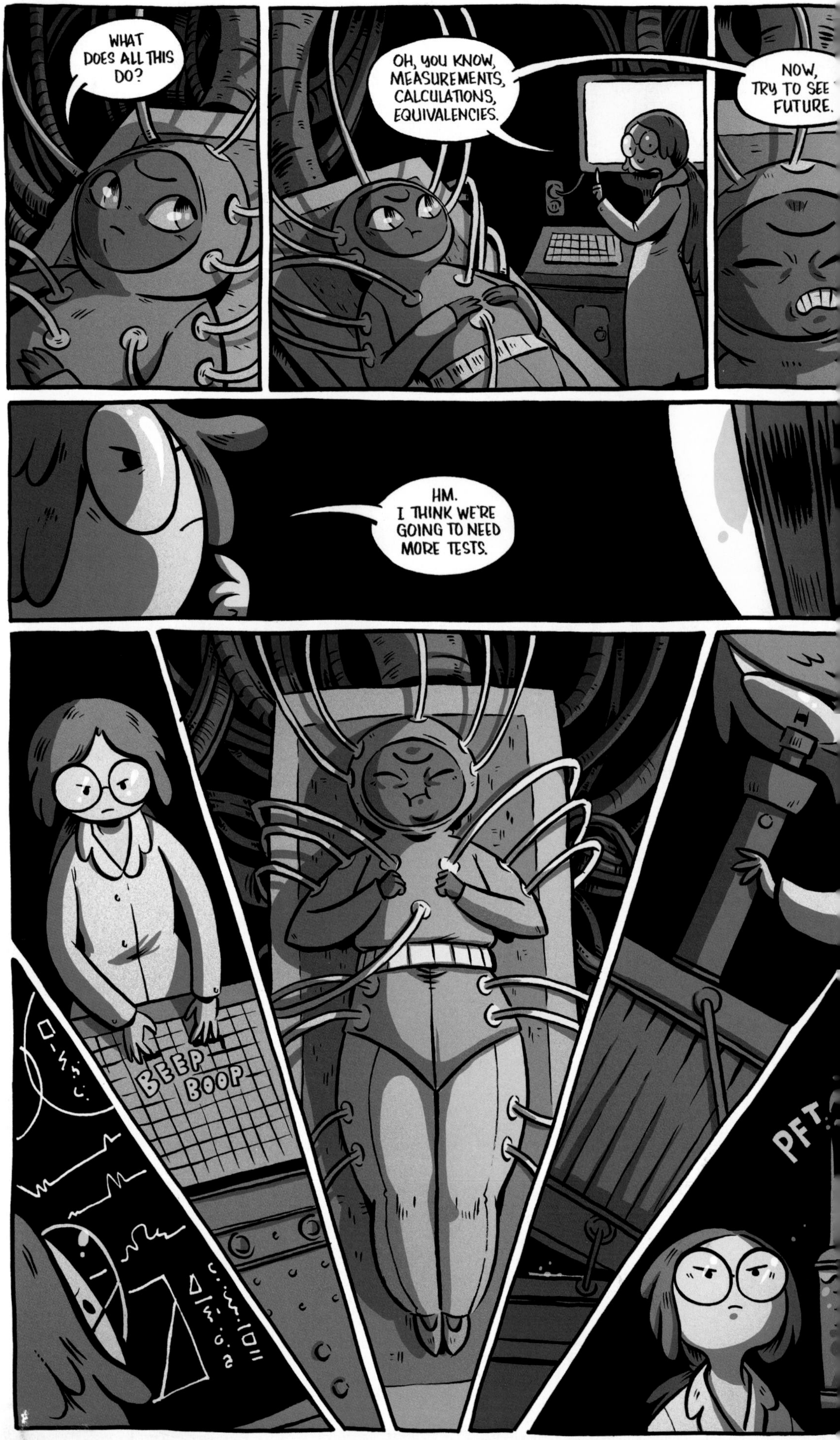
WHAT DOES ALL THIS DO?
OH, YOU KNOW, MEASUREMENTS, CALCULATIONS, EQUIVALENCIES.
NOW, TRY TO SEE FUTURE.
HM. I THINK WE'RE GOING TO NEED MORE TESTS.
BEEP BOOP
PFT

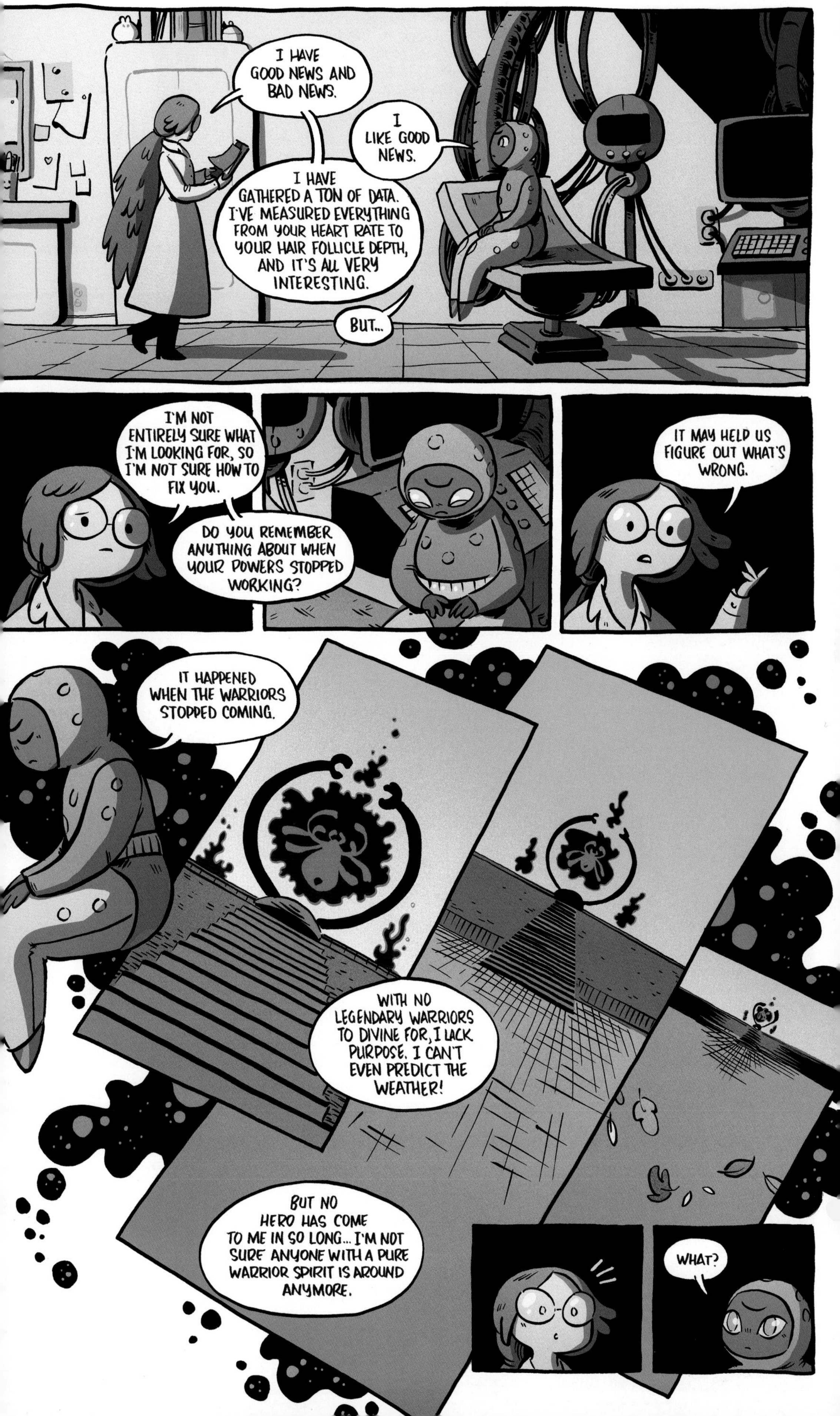
I HAVE GOOD NEWS AND BAD NEWS.
I LIKE GOOD NEWS.
I HAVE GATHERED A TON OF DATA. I'VE MEASURED EVERYTHING FROM YOUR HEART RATE TO YOUR HAIR FOLLICLE DEPTH, AND IT'S ALL VERY INTERESTING.
BUT...
I'M NOT ENTIRELY SURE WHAT I'M LOOKING FOR, SO I'M NOT SURE HOW TO FIX YOU.
DO YOU REMEMBER ANYTHING ABOUT WHEN YOUR POWERS STOPPED WORKING?
IT MAY HELP US FIGURE OUT WHAT'S WRONG.
IT HAPPENED WHEN THE WARRIORS STOPPED COMING.
WITH NO LEGENDARY WARRIORS TO DIVINE FOR, I LACK PURPOSE. I CAN'T EVEN PREDICT THE WEATHER!
BUT NO HERO HAS COME TO ME IN SO LONG... I'M NOT SURE ANYONE WITH A PURE WARRIOR SPIRIT IS AROUND ANYMORE.
WHAT?

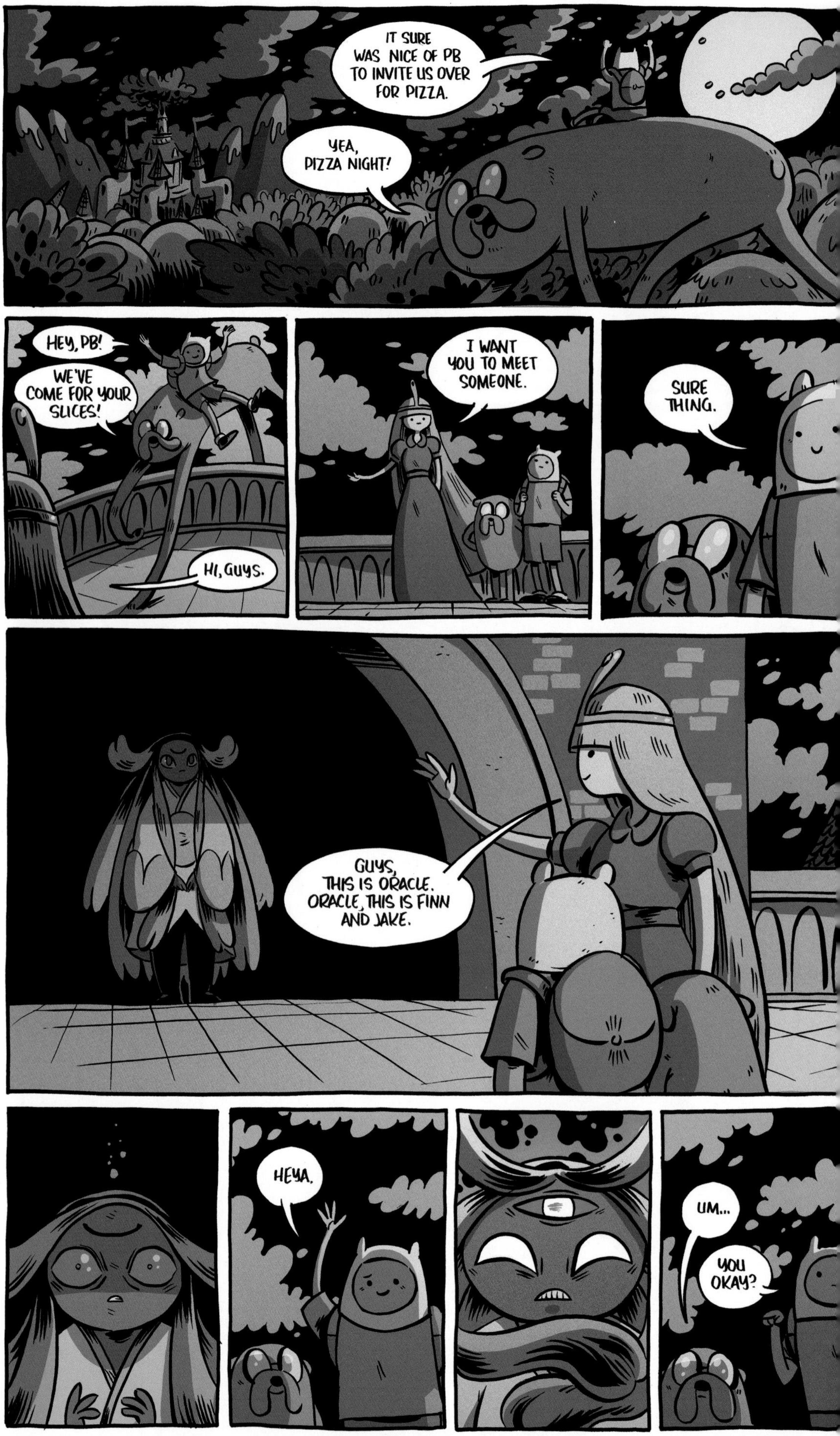
IT SURE WAS NICE OF PB TO INVITE US OVER FOR PIZZA.
YEA, PIZZA NIGHT!
HEY, PB!
WE'VE COME FOR YOUR SLICES!
HI, GUYS.
I WANT YOU TO MEET SOMEONE.
SURE THING.
GUYS, THIS IS ORACLE. ORACLE, THIS IS FINN AND JAKE.
HEYA.
UM...
YOU OKAY?

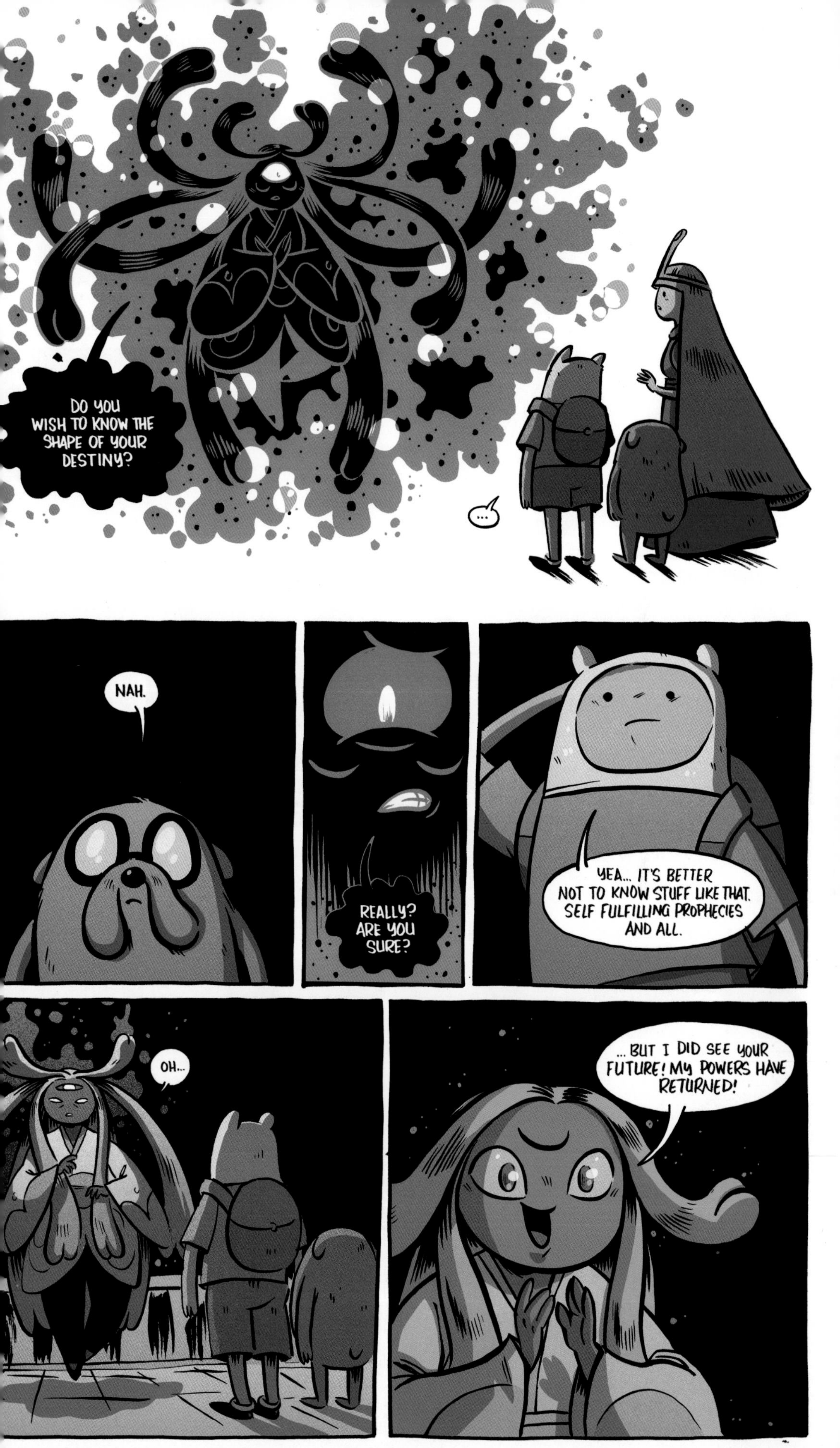
DO YOU WISH TO KNOW THE SHAPE OF YOUR DESTINY?
...
NAH.
REALLY? ARE YOU SURE?
YEA... IT'S BETTER NOT TO KNOW STUFF LIKE THAT. SELF FULFILLING PROPHECIES AND ALL.
OH...
... BUT I DID SEE YOUR FUTURE! MY POWERS HAVE RETURNED!

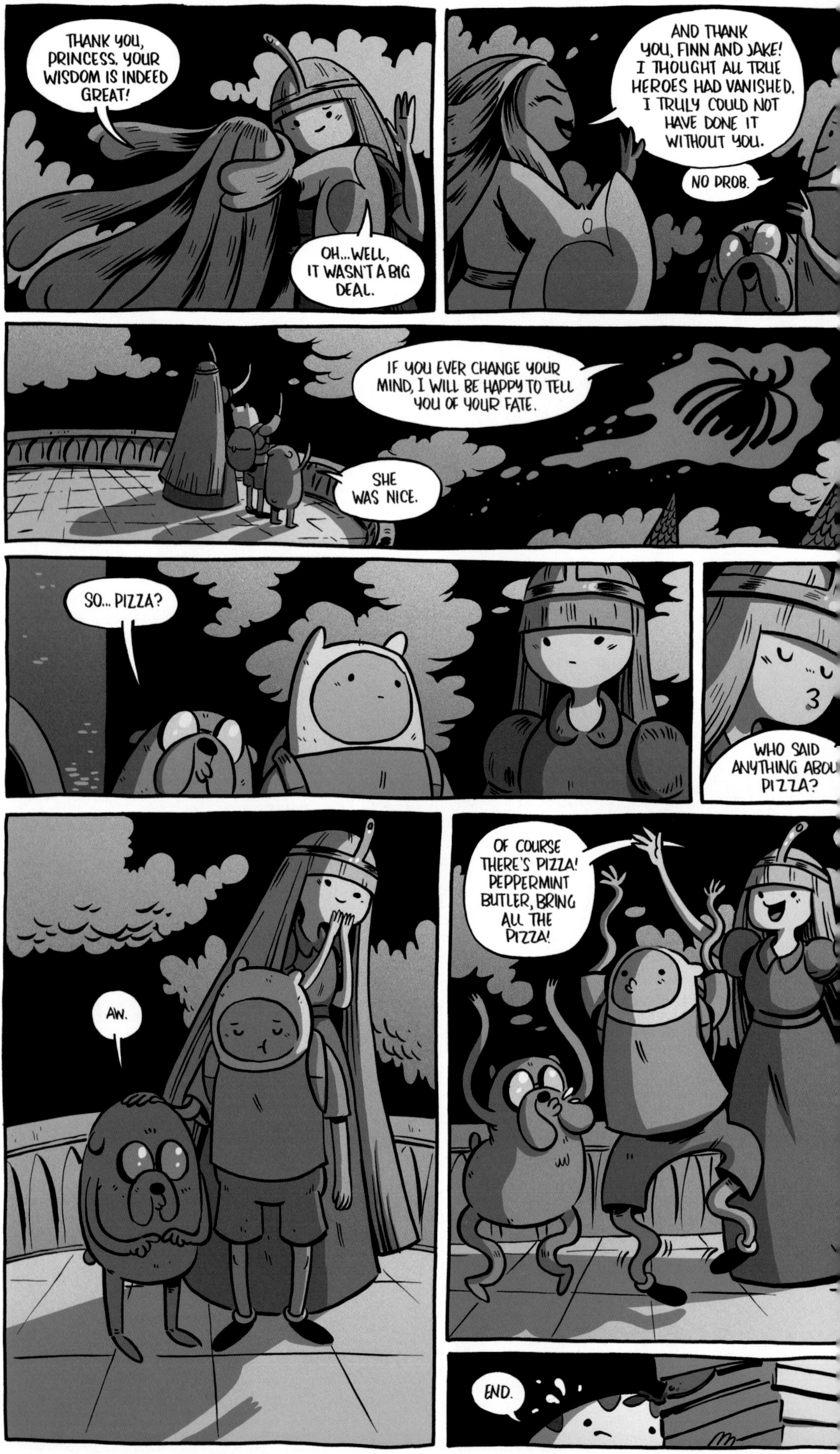
THANK YOU, PRINCESS. YOUR WISDOM IS INDEED GREAT!
OH...WELL, IT WASN'T A BIG DEAL.
AND THANK YOU, FINN AND JAKE! I THOUGHT ALL TRUE HEROES HAD VANISHED. I TRULY COULD NOT HAVE DONE IT WITHOUT YOU.
NO PROB.
IF YOU EVER CHANGE YOUR MIND, I WILL BE HAPPY TO TELL YOU OF YOUR FATE.
SHE WAS NICE.
SO... PIZZA?
WHO SAID ANYTHING ABOU PIZZA?
AW.
OF COURSE THERE'S PIZZA! PEPPERMINT BUTLER, BRING ALL THE PIZZA!
END.

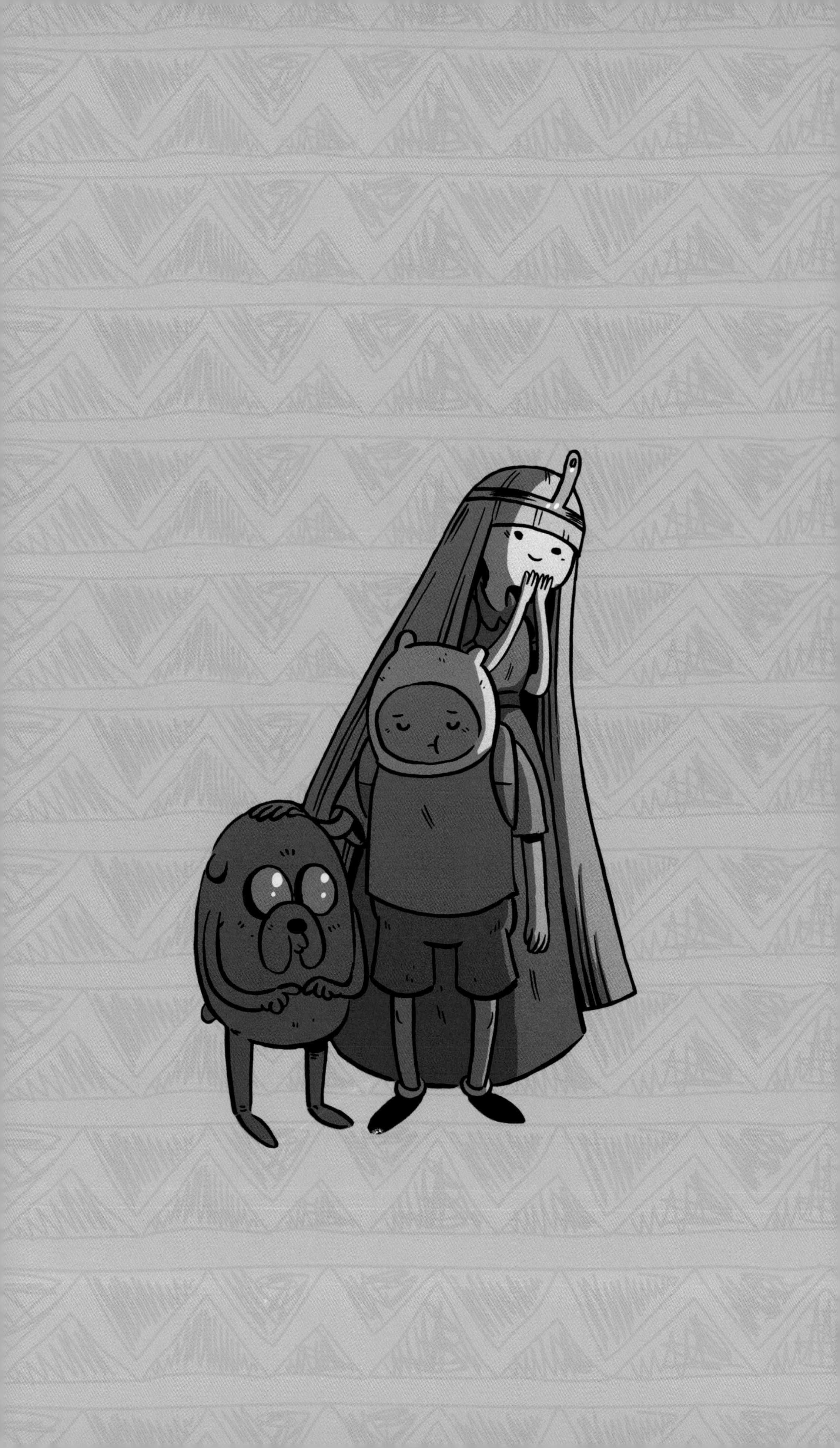

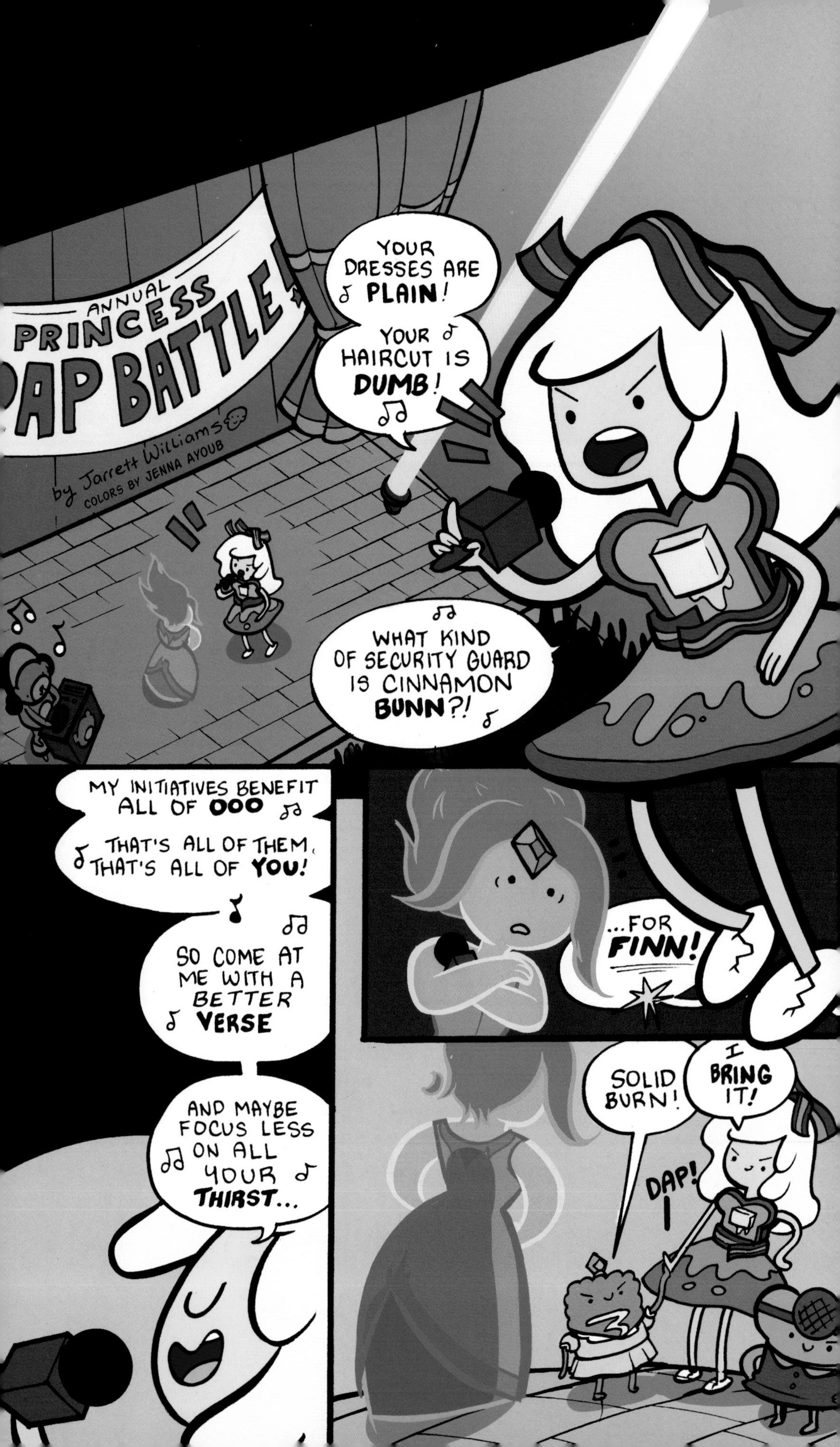
ANNUAL PRINCESS DAP BATTLE!
by Jarrett Williams
COLORS BY JENNA AYOUB
YOUR DRESSES ARE PLAIN!
YOUR HAIRCUT IS DUMB!
WHAT KIND OF SECURITY GUARD IS CINNAMON BUNN?!
MY INITIATIVES BENEFIT ALL OF OOO
THAT'S ALL OF THEM, THAT'S ALL OF YOU!
SO COME AT ME WITH A BETTER VERSE
AND MAYBE FOCUS LESS ON ALL YOUR THIRST...
...FOR FINN!
SOLID BURN!
I BRING IT!
DAP!

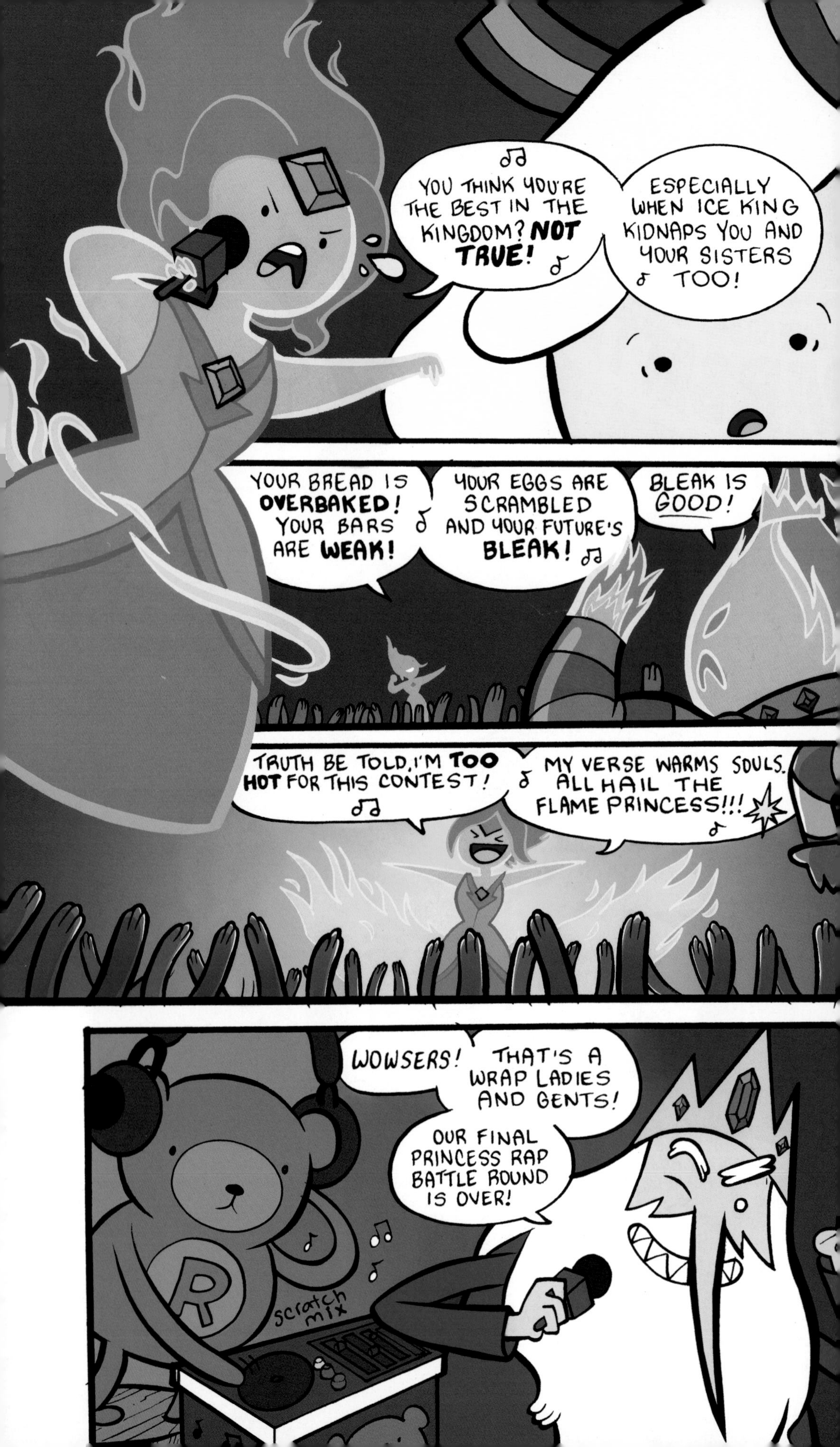
YOU THINK YOU'RE THE BEST IN THE KINGDOM? NOT TRUE!
ESPECIALLY WHEN ICE KING KIDNAPS YOU AND YOUR SISTERS TOO!
YOUR BREAD IS OVERBAKED! YOUR BARS ARE WEAK!
YOUR EGGS ARE SCRAMBLED AND YOUR FUTURE'S BLEAK!
BLEAK IS GOOD!
TRUTH BE TOLD, I'M TOO HOT FOR THIS CONTEST!
MY VERSE WARMS SOULS. ALL HAIL THE FLAME PRINCESS!!!
WOWSERS! THAT'S A WRAP LADIES AND GENTS!
OUR FINAL PRINCESS RAP BATTLE ROUND IS OVER!
scratch mix

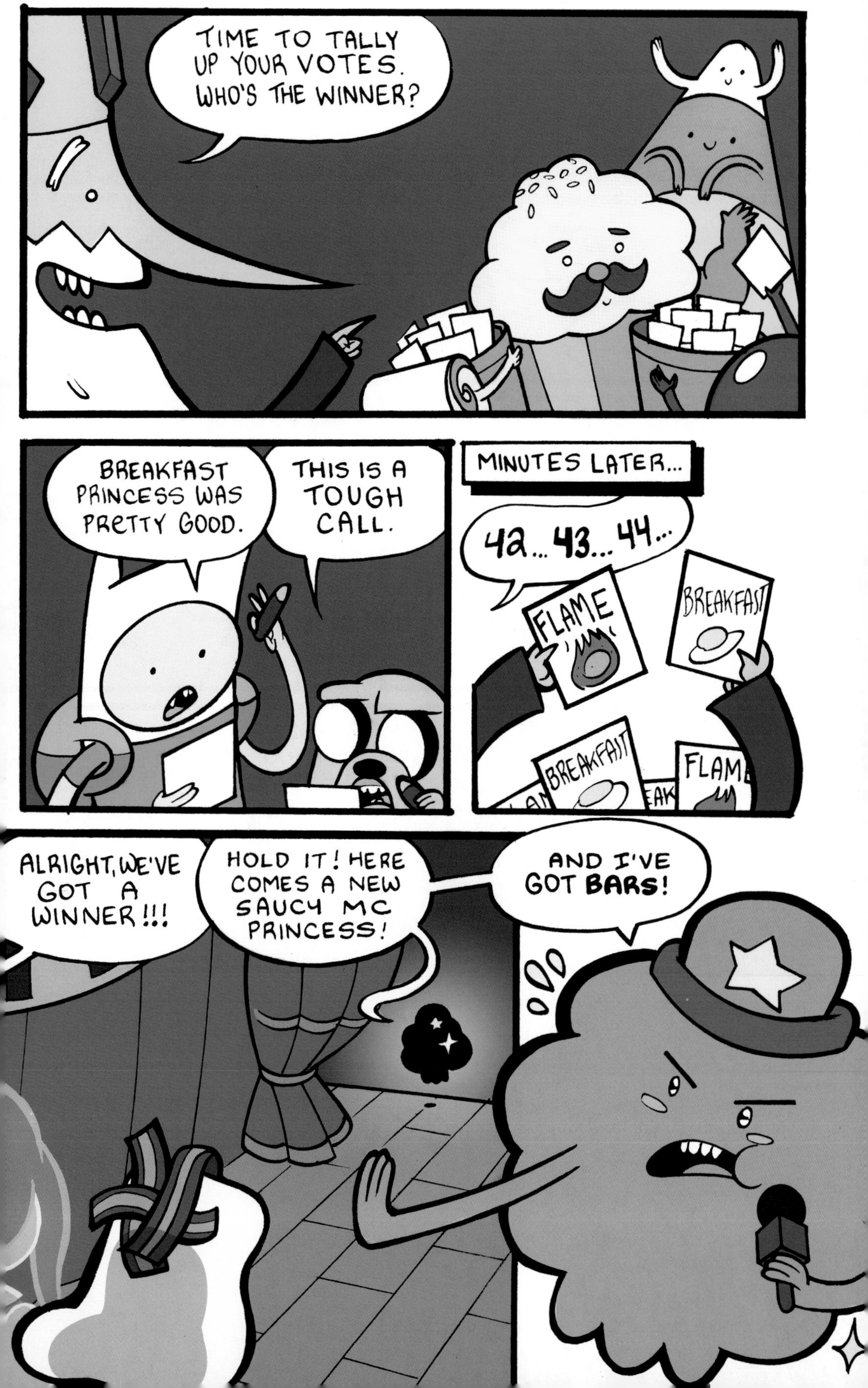
TIME TO TALLY UP YOUR VOTES. WHO'S THE WINNER?
BREAKFAST PRINCESS WAS PRETTY GOOD.
THIS IS A TOUGH CALL.
MINUTES LATER...
42... 43... 44...
FLAME
BREAKFAST
BREAKFAST
FLAME
ALRIGHT, WE'VE GOT A WINNER!!!
HOLD IT! HERE COMES A NEW SAUCY MC PRINCESS!
AND I'VE GOT **BARS**!

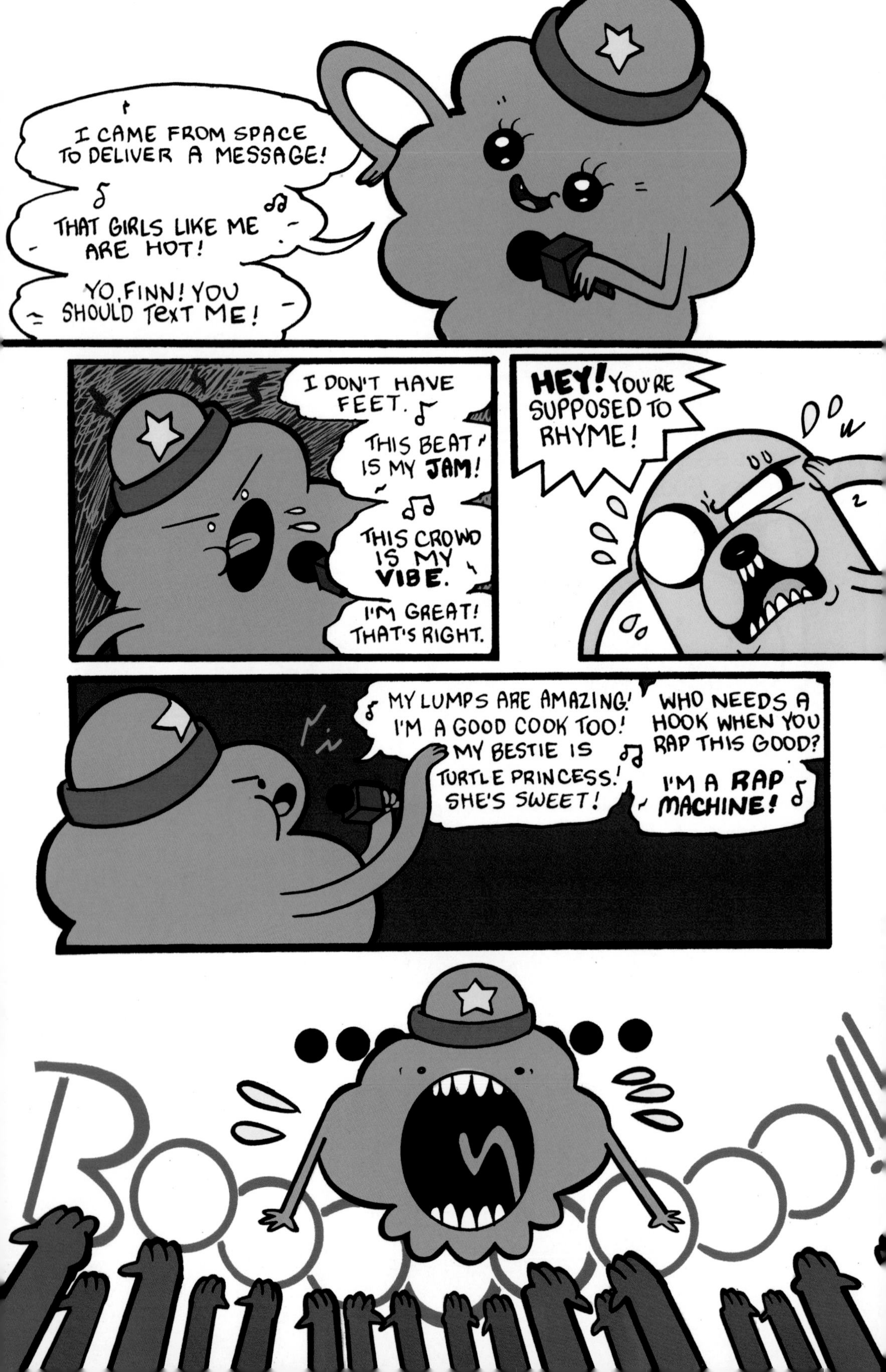
I CAME FROM SPACE TO DELIVER A MESSAGE!
THAT GIRLS LIKE ME ARE HOT!
YO, FINN! YOU SHOULD TEXT ME!
I DON'T HAVE FEET.
THIS BEAT IS MY JAM!
THIS CROWD IS MY VIBE.
I'M GREAT! THAT'S RIGHT.
HEY! YOU'RE SUPPOSED TO RHYME!
MY LUMPS ARE AMAZING! I'M A GOOD COOK TOO! MY BESTIE IS TURTLE PRINCESS! SHE'S SWEET!
WHO NEEDS A HOOK WHEN YOU RAP THIS GOOD?
I'M A RAP MACHINE!
BOOOOOOO!!

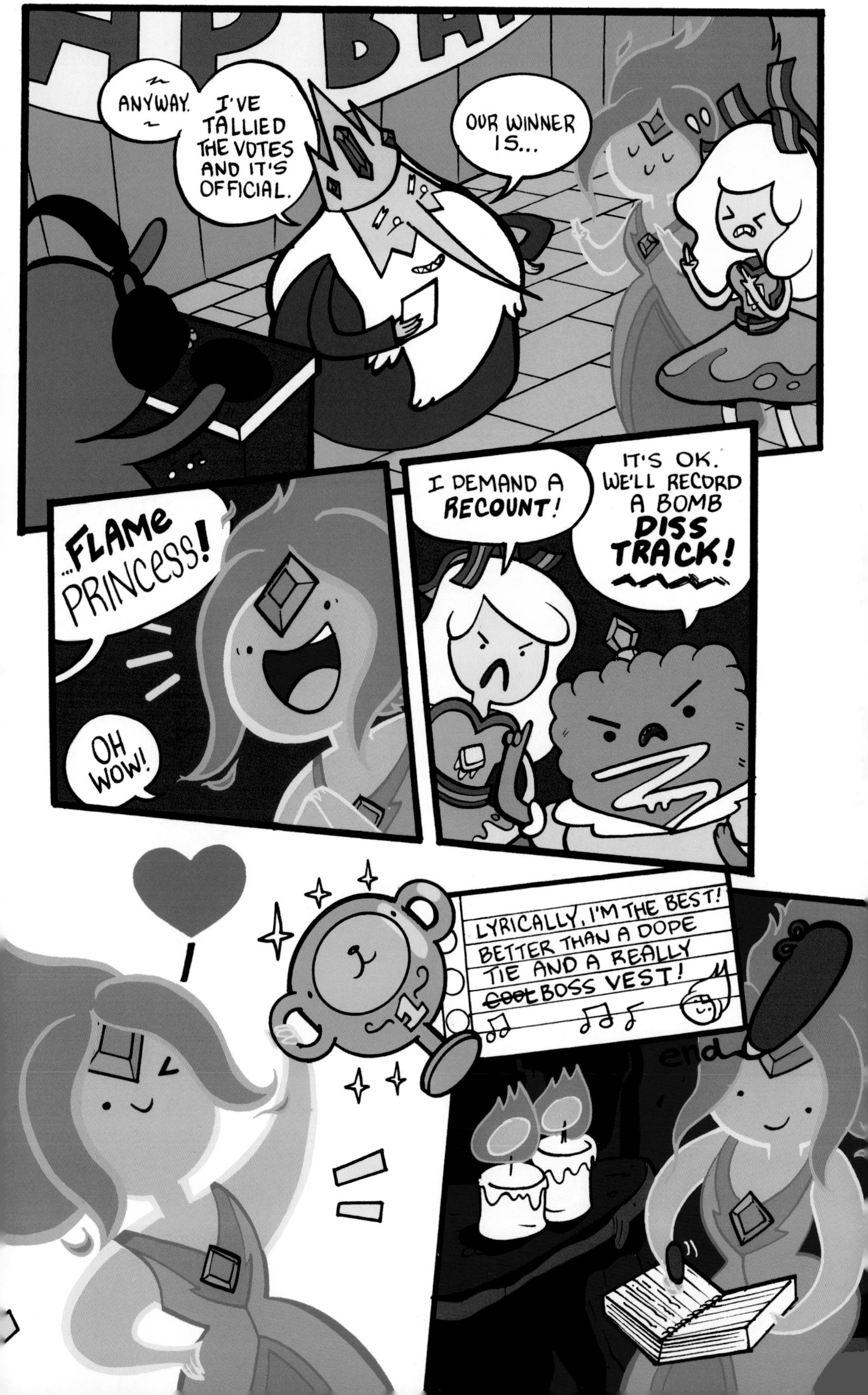
ANYWAY.
I'VE TALLIED THE VOTES AND IT'S OFFICIAL.
OUR WINNER IS...
...FLAME PRINCESS!
OH WOW!
I DEMAND A RECOUNT!
IT'S OK. WE'LL RECORD A BOMB DISS TRACK!
LYRICALLY, I'M THE BEST! BETTER THAN A DOPE TIE AND A REALLY cool BOSS VEST!
end

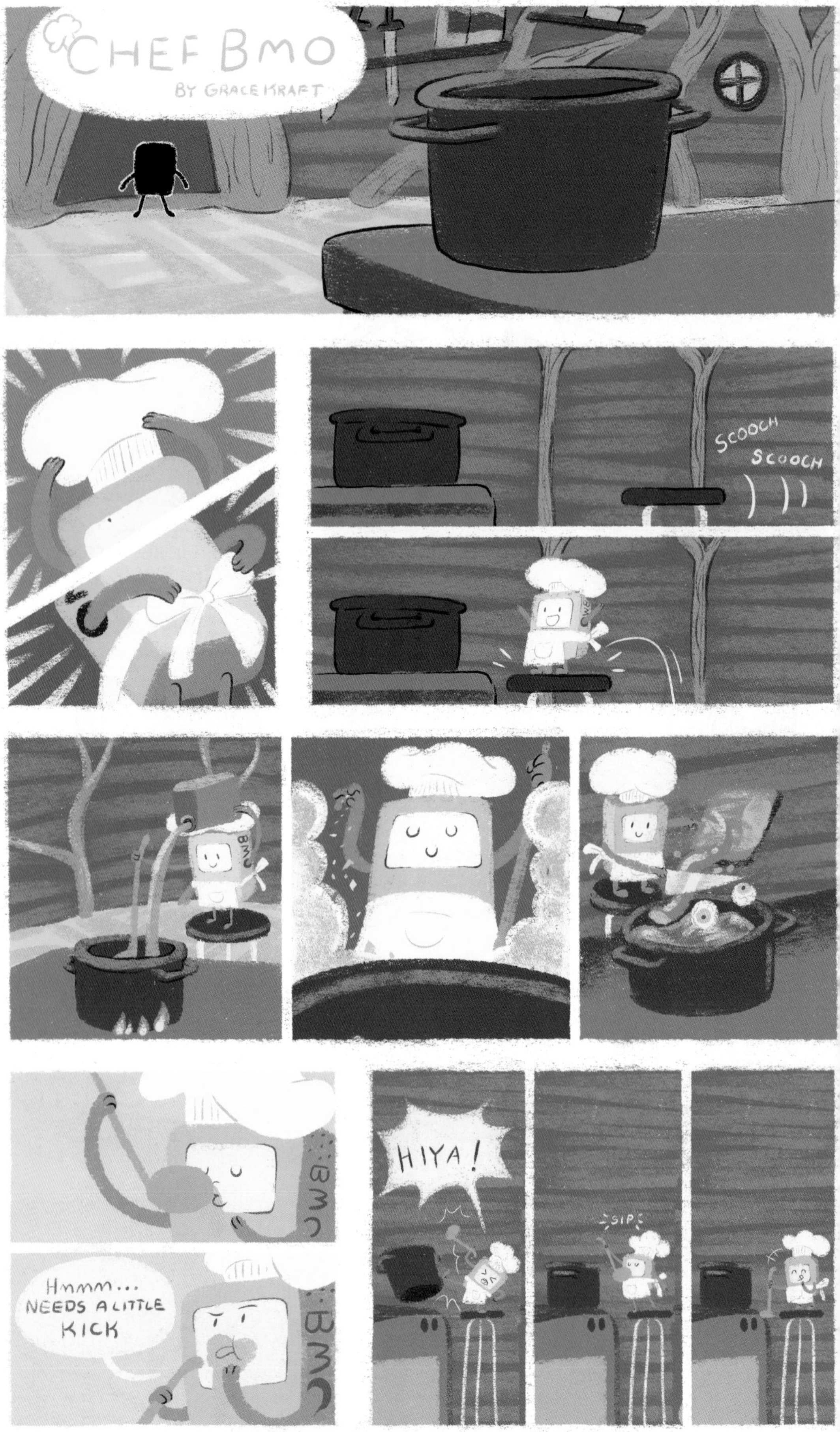
CHEF BMO
BY GRACE KRAFT
SCOOCH
SCOOCH
BMO
BMO
Hmmm... NEEDS A LITTLE KICK
HIYA!
SIP

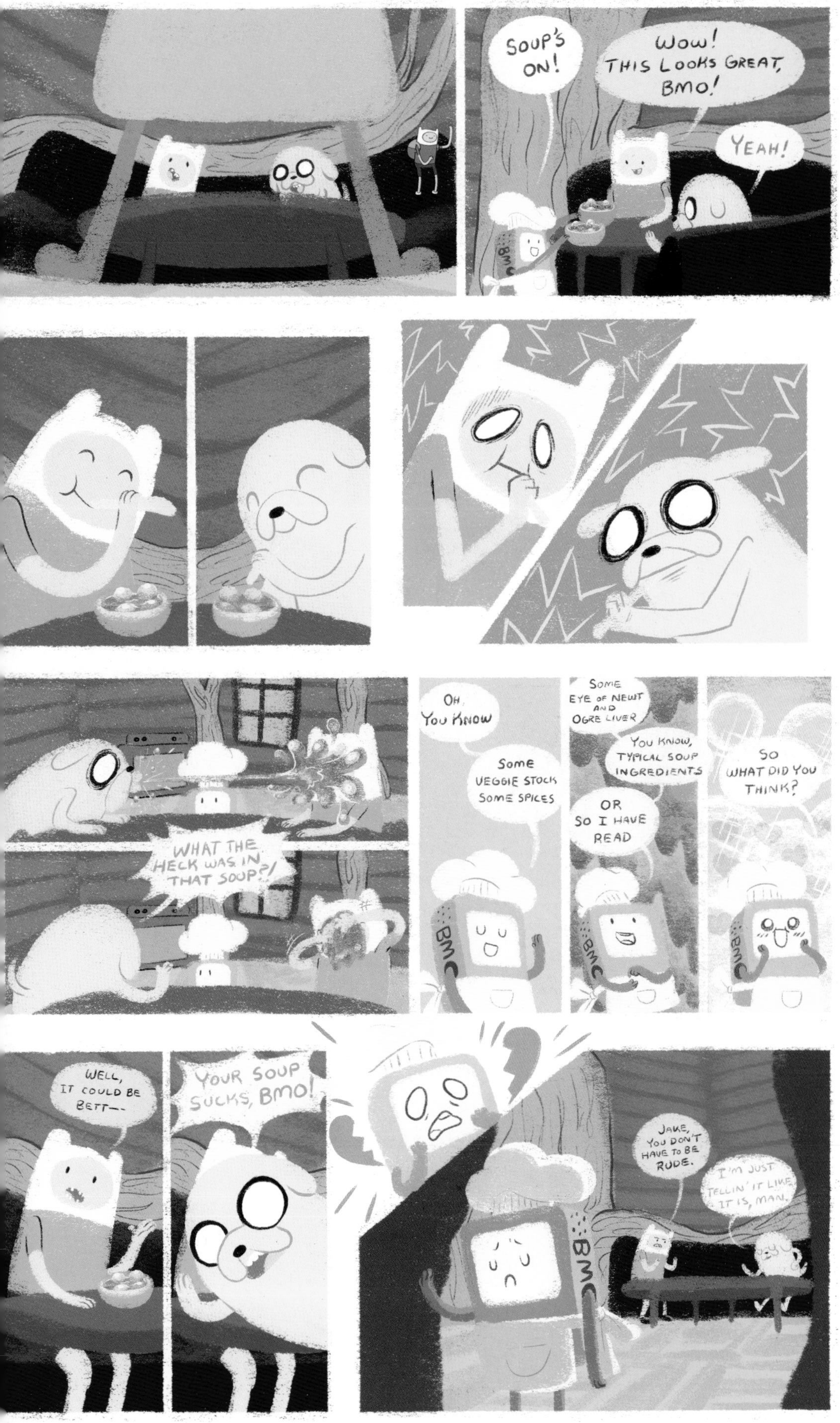

SOUP'S ON!
WOW! THIS LOOKS GREAT, BMO!
YEAH!
WHAT THE HECK WAS IN THAT SOUP?!
OH, YOU KNOW
SOME VEGGIE STOCK SOME SPICES
SOME EYE OF NEWT AND OGRE LIVER
YOU KNOW, TYPICAL SOUP INGREDIENTS
OR SO I HAVE READ
SO WHAT DID YOU THINK?
WELL, IT COULD BE BETT--
YOUR SOUP SUCKS, BMO!
JAKE, YOU DON'T HAVE TO BE RUDE.
I'M JUST TELLIN' IT LIKE IT IS, MAN.

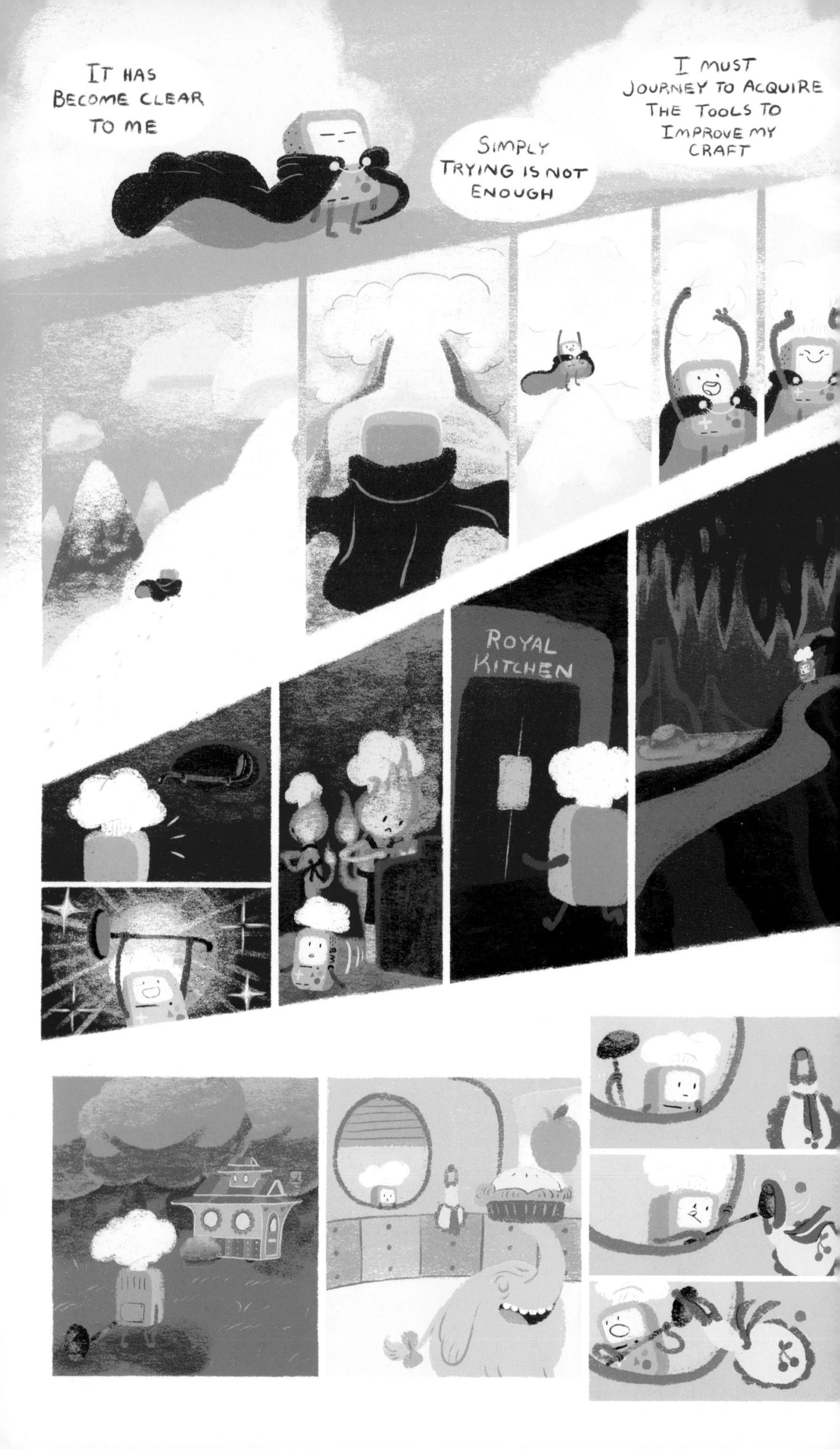
IT HAS BECOME CLEAR TO ME
SIMPLY TRYING IS NOT ENOUGH
I MUST JOURNEY TO ACQUIRE THE TOOLS TO IMPROVE MY CRAFT
ROYAL KITCHEN

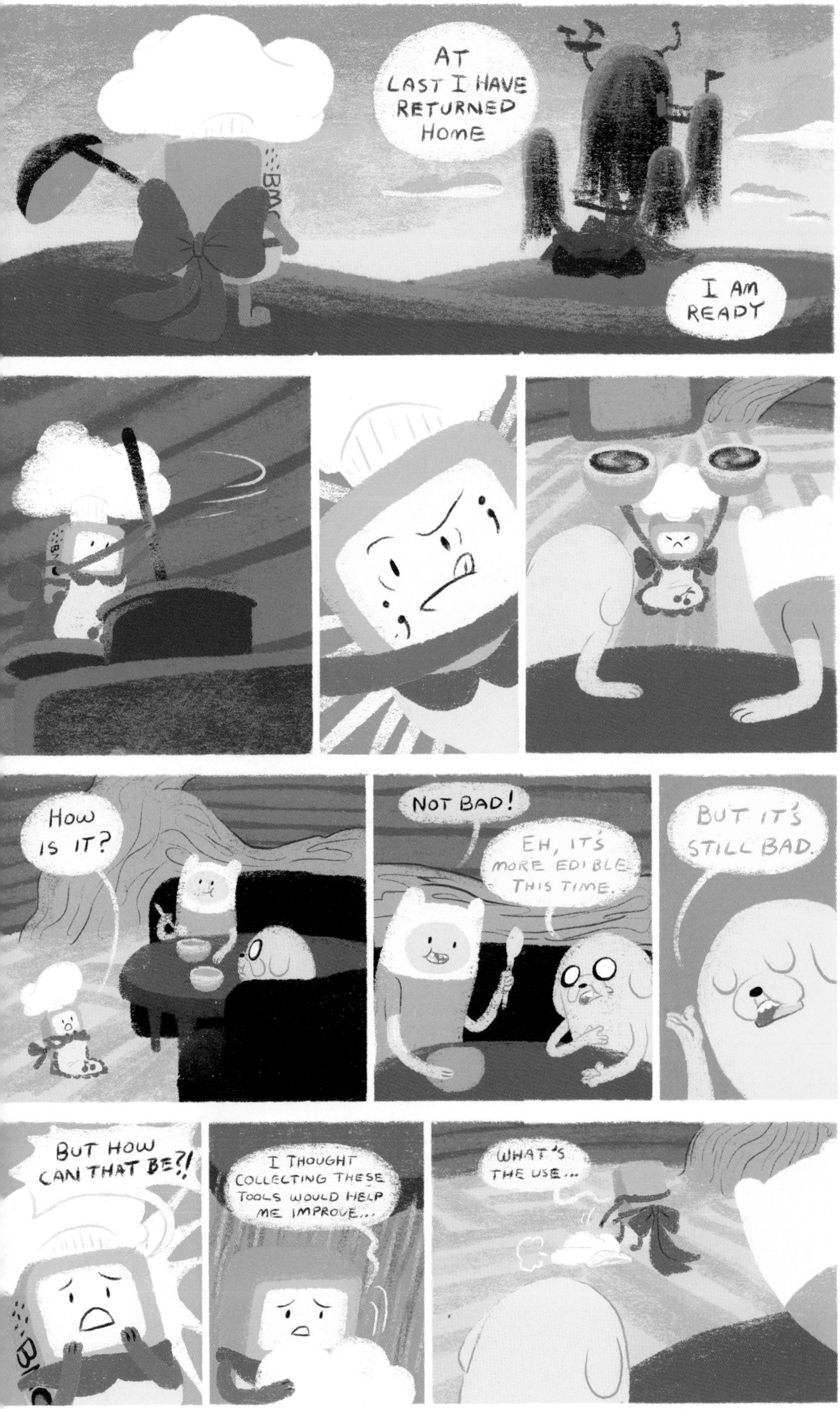
AT LAST I HAVE RETURNED HOME
BMO
I AM READY
BMO
HOW IS IT?
NOT BAD!
EH, IT'S MORE EDIBLE THIS TIME.
BUT IT'S STILL BAD.
BUT HOW CAN THAT BE?!
I THOUGHT COLLECTING THESE TOOLS WOULD HELP ME IMPROVE...
WHAT'S THE USE...

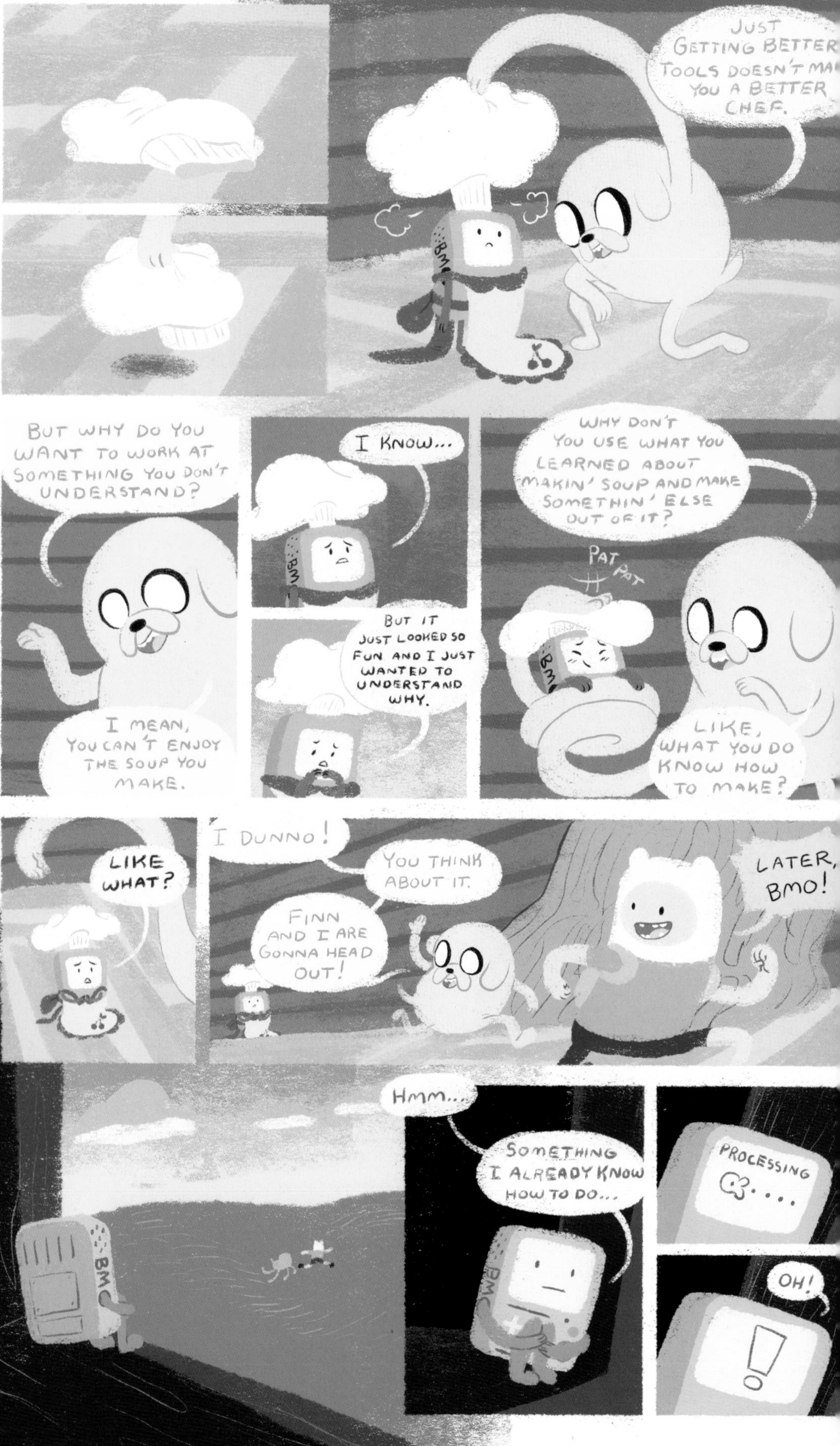

JUST GETTING BETTER TOOLS DOESN'T MA[KE] YOU A BETTER CHEF.
BUT WHY DO YOU WANT TO WORK AT SOMETHING YOU DON'T UNDERSTAND?
I MEAN, YOU CAN'T ENJOY THE SOUP YOU MAKE.
I KNOW...
BUT IT JUST LOOKED SO FUN AND I JUST WANTED TO UNDERSTAND WHY.
WHY DON'T YOU USE WHAT YOU LEARNED ABOUT MAKIN' SOUP AND MAKE SOMETHIN' ELSE OUT OF IT?
PAT PAT
LIKE, WHAT YOU DO KNOW HOW TO MAKE?
LIKE WHAT?
I DUNNO!
YOU THINK ABOUT IT.
FINN AND I ARE GONNA HEAD OUT!
LATER, BMO!
HMM...
SOMETHING I ALREADY KNOW HOW TO DO...
PROCESSING
OH!
!

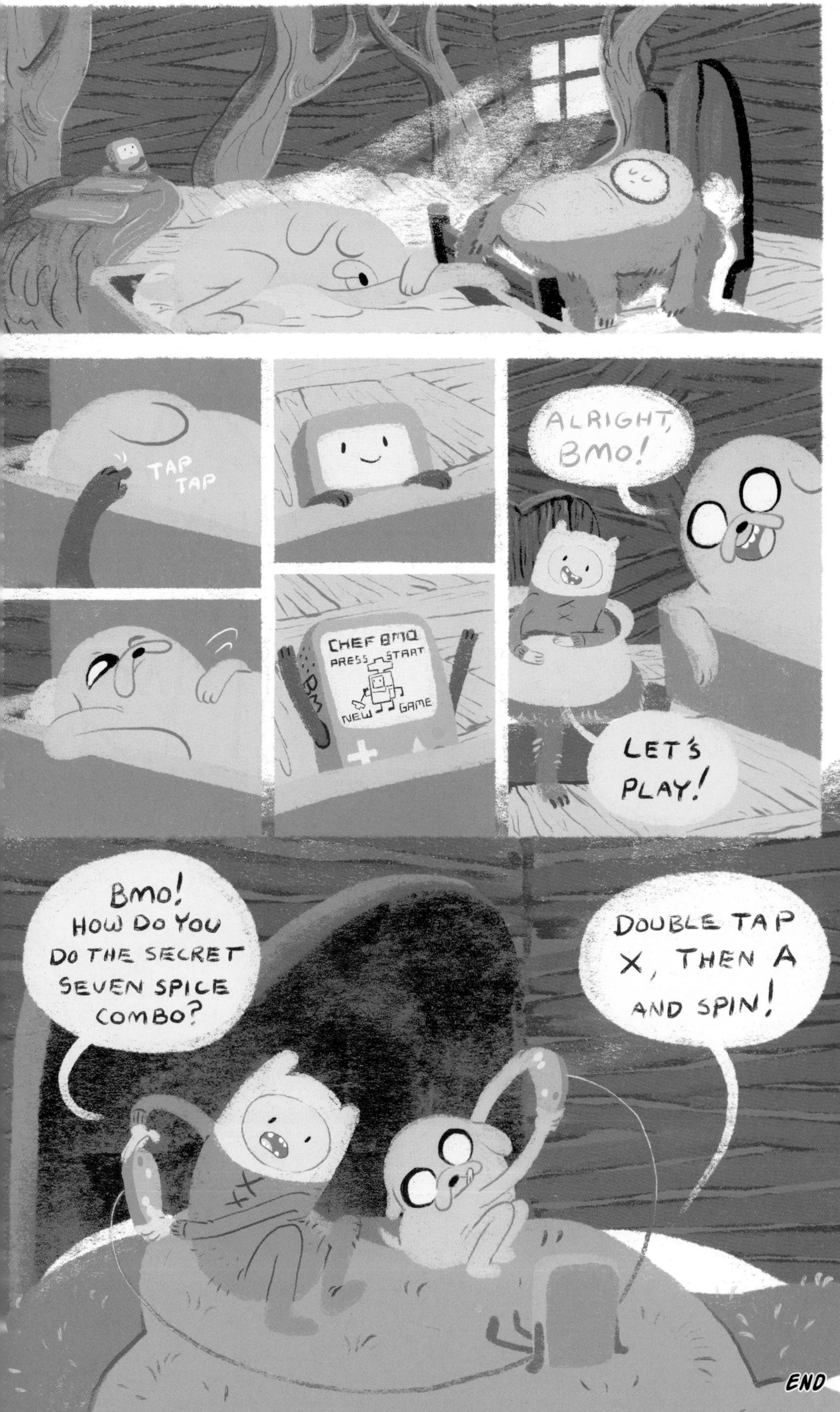
TAP TAP
CHEF BMO
PRESS START
NEW GAME
BMO
ALRIGHT, BMO!
LET'S PLAY!
BMO! HOW DO YOU DO THE SECRET SEVEN SPICE COMBO?
DOUBLE TAP X, THEN A AND SPIN!
END

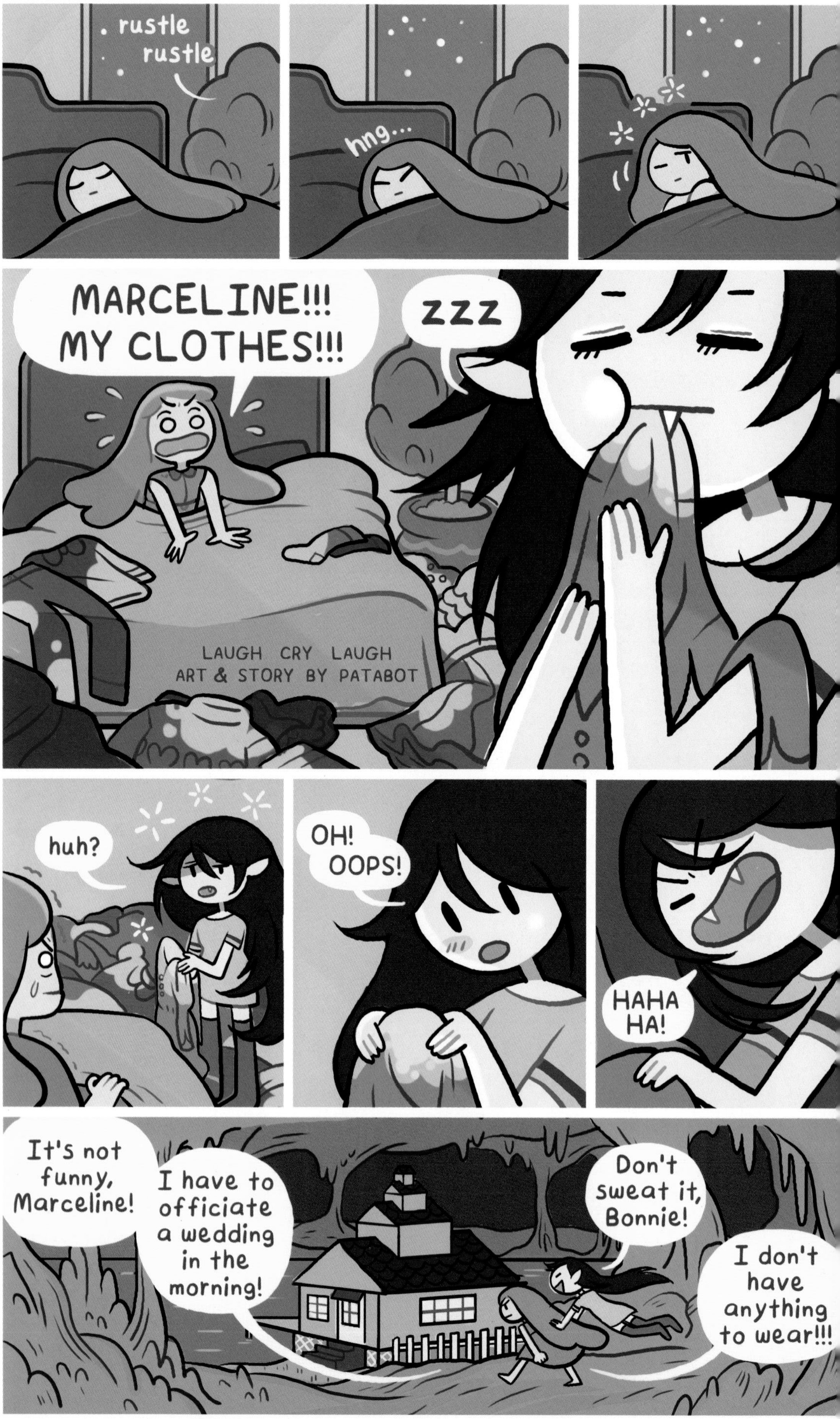
rustle
rustle
hng...
MARCELINE!!! MY CLOTHES!!!
ZZZ
LAUGH CRY LAUGH
ART & STORY BY PATABOT
huh?
OH! OOPS!
HAHA HA!
It's not funny, Marceline!
I have to officiate a wedding in the morning!
Don't sweat it, Bonnie!
I don't have anything to wear!!!

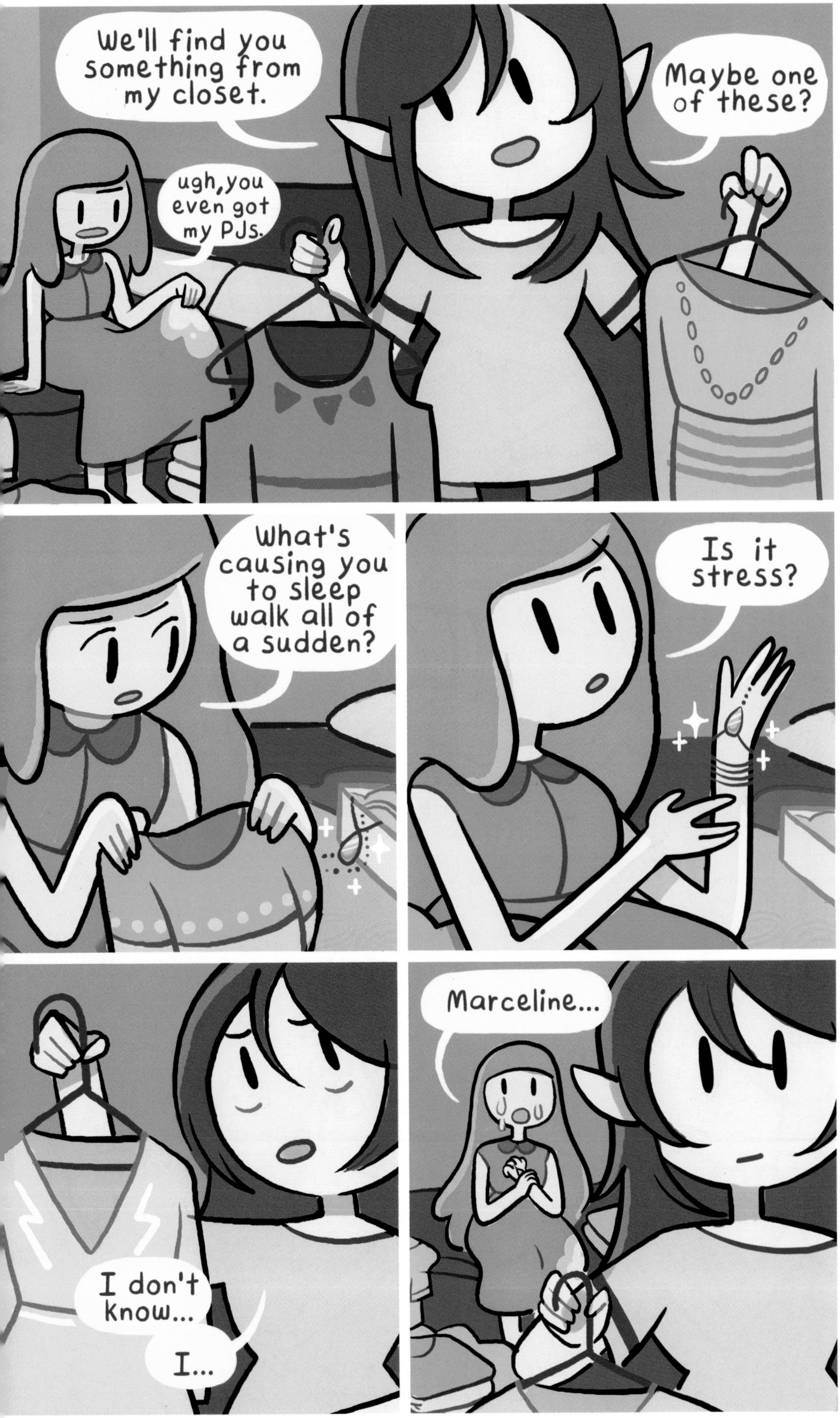
We'll find you something from my closet.
ugh,you even got my PJs.
Maybe one of these?
What's causing you to sleep walk all of a sudden?
Is it stress?
I don't know...
I...
Marceline...

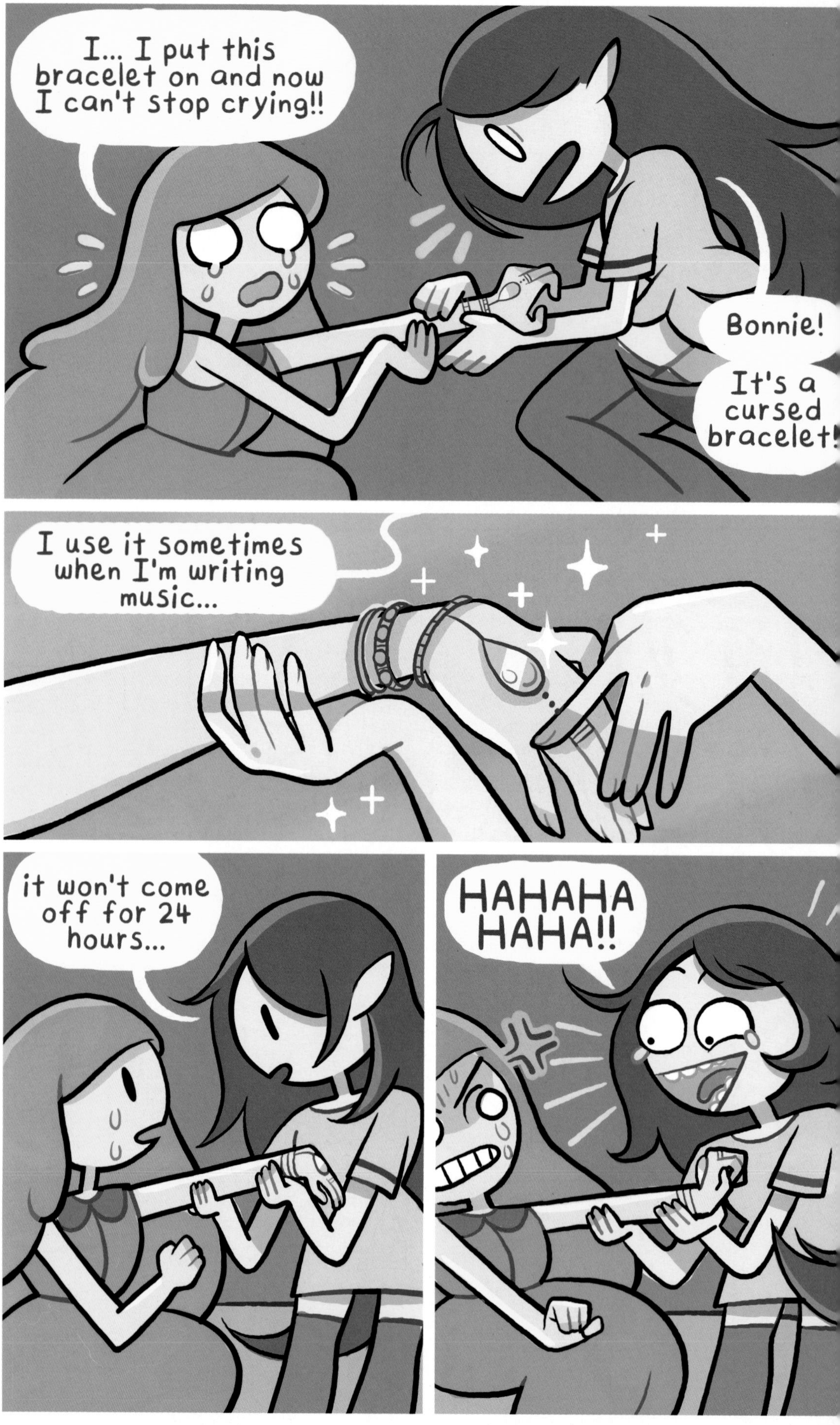
I... I put this bracelet on and now I can't stop crying!!
Bonnie!
It's a cursed bracelet!
I use it sometimes when I'm writing music...
it won't come off for 24 hours...
HAHAHA HAHA!!

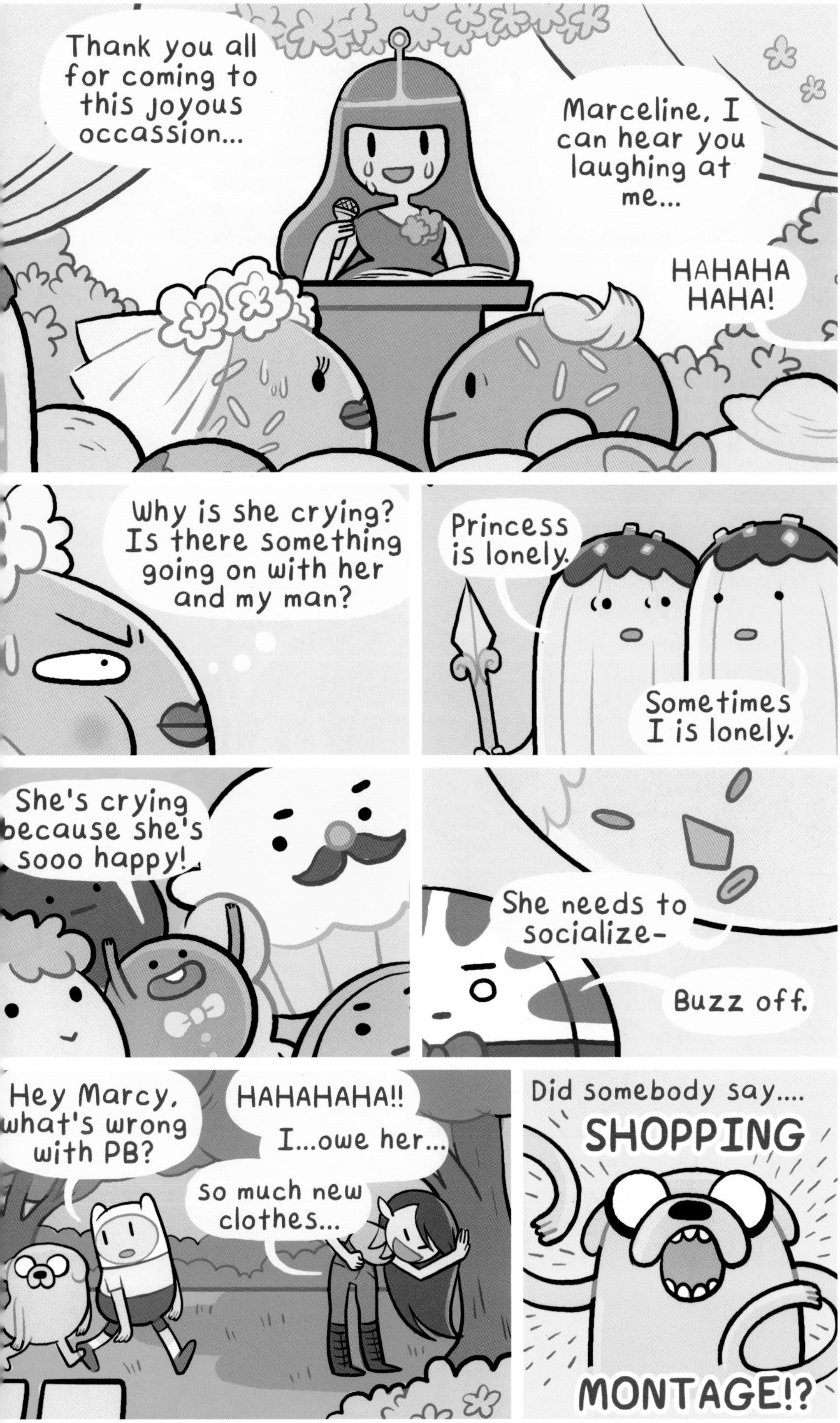
Thank you all for coming to this joyous occassion...
Marceline, I can hear you laughing at me...
HAHAHA HAHA!
Why is she crying? Is there something going on with her and my man?
Princess is lonely.
Sometimes I is lonely.
She's crying because she's sooo happy!
She needs to socialize-
Buzz off.
Hey Marcy, what's wrong with PB?
HAHAHAHA!!
I...owe her...
so much new clothes...
Did somebody say....
SHOPPING
MONTAGE!?

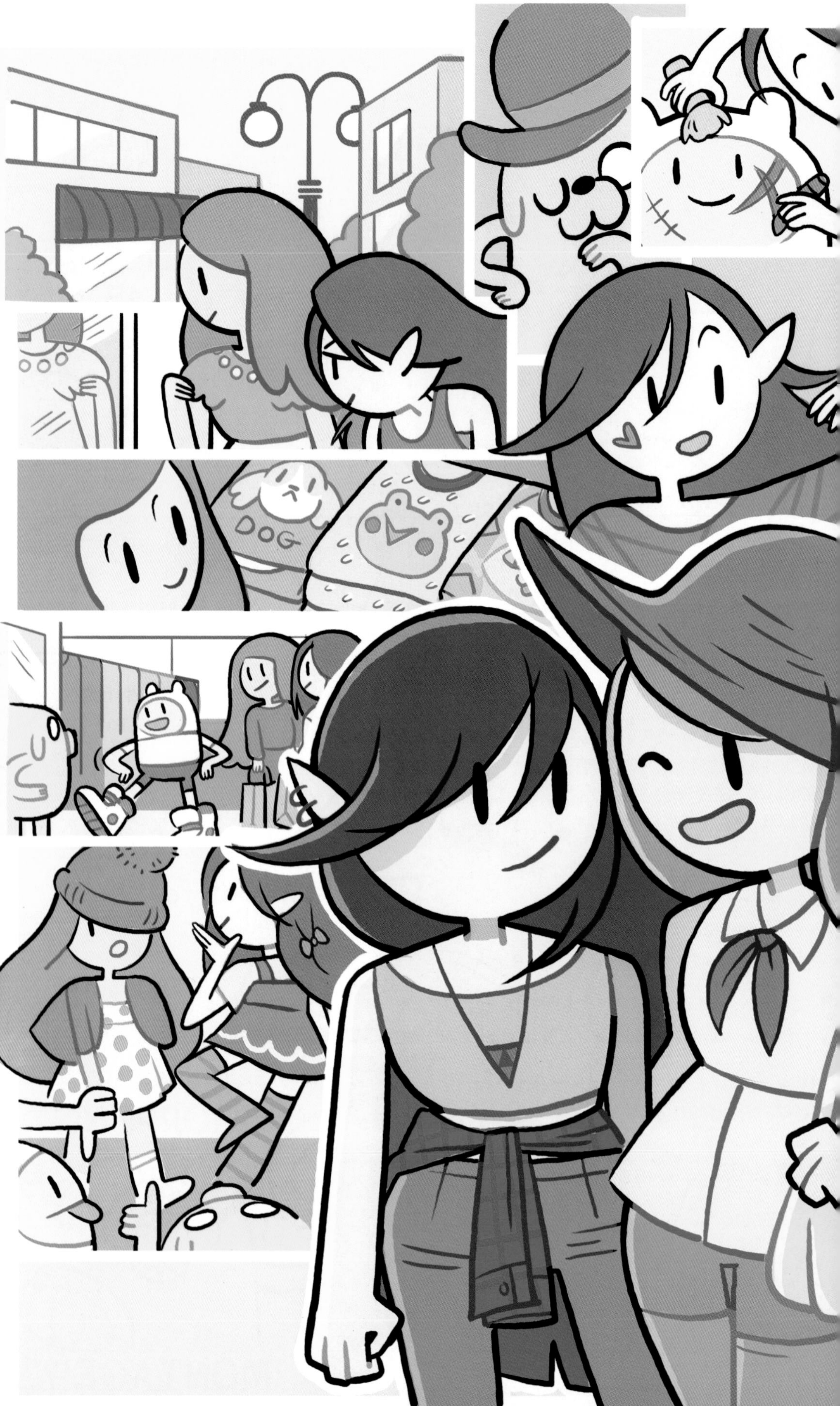
DOG

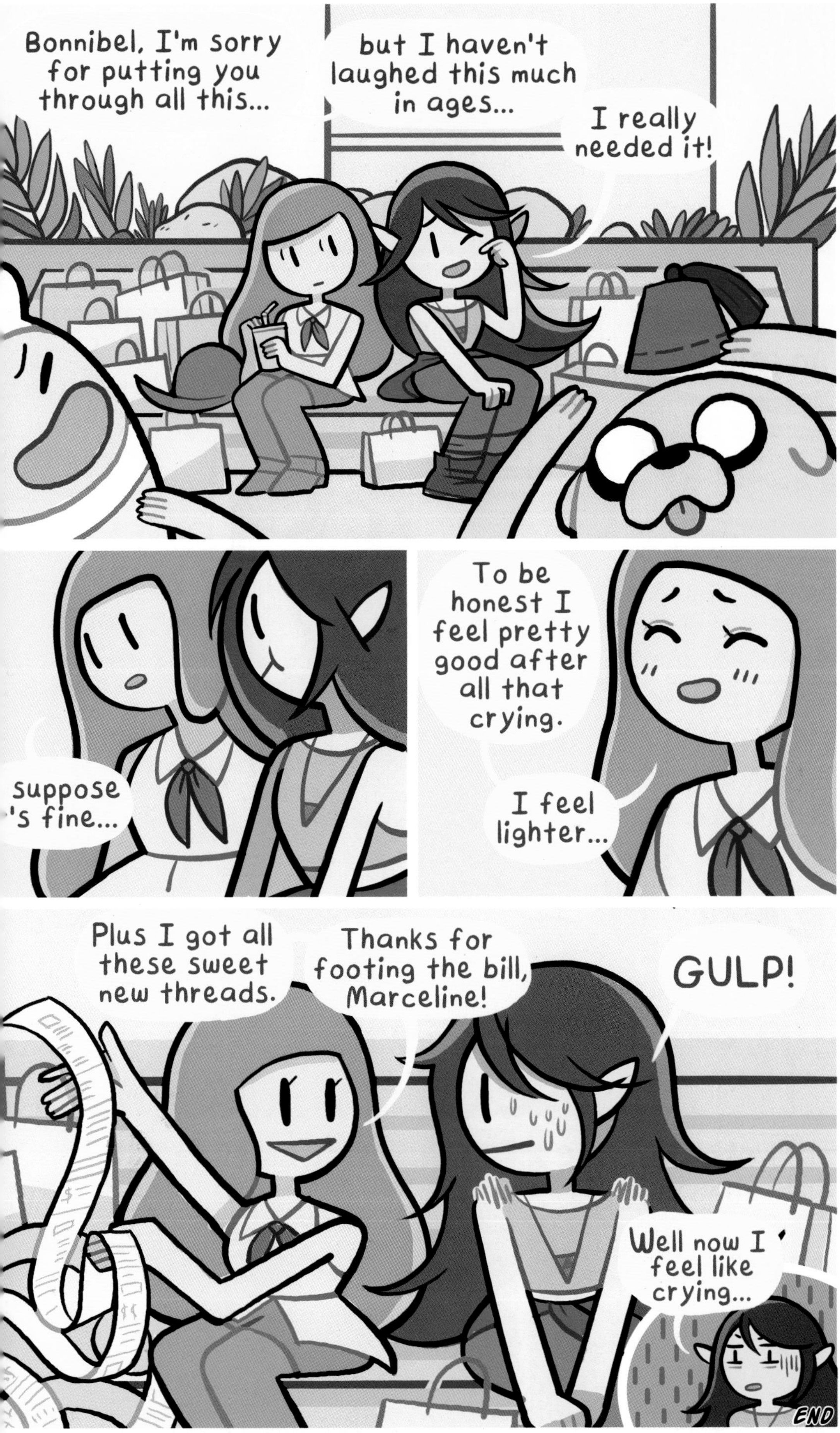
Bonnibel, I'm sorry for putting you through all this...
but I haven't laughed this much in ages...
I really needed it!
suppose 's fine...
To be honest I feel pretty good after all that crying.
I feel lighter...
Plus I got all these sweet new threads.
Thanks for footing the bill, Marceline!
GULP!
Well now I feel like crying...
END

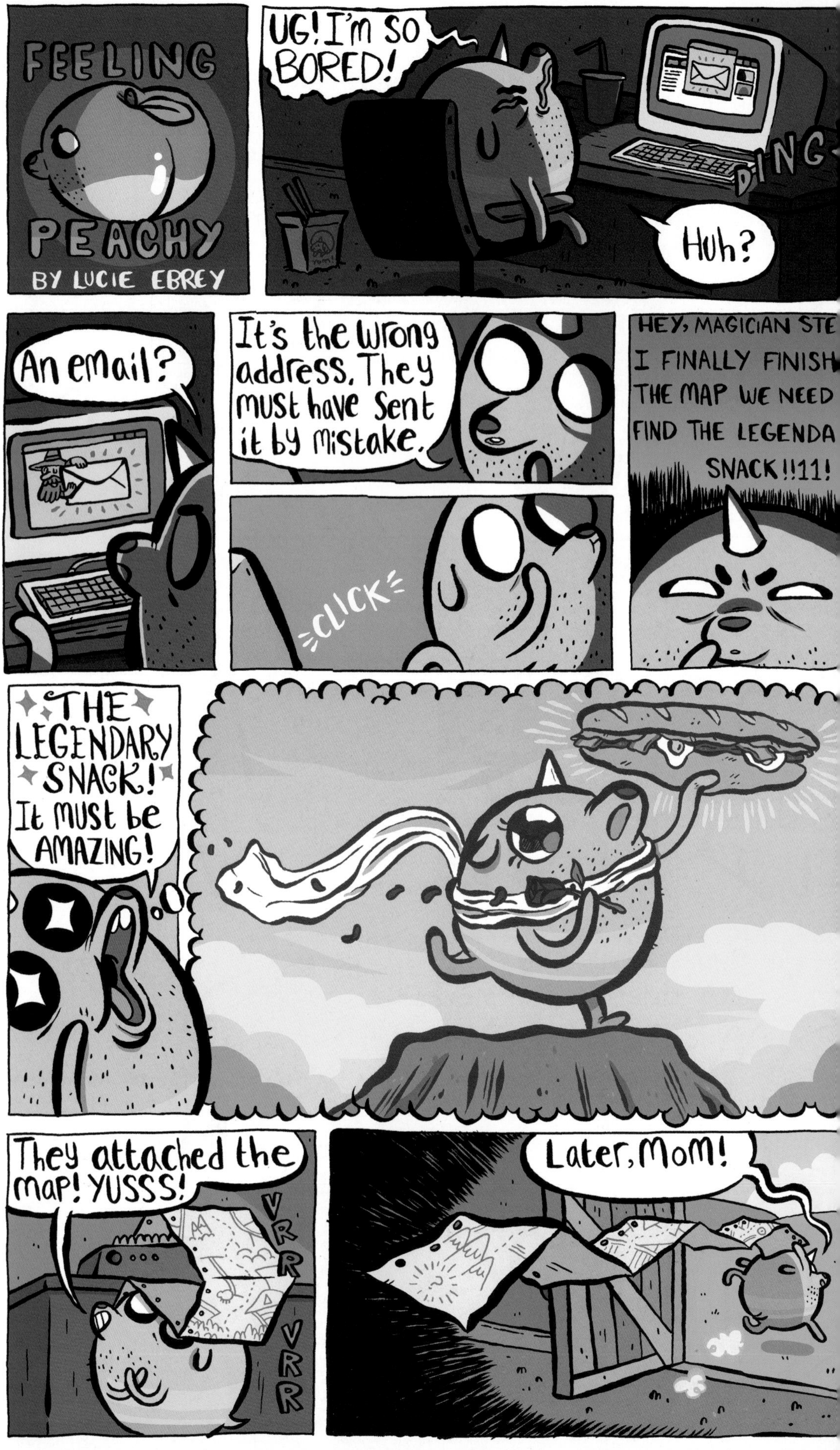
FEELING PEACHY
BY LUCIE EBREY
UG! I'm SO BORED!
DING
Huh?
An email?
It's the wrong address. They must have sent it by mistake.
HEY, MAGICIAN STE
I FINALLY FINISH
THE MAP WE NEED
FIND THE LEGENDA
SNACK!!11!
CLICK
THE LEGENDARY SNACK! It must be AMAZING!
They attached the map! YUSSS!
VRR
VRR
Later, Mom!

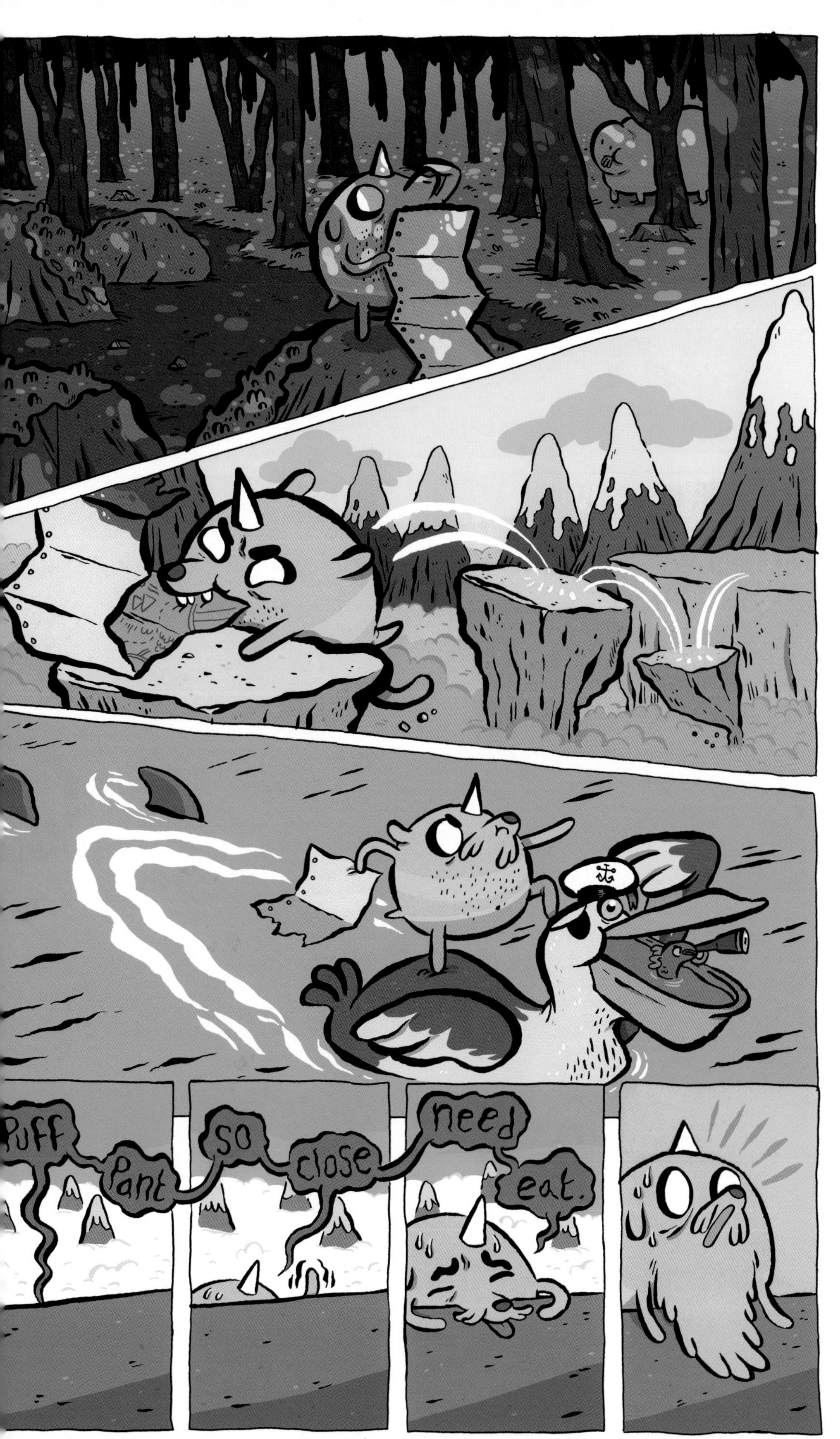

Puff
Pant
so
close
need
eat.

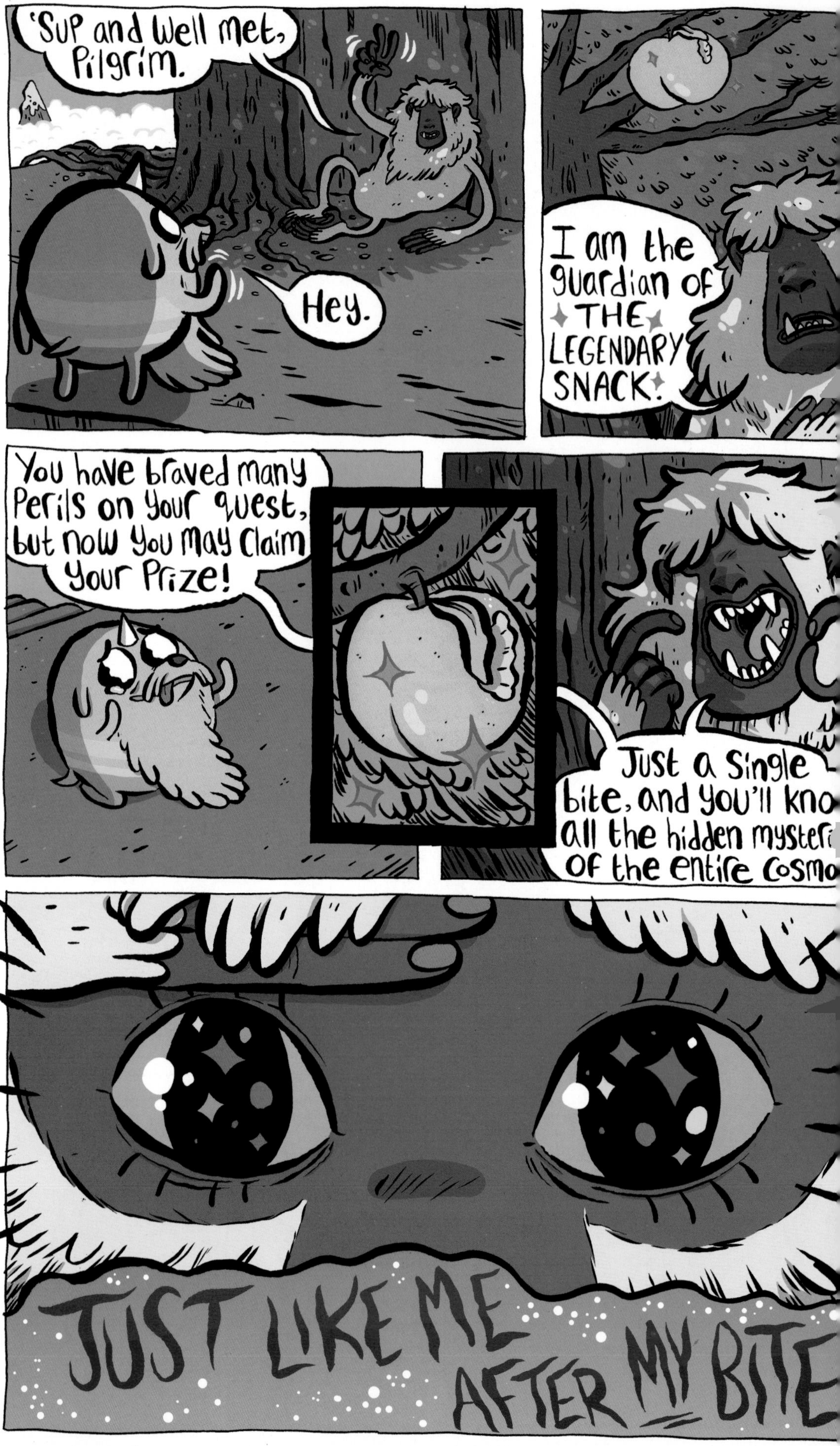
'Sup and Well met, Pilgrim.
Hey.
I am the guardian of THE LEGENDARY SNACK!
You have braved many Perils on your quest, but now you may Claim your Prize!
Just a Single bite, and you'll kno
all the hidden mysteri
of the entire cosmo
JUST LIKE ME
AFTER MY BITE

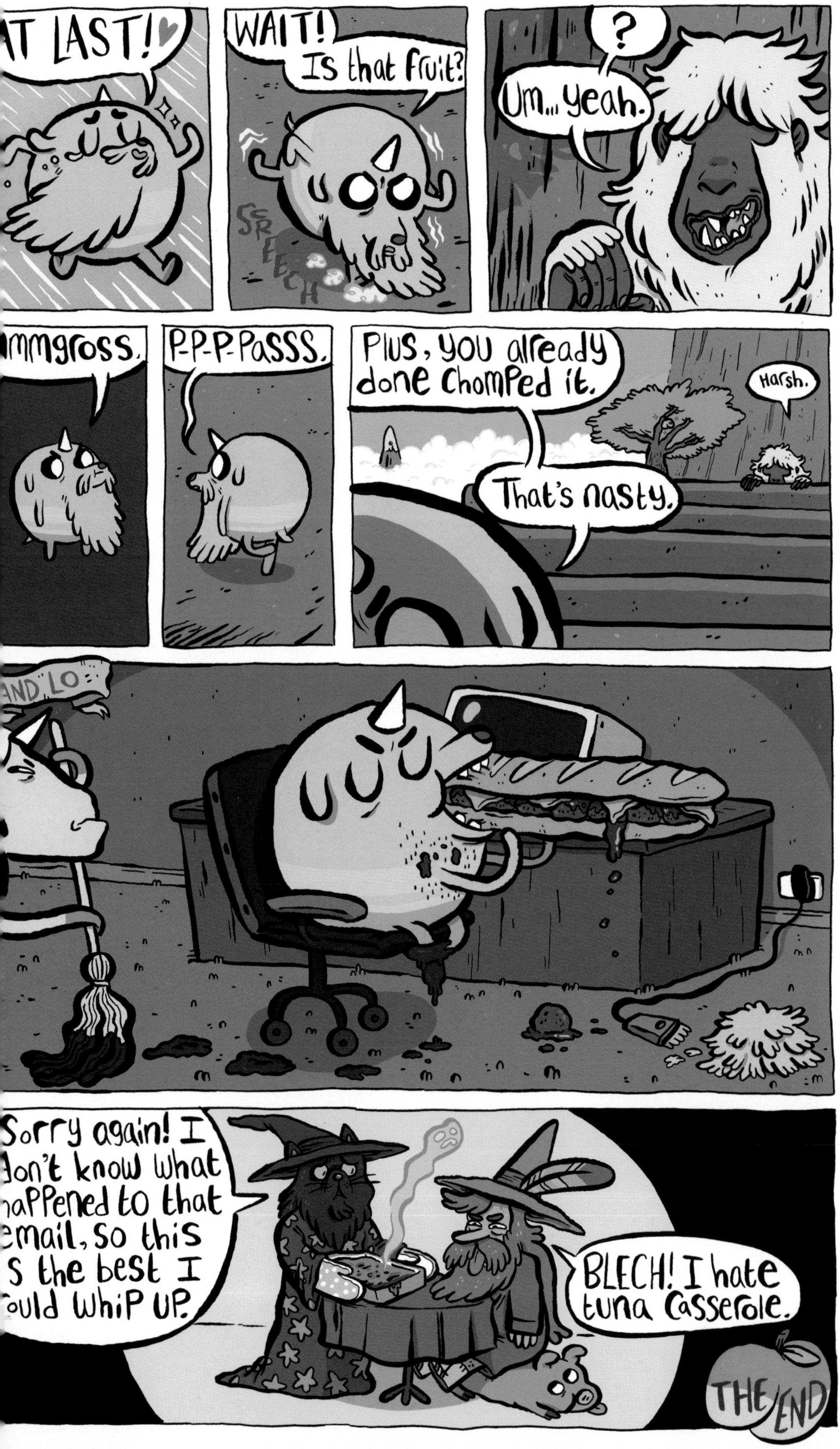
AT LAST!♥
WAIT! Is that fruit?
?
Um... yeah.
MMMgross.
P-P-P-PASSS.
SCREECH
Plus, you already done chomped it.
That's nasty.
Harsh.
AND LO
Sorry again! I don't know what happened to that email, so this is the best I could whip up.
BLECH! I hate tuna casserole.
THE END

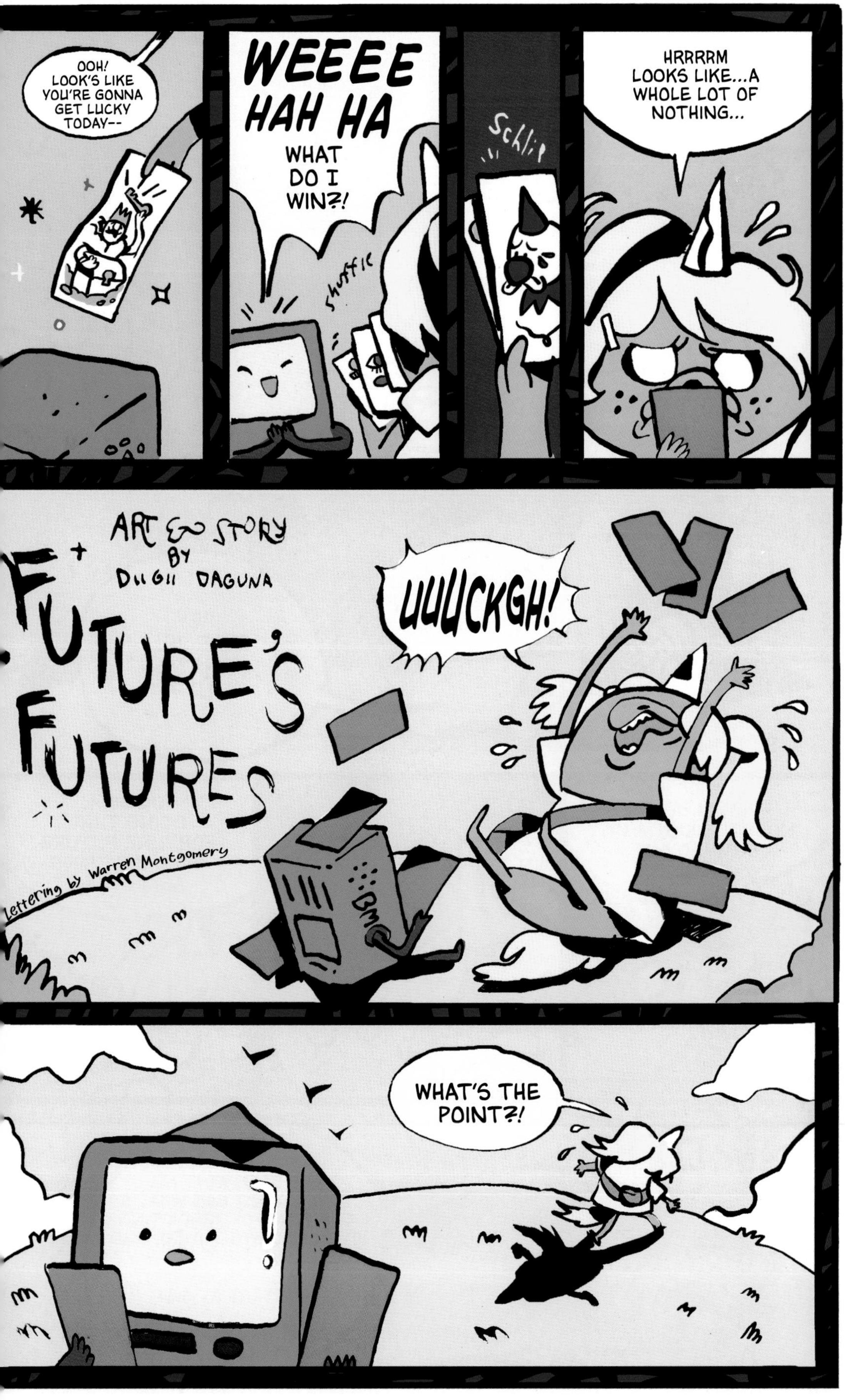
OOH! LOOK'S LIKE YOU'RE GONNA GET LUCKY TODAY--
WEEEE HAH HA
WHAT DO I WIN?!
shuffle
Schlip
HRRRRM LOOKS LIKE...A WHOLE LOT OF NOTHING...
ART & STORY BY DUGII DAGUNA
FUTURE'S FUTURES
Lettering by Warren Montgomery
UUUCKGH!
BMO
WHAT'S THE POINT?!

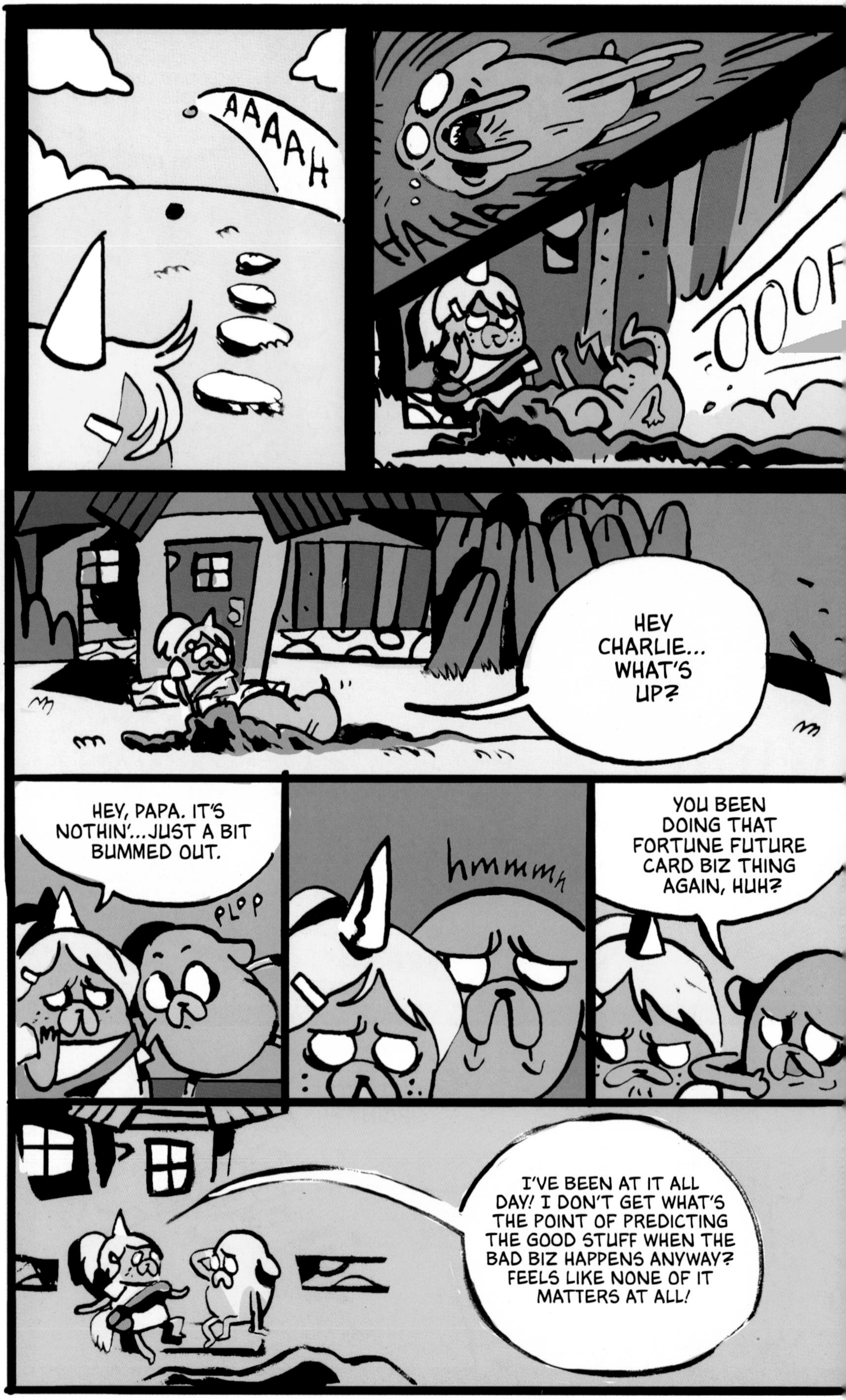
AAAAAH
AHHH
OOOF
HEY CHARLIE... WHAT'S UP?
HEY, PAPA. IT'S NOTHIN'...JUST A BIT BUMMED OUT.
PLOP
hmmmm
YOU BEEN DOING THAT FORTUNE FUTURE CARD BIZ THING AGAIN, HUH?
I'VE BEEN AT IT ALL DAY! I DON'T GET WHAT'S THE POINT OF PREDICTING THE GOOD STUFF WHEN THE BAD BIZ HAPPENS ANYWAY? FEELS LIKE NONE OF IT MATTERS AT ALL!

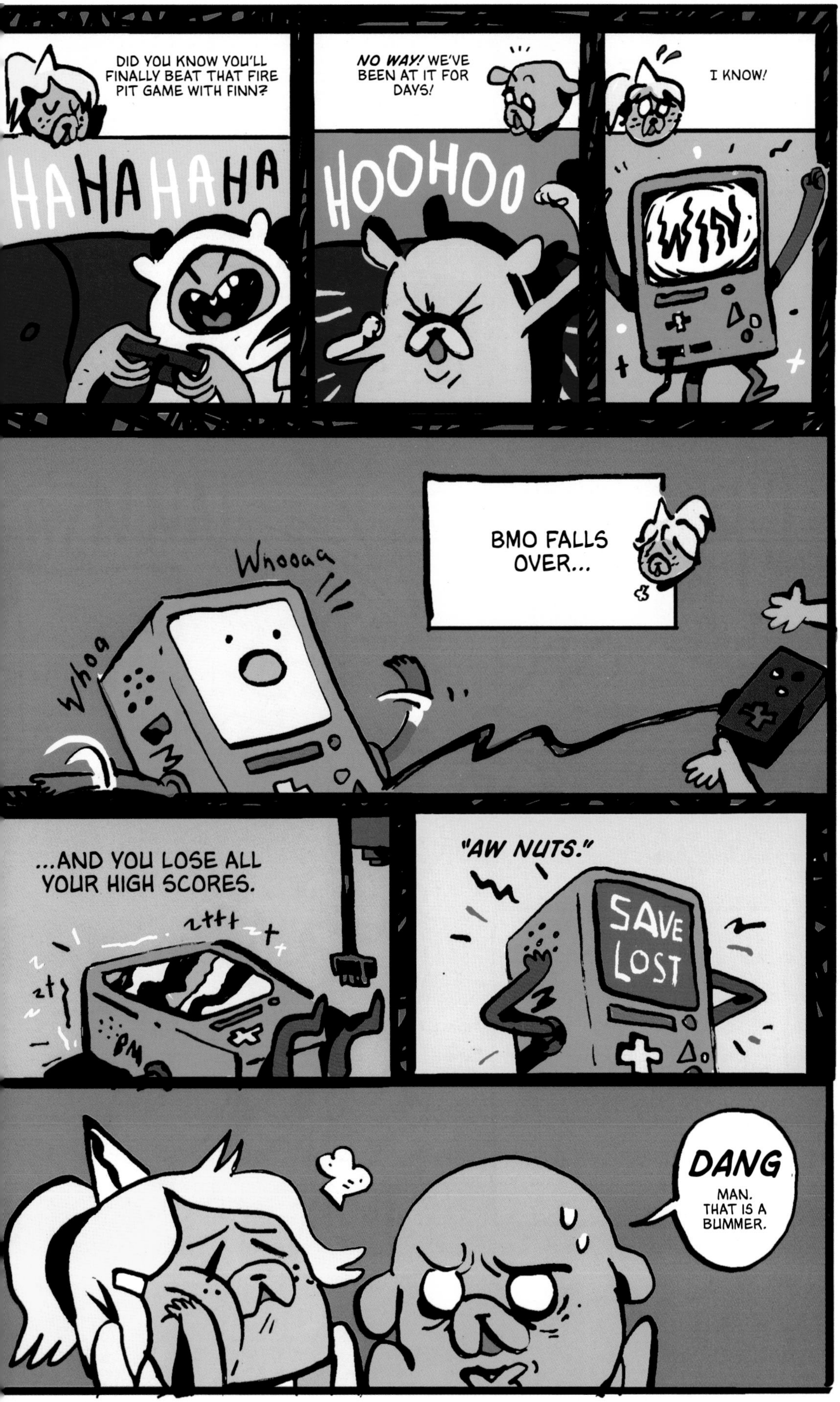
DID YOU KNOW YOU'LL FINALLY BEAT THAT FIRE PIT GAME WITH FINN?
HAHAHAHAHA
NO WAY! WE'VE BEEN AT IT FOR DAYS!
HOOHOO
I KNOW!
BMO FALLS OVER...
Whooaa
Whoa
...AND YOU LOSE ALL YOUR HIGH SCORES.
"AW NUTS."
SAVE LOST
DANG MAN. THAT IS A BUMMER.

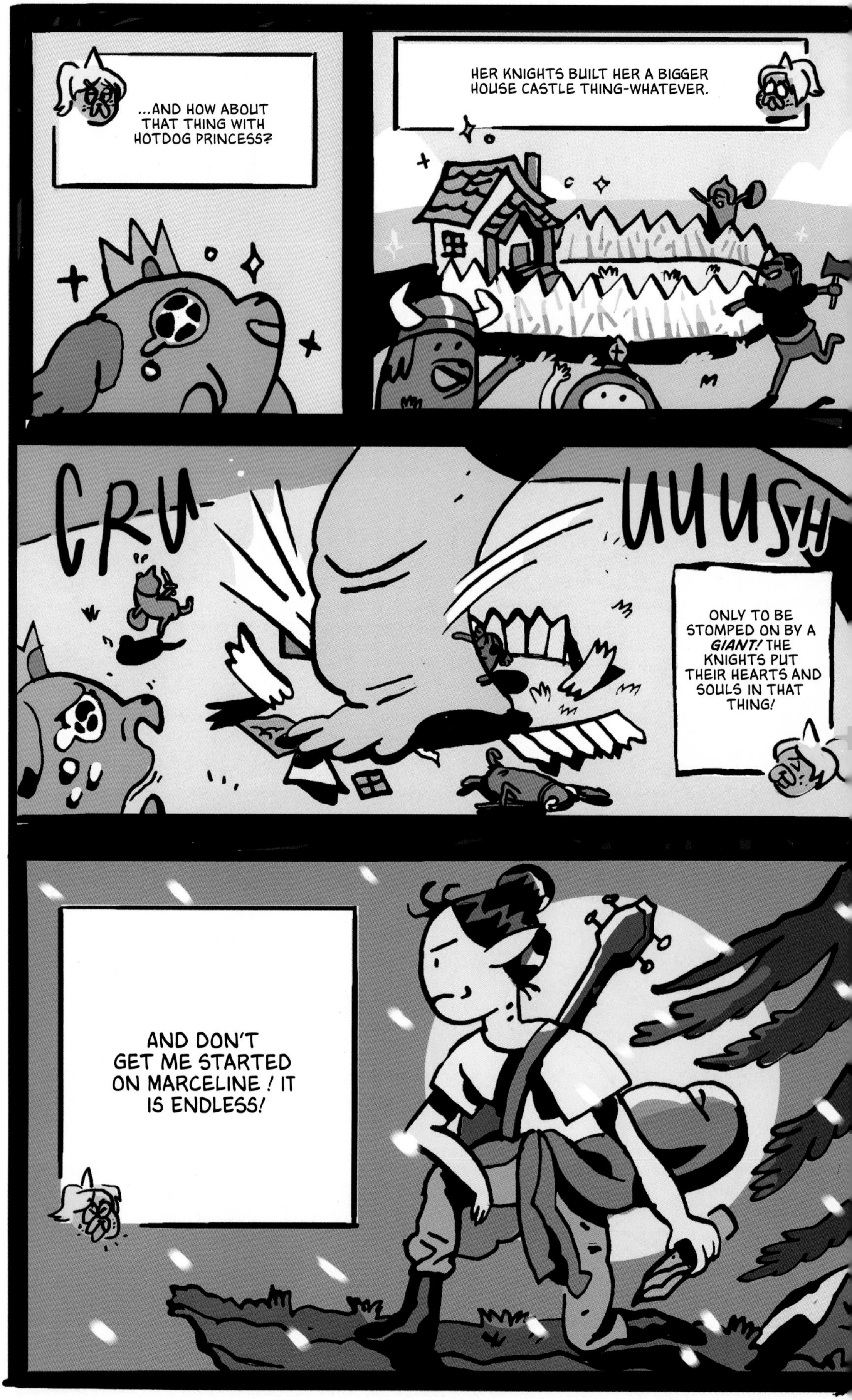
...AND HOW ABOUT THAT THING WITH HOTDOG PRINCESS?
HER KNIGHTS BUILT HER A BIGGER HOUSE CASTLE THING-WHATEVER.
CRU
UUUSH
ONLY TO BE STOMPED ON BY A GIANT! THE KNIGHTS PUT THEIR HEARTS AND SOULS IN THAT THING!
AND DON'T GET ME STARTED ON MARCELINE! IT IS ENDLESS!

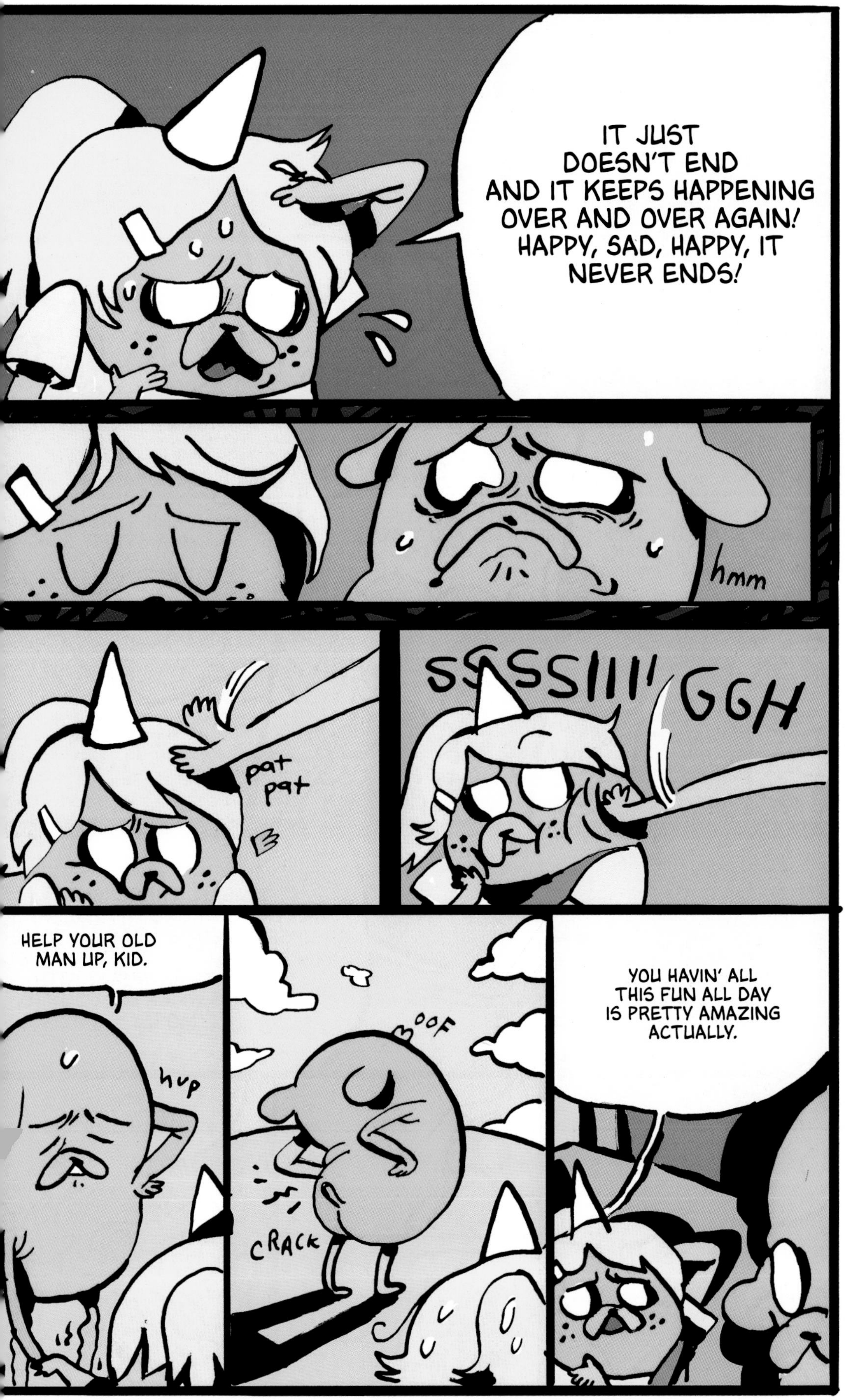
IT JUST DOESN'T END AND IT KEEPS HAPPENING OVER AND OVER AGAIN! HAPPY, SAD, HAPPY, IT NEVER ENDS!
hmm
pat pat
SSSSIII'GGH
HELP YOUR OLD MAN UP, KID.
hup
OOF
CRACK
YOU HAVIN' ALL THIS FUN ALL DAY IS PRETTY AMAZING ACTUALLY.

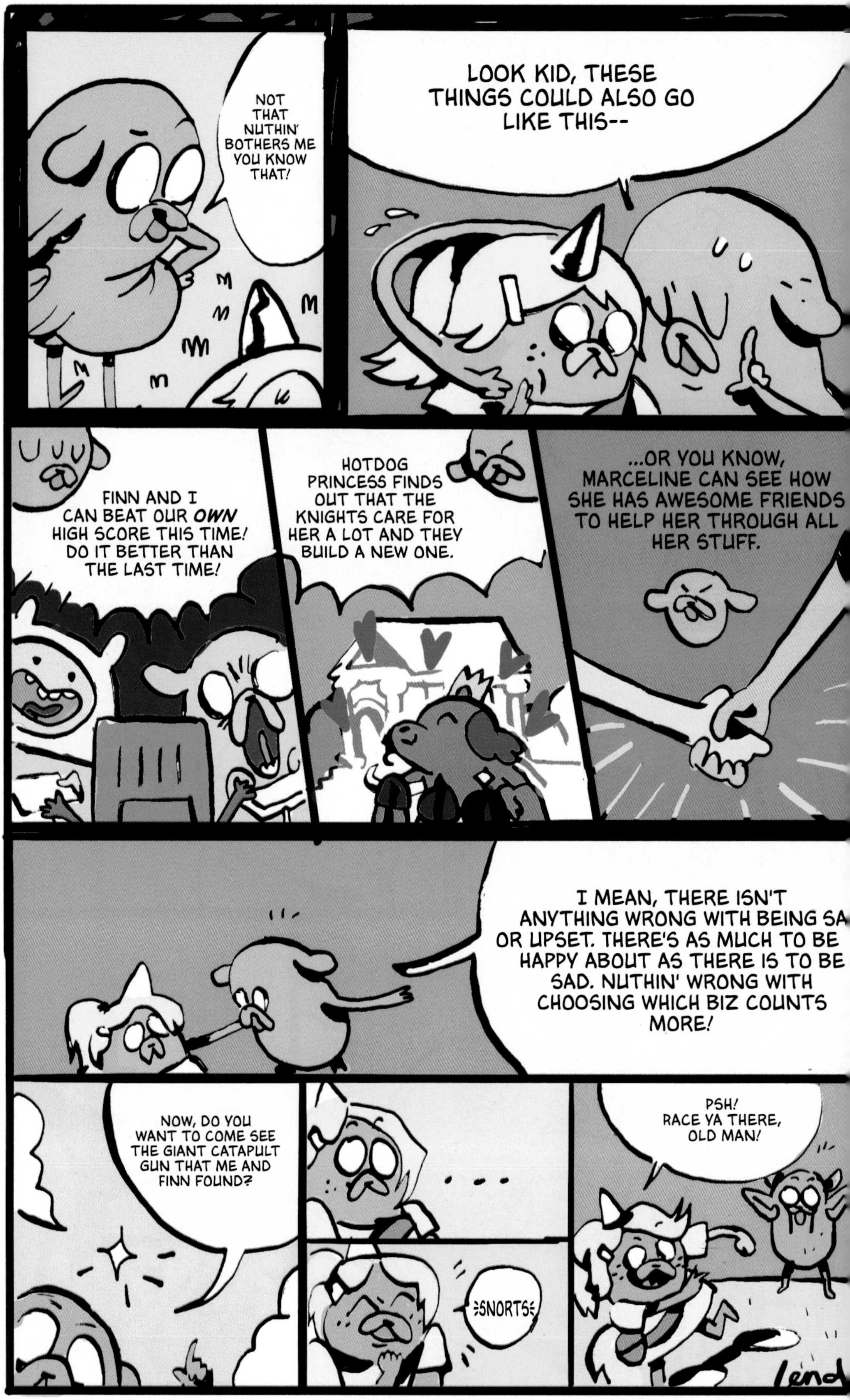
NOT THAT NUTHIN' BOTHERS ME YOU KNOW THAT!
LOOK KID, THESE THINGS COULD ALSO GO LIKE THIS--
FINN AND I CAN BEAT OUR *OWN* HIGH SCORE THIS TIME! DO IT BETTER THAN THE LAST TIME!
HOTDOG PRINCESS FINDS OUT THAT THE KNIGHTS CARE FOR HER A LOT AND THEY BUILD A NEW ONE.
...OR YOU KNOW, MARCELINE CAN SEE HOW SHE HAS AWESOME FRIENDS TO HELP HER THROUGH ALL HER STUFF.
I MEAN, THERE ISN'T ANYTHING WRONG WITH BEING SA OR UPSET. THERE'S AS MUCH TO BE HAPPY ABOUT AS THERE IS TO BE SAD. NUTHIN' WRONG WITH CHOOSING WHICH BIZ COUNTS MORE!
NOW, DO YOU WANT TO COME SEE THE GIANT CATAPULT GUN THAT ME AND FINN FOUND?
. . .
SNORTS
PSH! RACE YA THERE, OLD MAN!

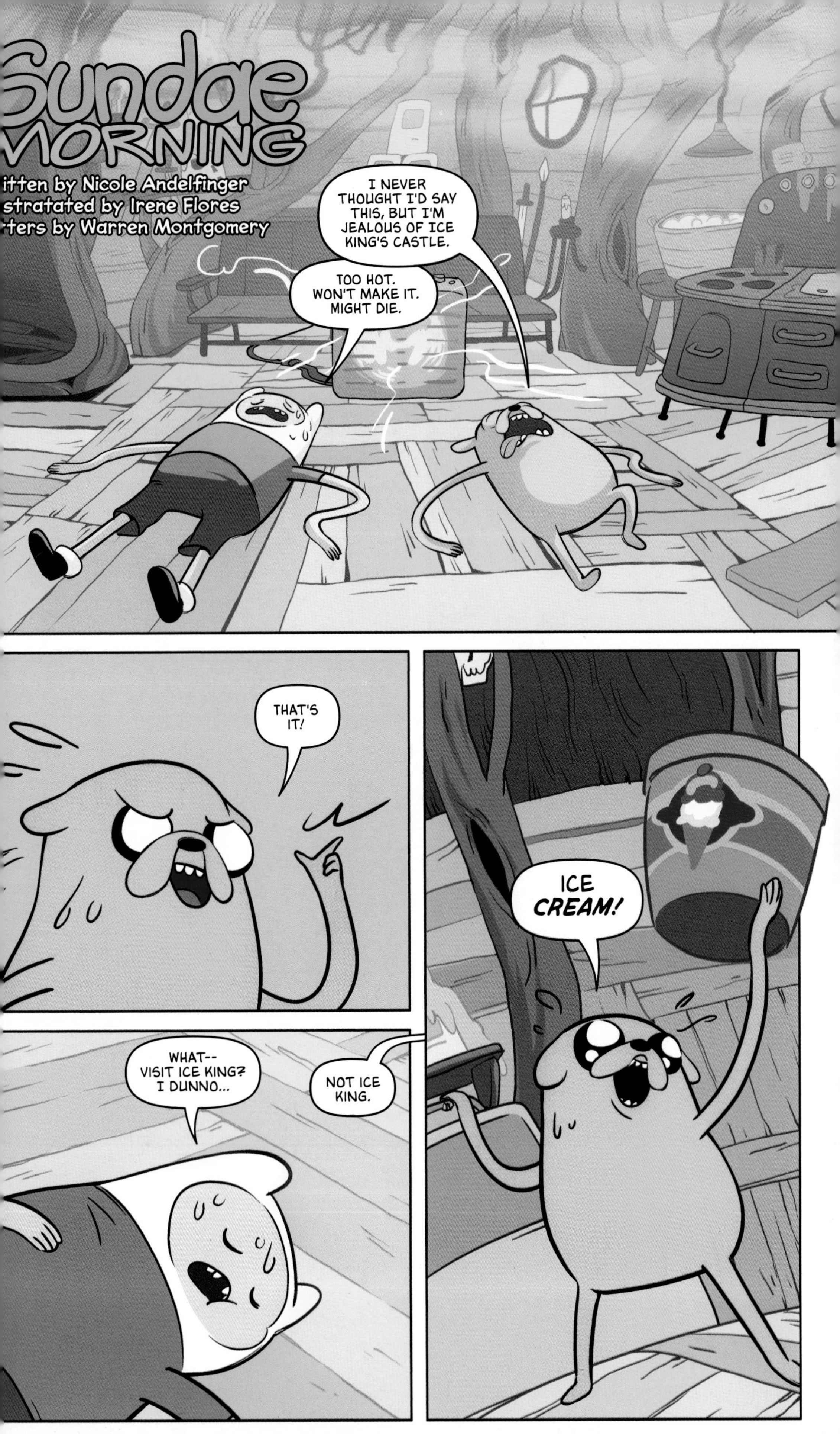

Sundae Morning
itten by Nicole Andelfinger
strated by Irene Flores
-ters by Warren Montgomery
I NEVER THOUGHT I'D SAY THIS, BUT I'M JEALOUS OF ICE KING'S CASTLE.
TOO HOT. WON'T MAKE IT. MIGHT DIE.
THAT'S IT!
ICE CREAM!
WHAT-- VISIT ICE KING? I DUNNO...
NOT ICE KING.

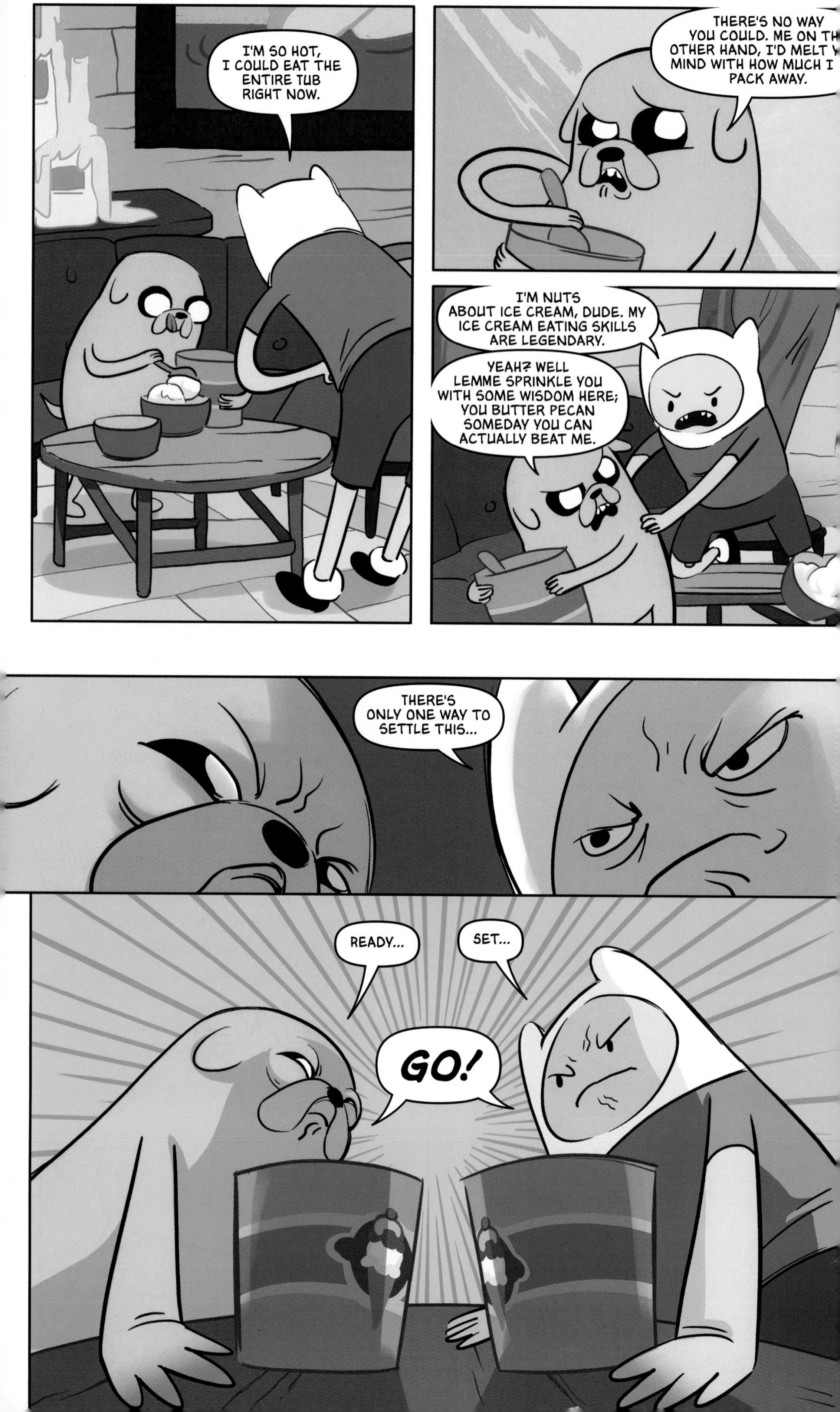
I'M SO HOT, I COULD EAT THE ENTIRE TUB RIGHT NOW.
THERE'S NO WAY YOU COULD. ME ON TH OTHER HAND, I'D MELT Y MIND WITH HOW MUCH I PACK AWAY.
I'M NUTS ABOUT ICE CREAM, DUDE. MY ICE CREAM EATING SKILLS ARE LEGENDARY.
YEAH? WELL LEMME SPRINKLE YOU WITH SOME WISDOM HERE; YOU BUTTER PECAN SOMEDAY YOU CAN ACTUALLY BEAT ME.
THERE'S ONLY ONE WAY TO SETTLE THIS...
READY...
SET...
GO!

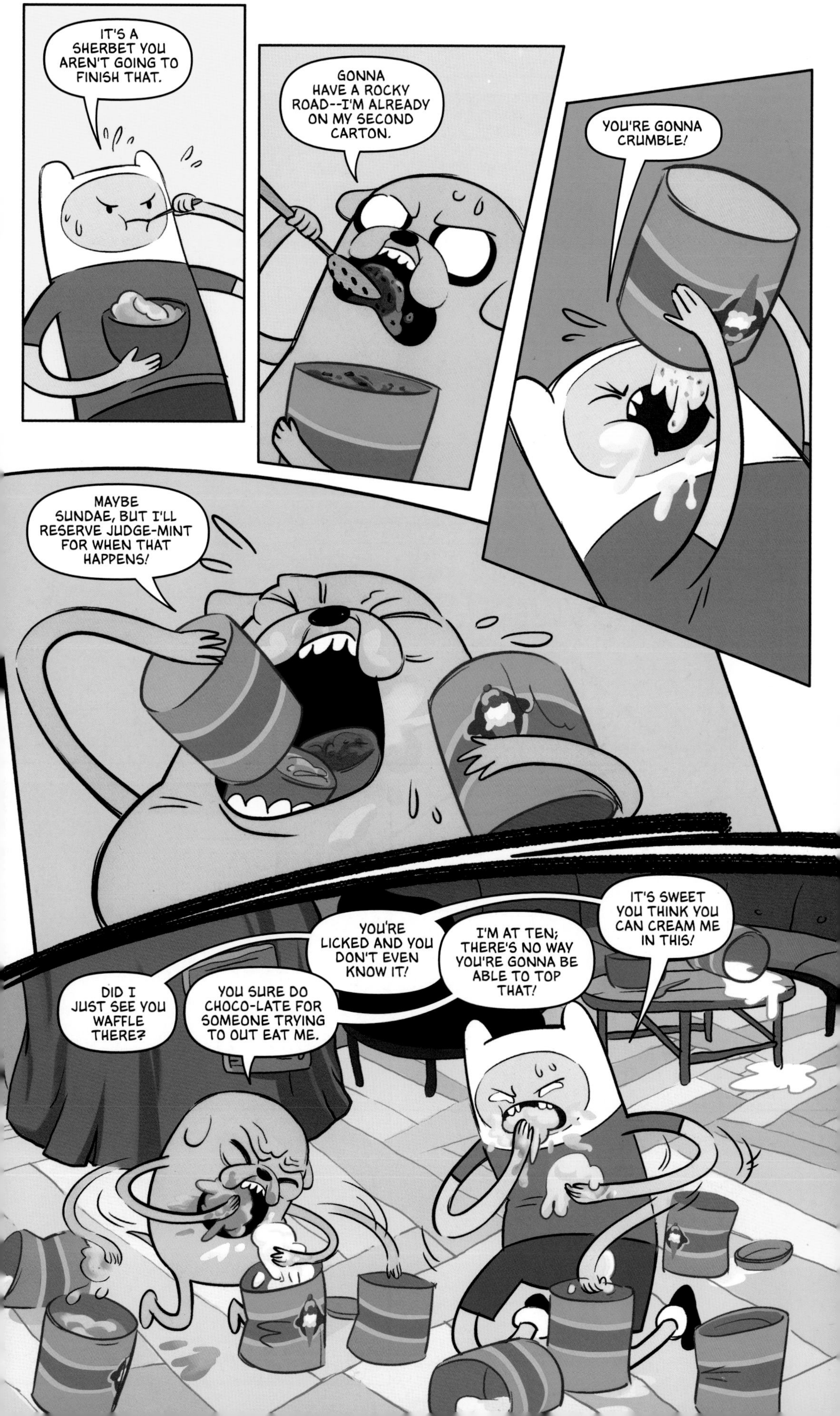
IT'S A SHERBET YOU AREN'T GOING TO FINISH THAT.
GONNA HAVE A ROCKY ROAD--I'M ALREADY ON MY SECOND CARTON.
YOU'RE GONNA CRUMBLE!
MAYBE SUNDAE, BUT I'LL RESERVE JUDGE-MINT FOR WHEN THAT HAPPENS!
DID I JUST SEE YOU WAFFLE THERE?
YOU SURE DO CHOCO-LATE FOR SOMEONE TRYING TO OUT EAT ME.
YOU'RE LICKED AND YOU DON'T EVEN KNOW IT!
I'M AT TEN; THERE'S NO WAY YOU'RE GONNA BE ABLE TO TOP THAT!
IT'S SWEET YOU THINK YOU CAN CREAM ME IN THIS!

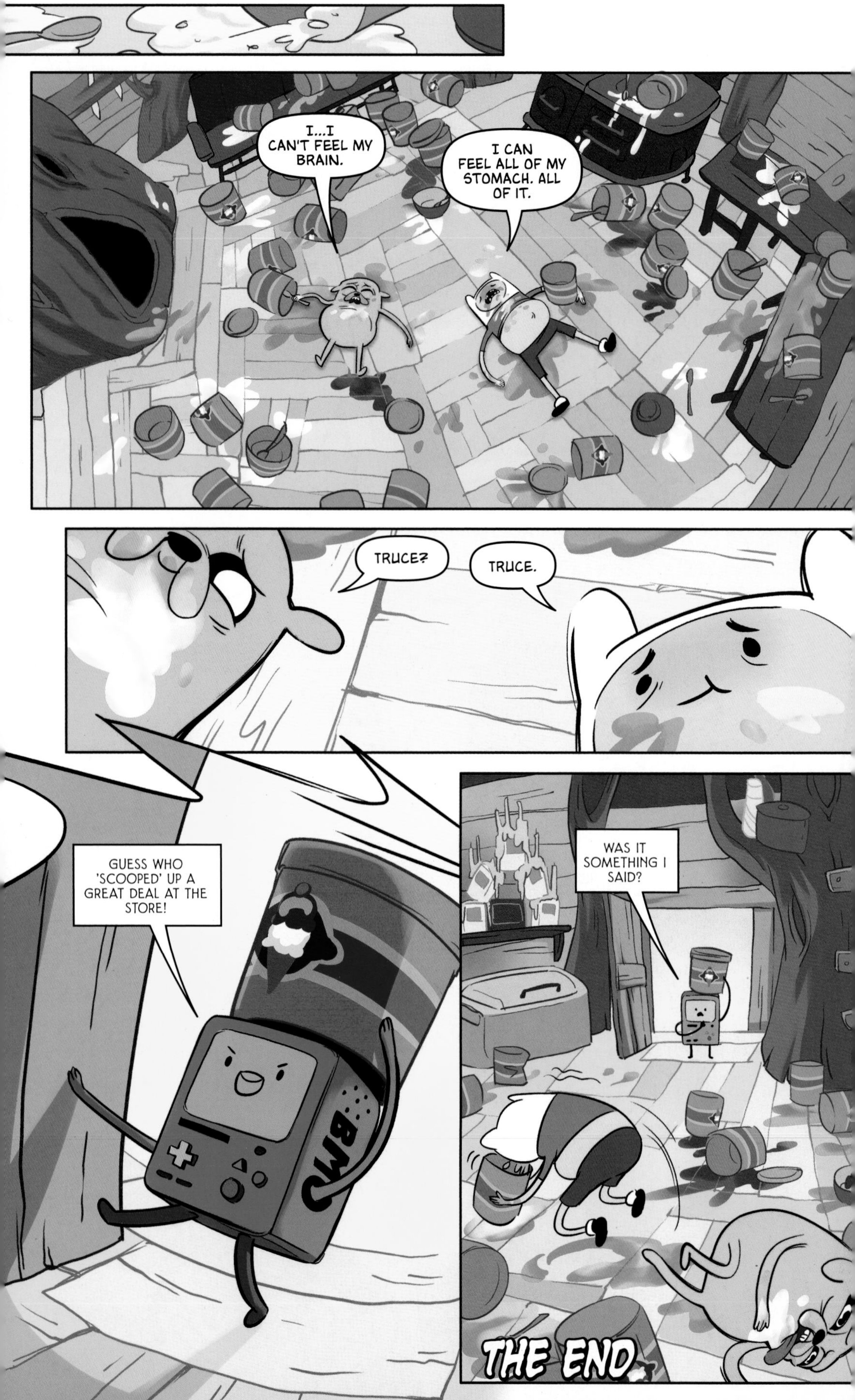
I...I CAN'T FEEL MY BRAIN.
I CAN FEEL ALL OF MY STOMACH. ALL OF IT.
TRUCE?
TRUCE.
GUESS WHO 'SCOOPED' UP A GREAT DEAL AT THE STORE!
WAS IT SOMETHING I SAID?
BMO
THE END

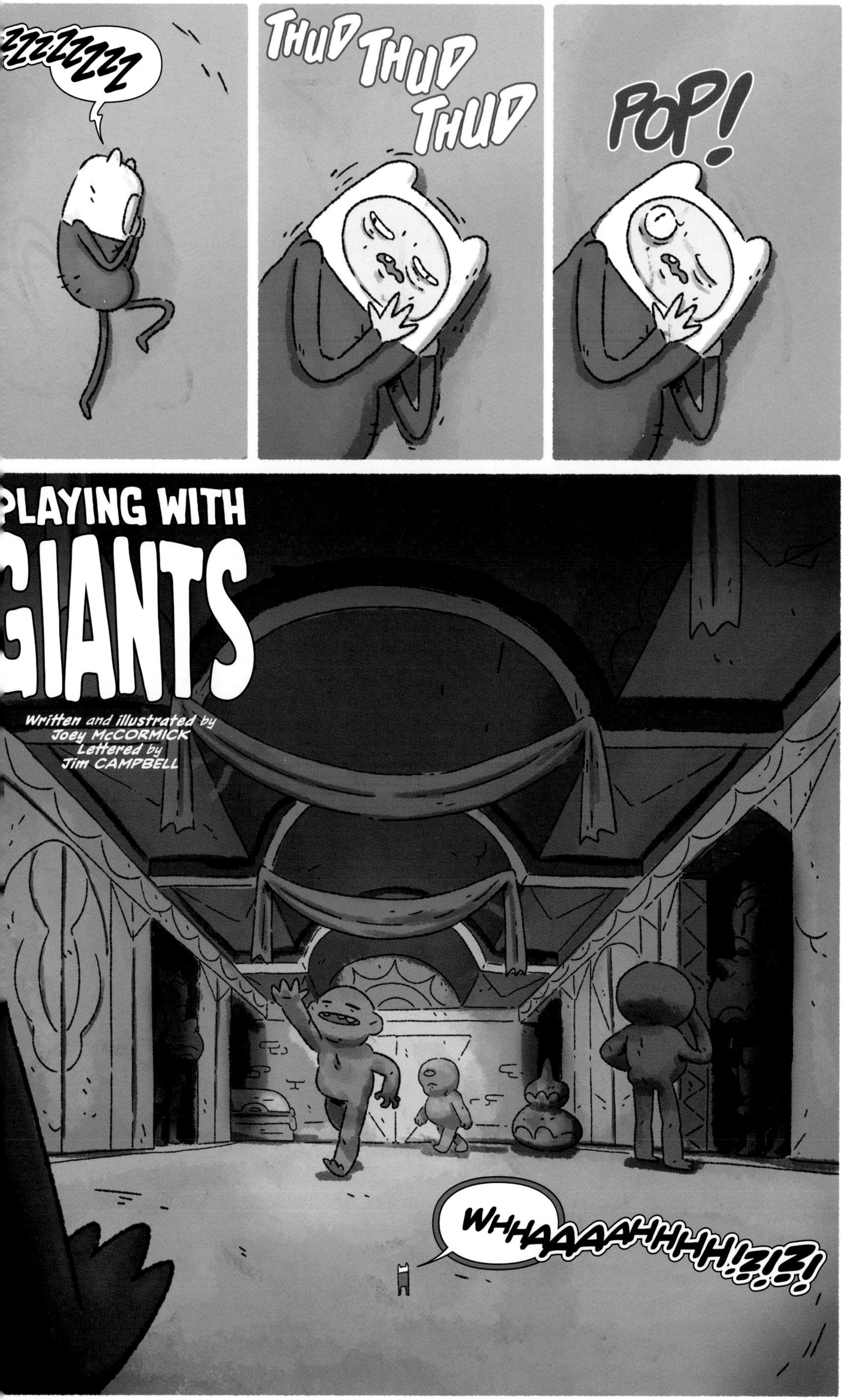
ZZZZZZZZ
THUD THUD THUD
POP!
PLAYING WITH GIANTS
Written and illustrated by Joey McCORMICK
Lettered by Jim CAMPBELL
WHHAAAAHHHH!?!?!

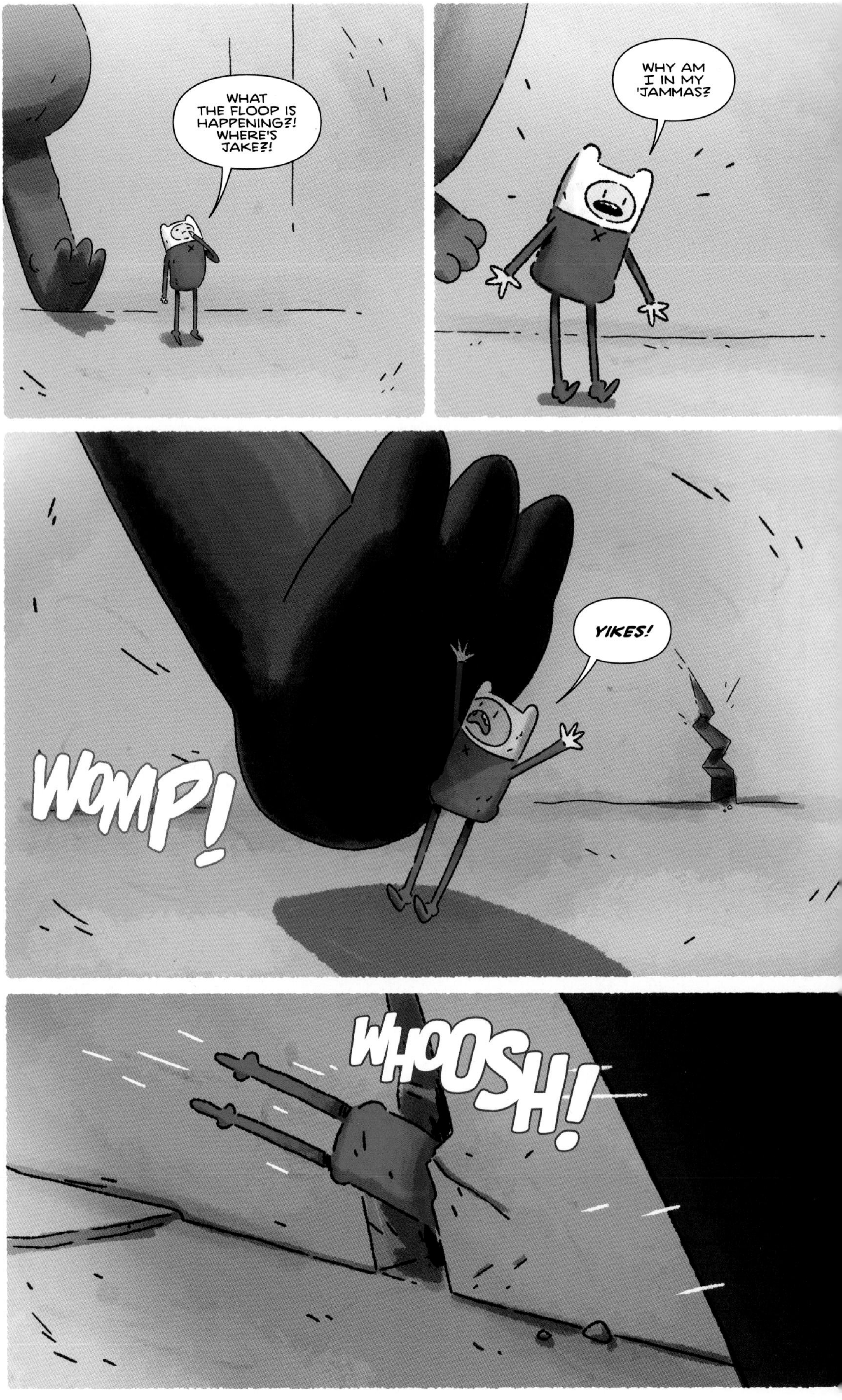
WHAT THE FLOOP IS HAPPENING?! WHERE'S JAKE?!
WHY AM I IN MY 'JAMMAS?
YIKES!
WOMP!
WHOOSH!

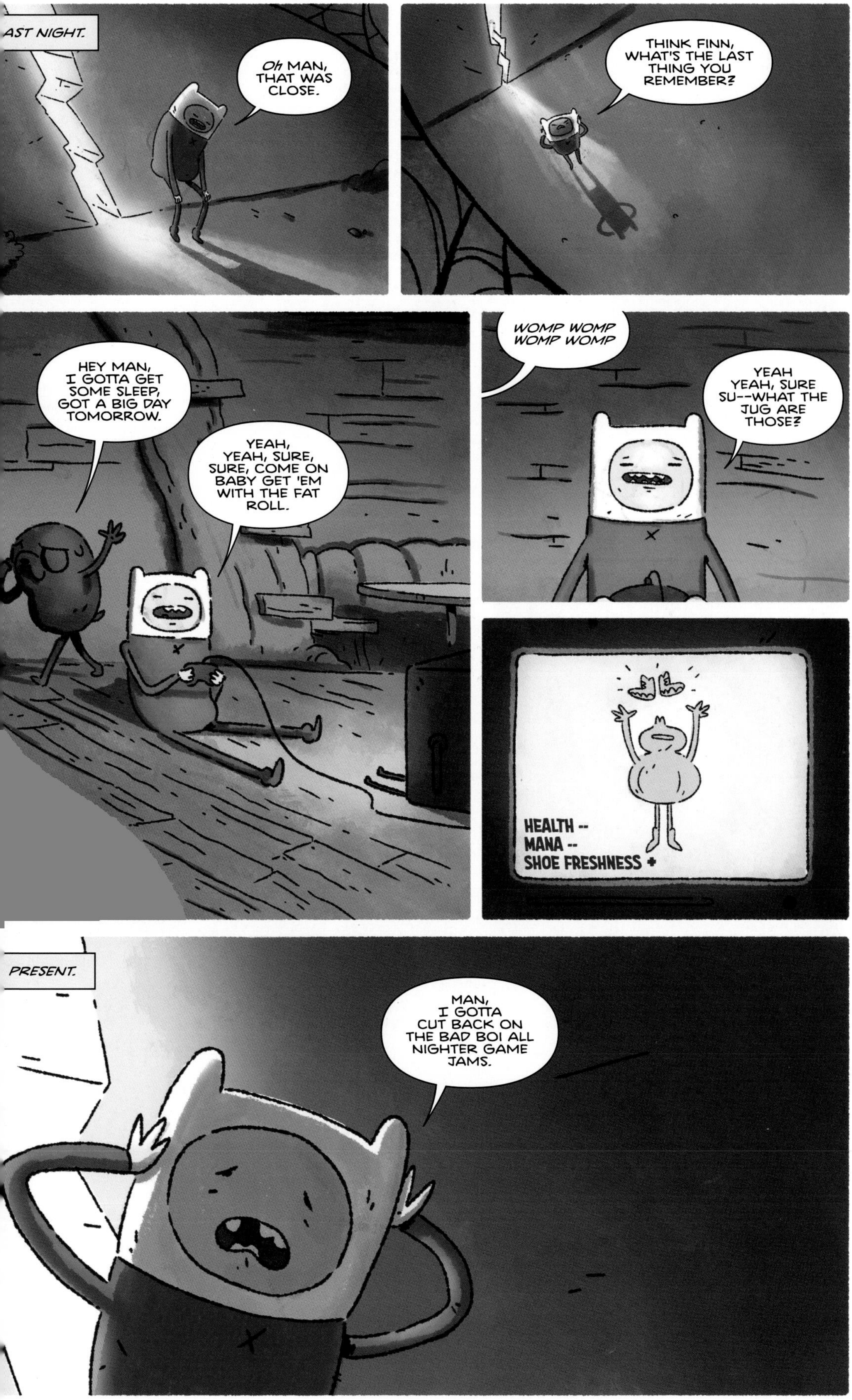
AST NIGHT.
Oh MAN, THAT WAS CLOSE.
THINK FINN, WHAT'S THE LAST THING YOU REMEMBER?
HEY MAN, I GOTTA GET SOME SLEEP, GOT A BIG DAY TOMORROW.
YEAH, YEAH, SURE, SURE, COME ON BABY GET 'EM WITH THE FAT ROLL.
WOMP WOMP WOMP WOMP
YEAH YEAH, SURE SU--WHAT THE JUG ARE THOSE?
HEALTH --
MANA --
SHOE FRESHNESS +
PRESENT.
MAN, I GOTTA CUT BACK ON THE BAD BOI ALL NIGHTER GAME JAMS.

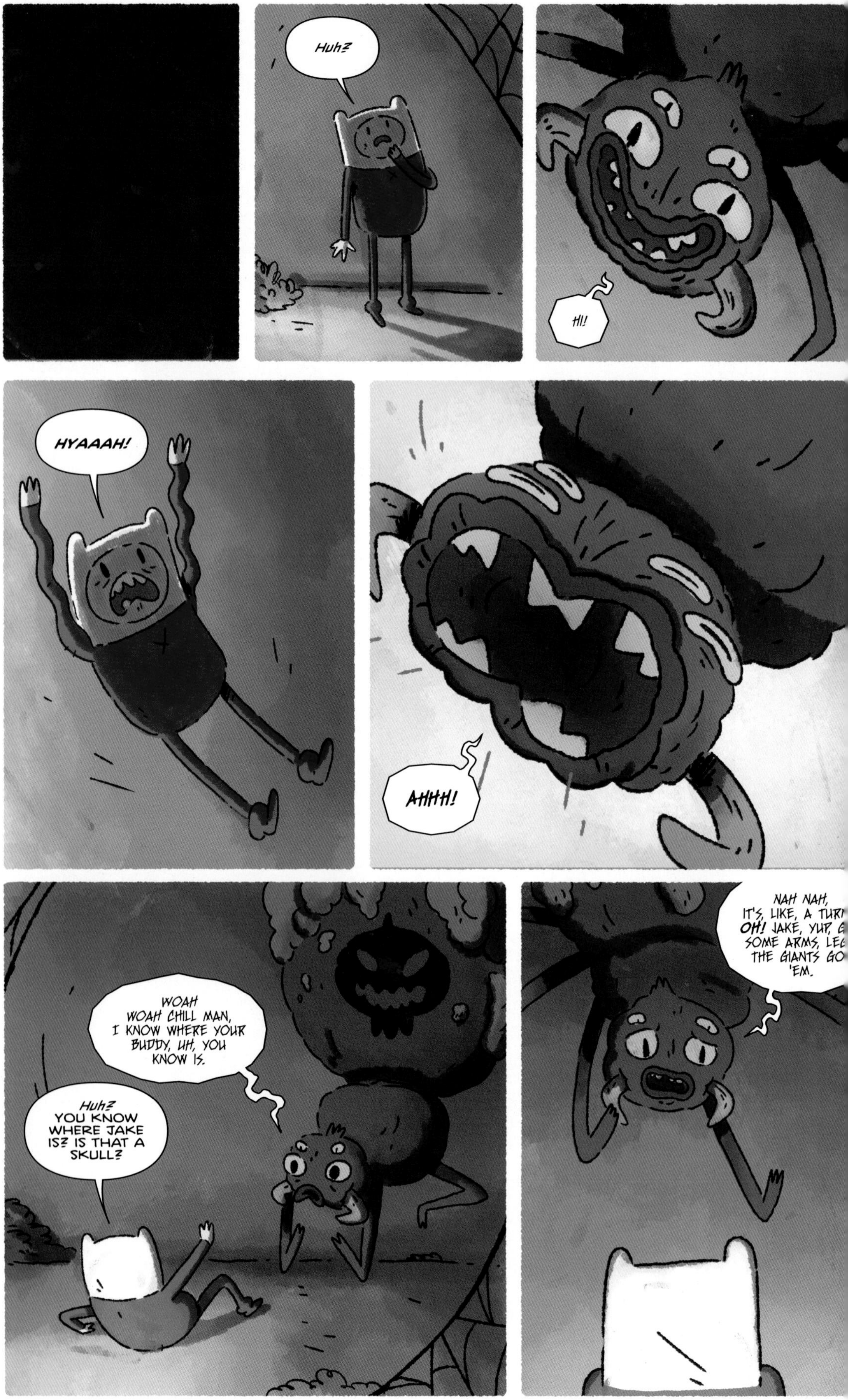
Huh?
HI!
HYAAAH!
AHHH!
WOAH WOAH CHILL MAN, I KNOW WHERE YOUR BUDDY, UH, YOU KNOW IS.
Huh? YOU KNOW WHERE JAKE IS? IS THAT A SKULL?
NAH NAH, IT'S, LIKE, A TUR
OH! JAKE, YUP,
SOME ARMS, LE
THE GIANTS GO
'EM.

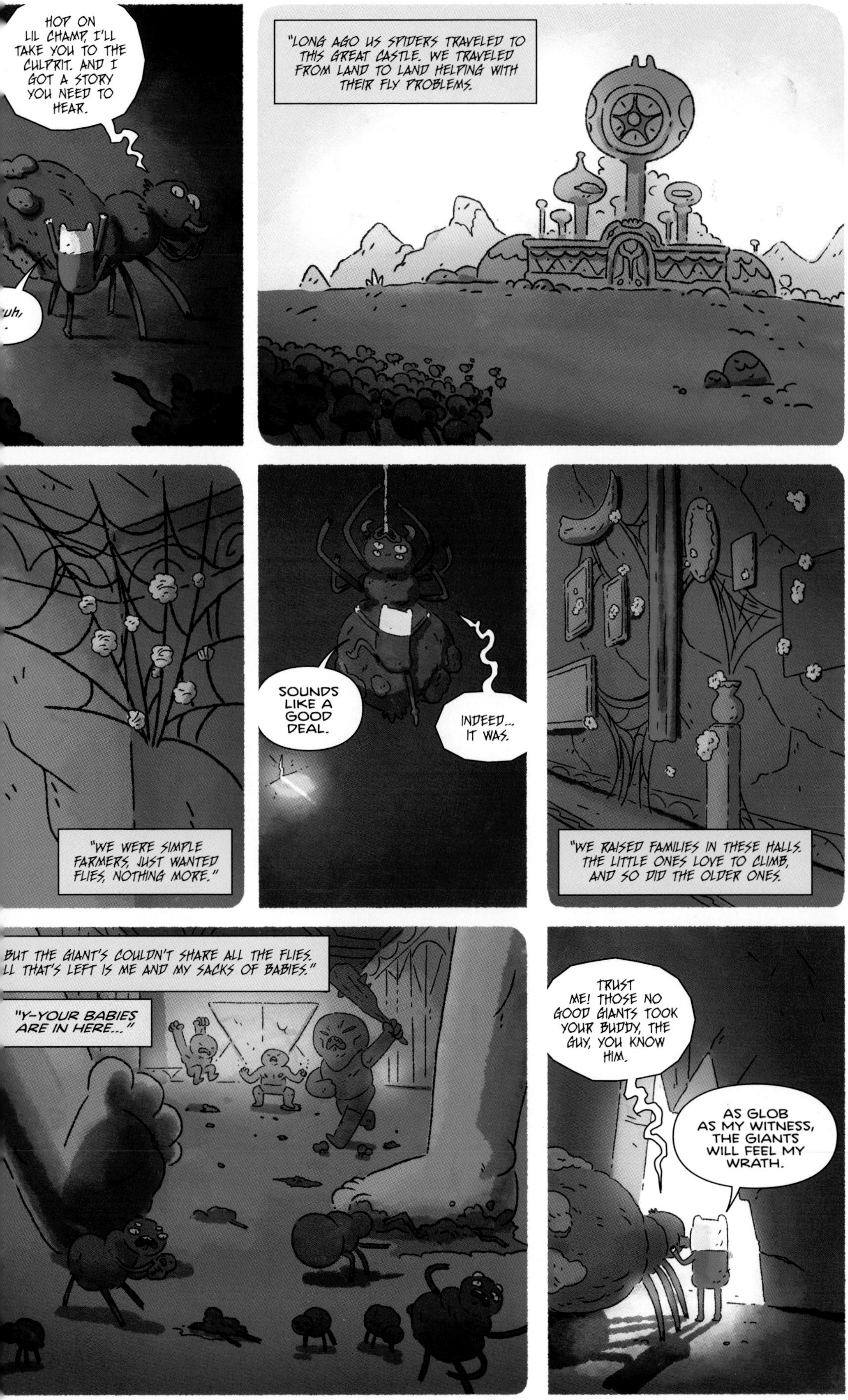

HOP ON LIL CHAMP, I'LL TAKE YOU TO THE CULPRIT. AND I GOT A STORY YOU NEED TO HEAR.
"LONG AGO US SPIDERS TRAVELED TO THIS GREAT CASTLE. WE TRAVELED FROM LAND TO LAND HELPING WITH THEIR FLY PROBLEMS.
"WE WERE SIMPLE FARMERS, JUST WANTED FLIES, NOTHING MORE."
SOUNDS LIKE A GOOD DEAL.
INDEED... IT WAS.
"WE RAISED FAMILIES IN THESE HALLS. THE LITTLE ONES LOVE TO CLIMB, AND SO DID THE OLDER ONES.
BUT THE GIANT'S COULDN'T SHARE ALL THE FLIES.
LL THAT'S LEFT IS ME AND MY SACKS OF BABIES."
"Y-YOUR BABIES ARE IN HERE..."
TRUST ME! THOSE NO GOOD GIANTS TOOK YOUR BUDDY, THE GUY, YOU KNOW HIM.
AS GLOB AS MY WITNESS, THE GIANTS WILL FEEL MY WRATH.

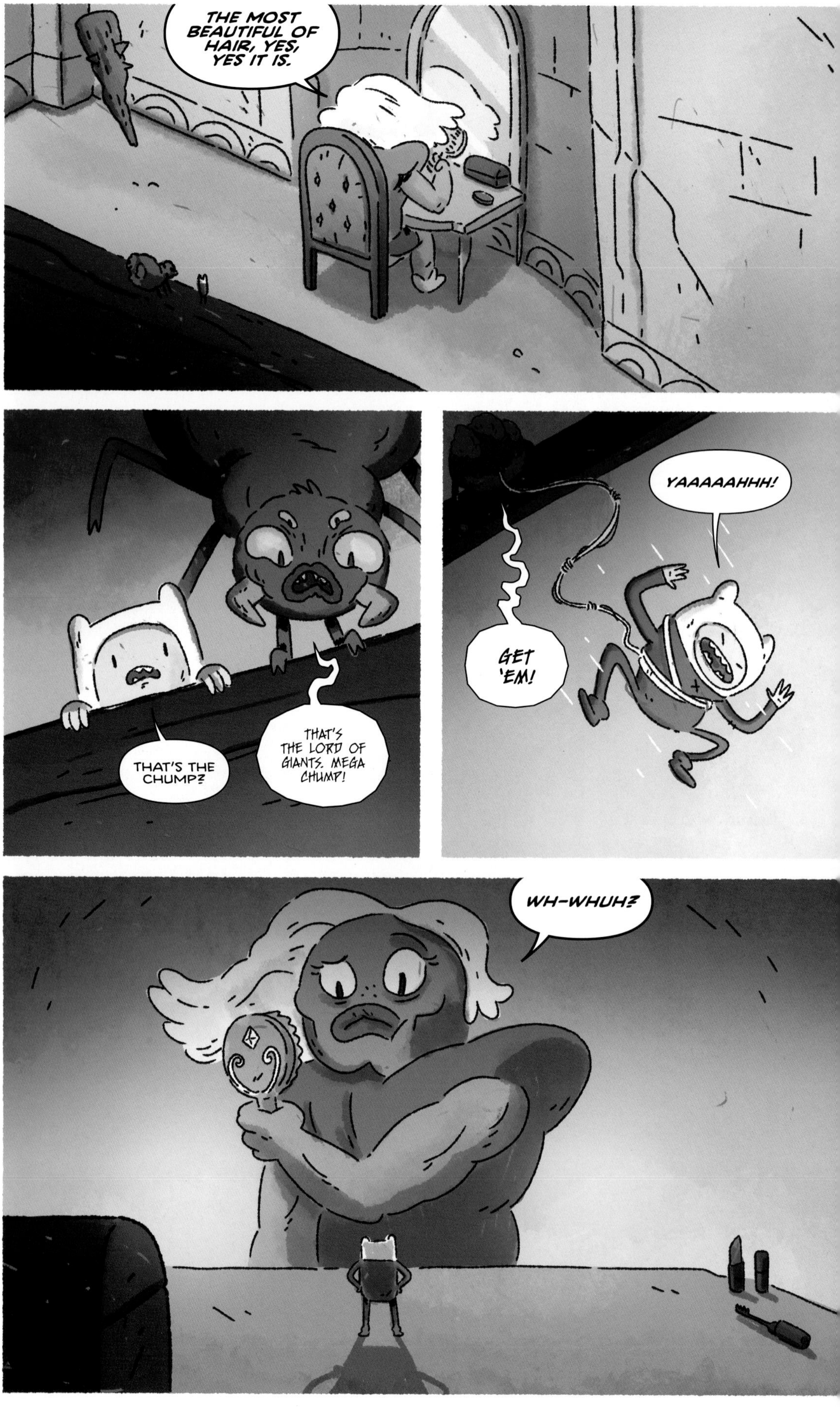
THE MOST BEAUTIFUL OF HAIR, YES, YES IT IS.
THAT'S THE CHUMP?
THAT'S THE LORD OF GIANTS. MEGA CHUMP!
YAAAAAHHH!
GET 'EM!
WH-WHUH?

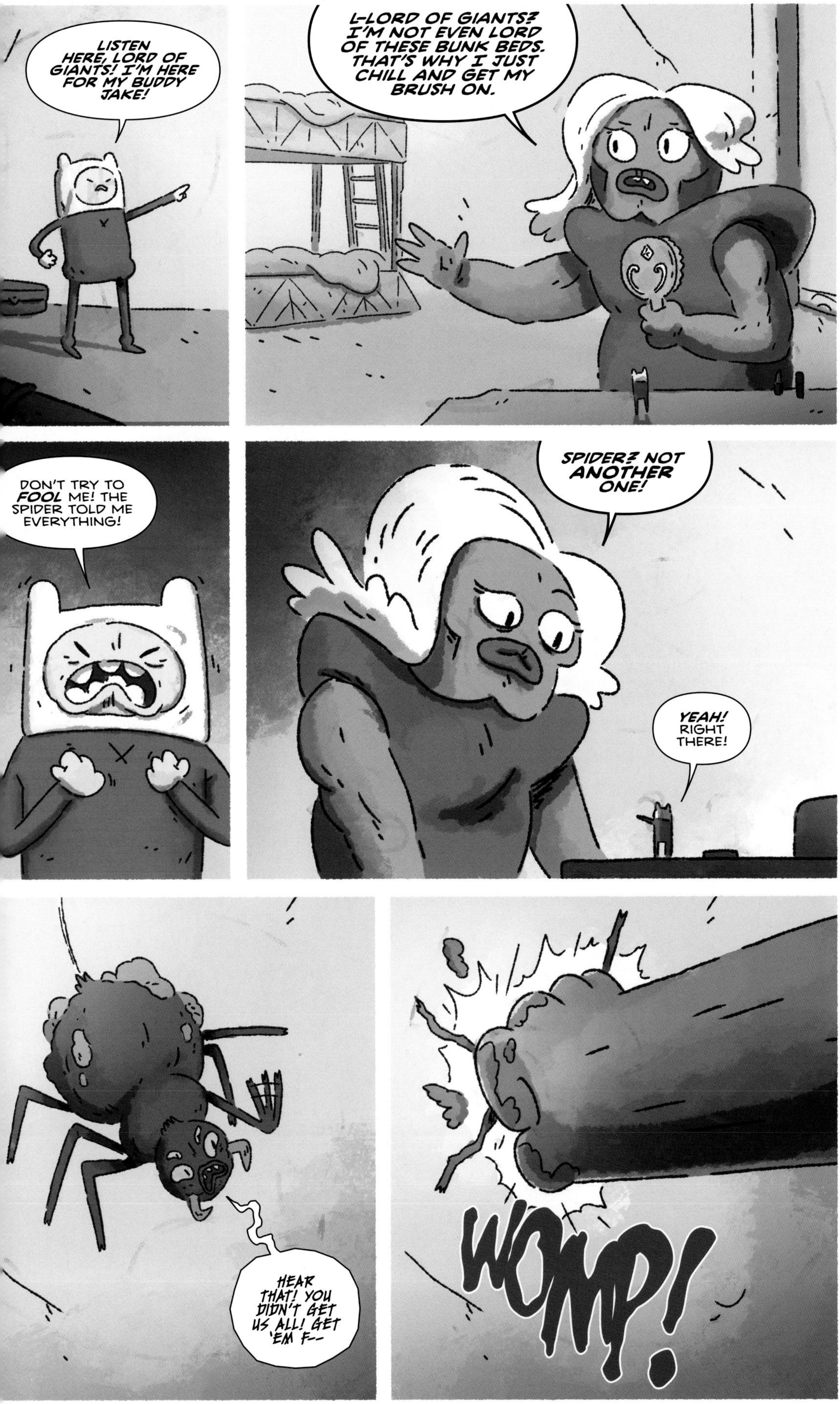
LISTEN HERE, LORD OF GIANTS! I'M HERE FOR MY BUDDY JAKE!
L-LORD OF GIANTS? I'M NOT EVEN LORD OF THESE BUNK BEDS. THAT'S WHY I JUST CHILL AND GET MY BRUSH ON.
DON'T TRY TO FOOL ME! THE SPIDER TOLD ME EVERYTHING!
SPIDER? NOT ANOTHER ONE!
YEAH! RIGHT THERE!
HEAR THAT! YOU DIDN'T GET US ALL! GET 'EM F--
WOMP!

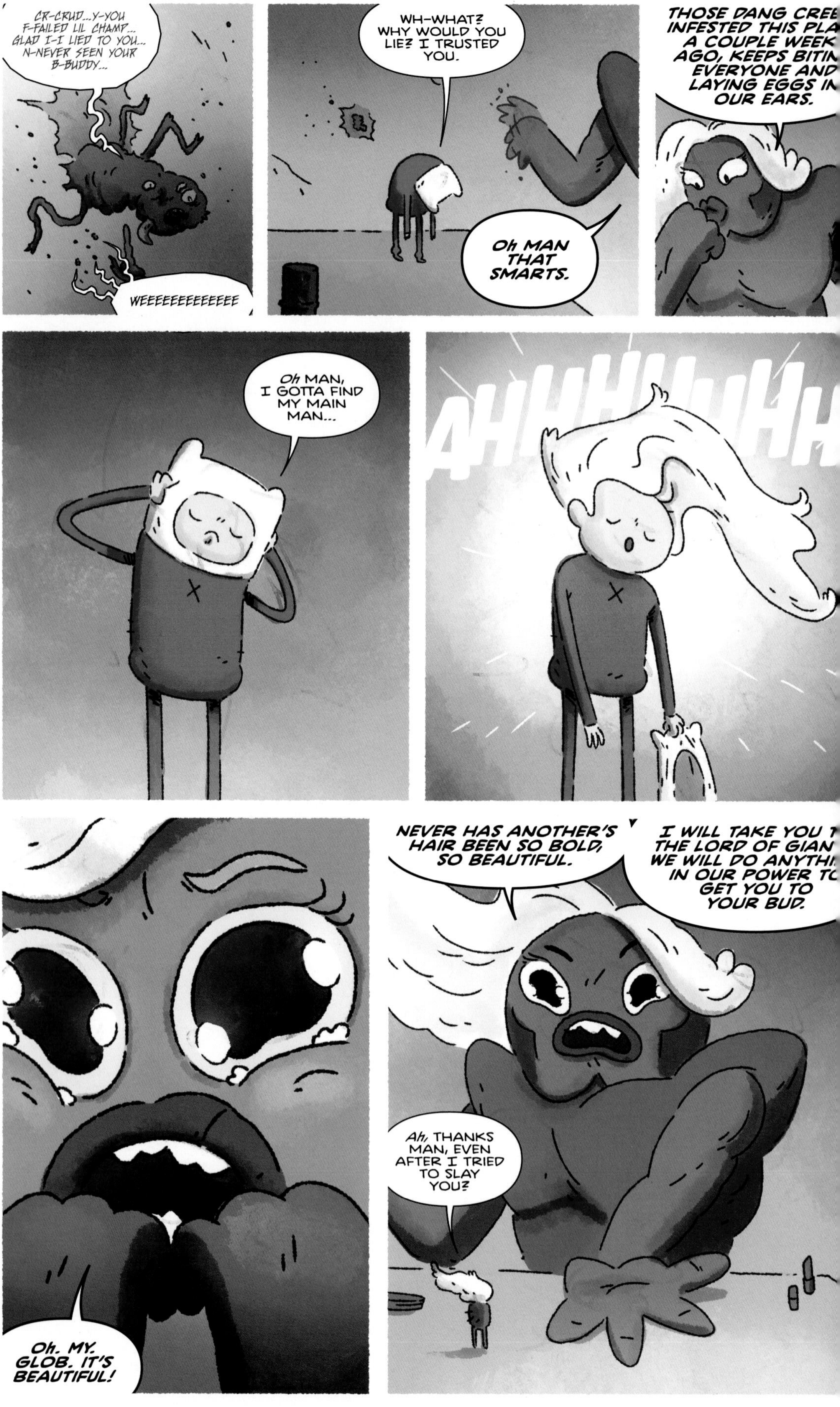
CR-CRUD... Y-YOU F-FAILED LIL CHAMP... GLAD I-I LIED TO YOU... N-NEVER SEEN YOUR B-BUDDY...
WEEEEEEEEEEEEE
WH-WHAT? WHY WOULD YOU LIE? I TRUSTED YOU.
Oh MAN THAT SMARTS.
THOSE DANG CREE
INFESTED THIS PLA
A COUPLE WEEK
AGO, KEEPS BITIN
EVERYONE AND
LAYING EGGS IN
OUR EARS.
Oh MAN, I GOTTA FIND MY MAIN MAN...
AHHHHHHHH
Oh. MY. GLOB. IT'S BEAUTIFUL!
NEVER HAS ANOTHER'S HAIR BEEN SO BOLD, SO BEAUTIFUL.
I WILL TAKE YOU T
THE LORD OF GIAN
WE WILL DO ANYTHI
IN OUR POWER TO
GET YOU TO YOUR BUD.
Ah, THANKS MAN, EVEN AFTER I TRIED TO SLAY YOU?

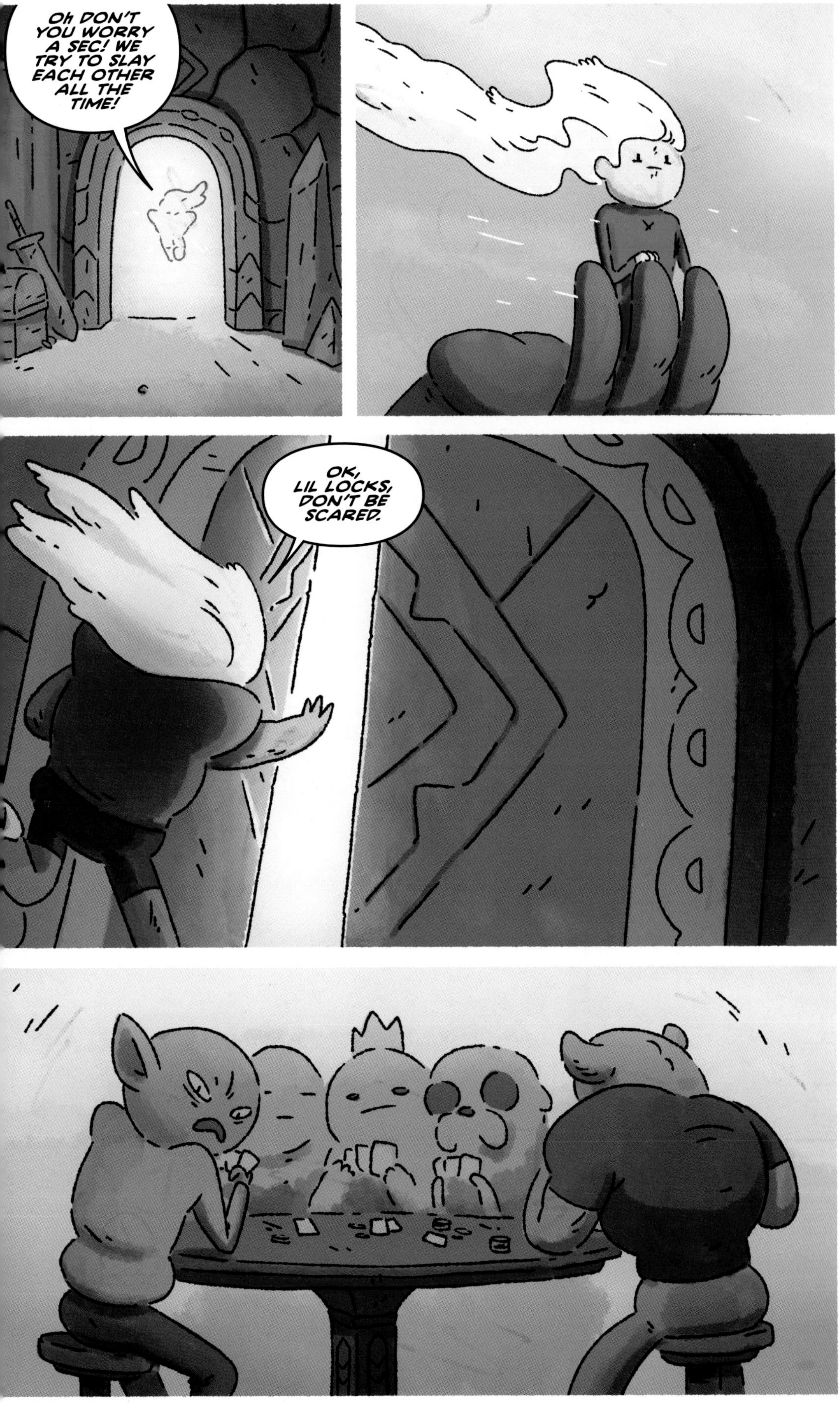
Oh DON'T YOU WORRY A SEC! WE TRY TO SLAY EACH OTHER ALL THE TIME!
OK, LIL LOCKS, DON'T BE SCARED.

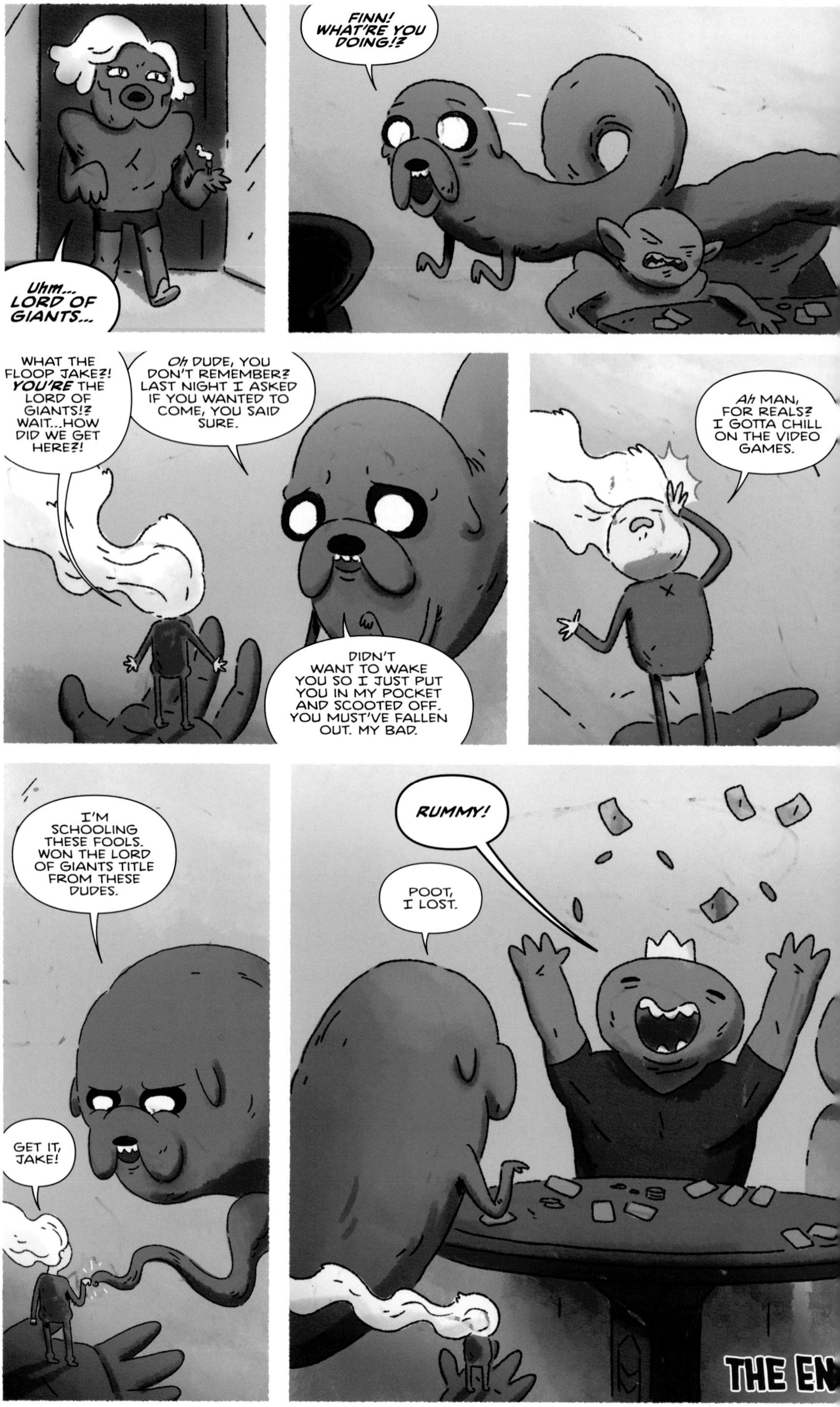

Uhm... LORD OF GIANTS...
FINN! WHAT'RE YOU DOING!?
WHAT THE FLOOP JAKE?! YOU'RE THE LORD OF GIANTS!? WAIT...HOW DID WE GET HERE?!
Oh DUDE, YOU DON'T REMEMBER? LAST NIGHT I ASKED IF YOU WANTED TO COME, YOU SAID SURE.
DIDN'T WANT TO WAKE YOU SO I JUST PUT YOU IN MY POCKET AND SCOOTED OFF. YOU MUST'VE FALLEN OUT. MY BAD.
Ah MAN, FOR REALS? I GOTTA CHILL ON THE VIDEO GAMES.
I'M SCHOOLING THESE FOOLS. WON THE LORD OF GIANTS TITLE FROM THESE DUDES.
GET IT, JAKE!
RUMMY!
POOT, I LOST.

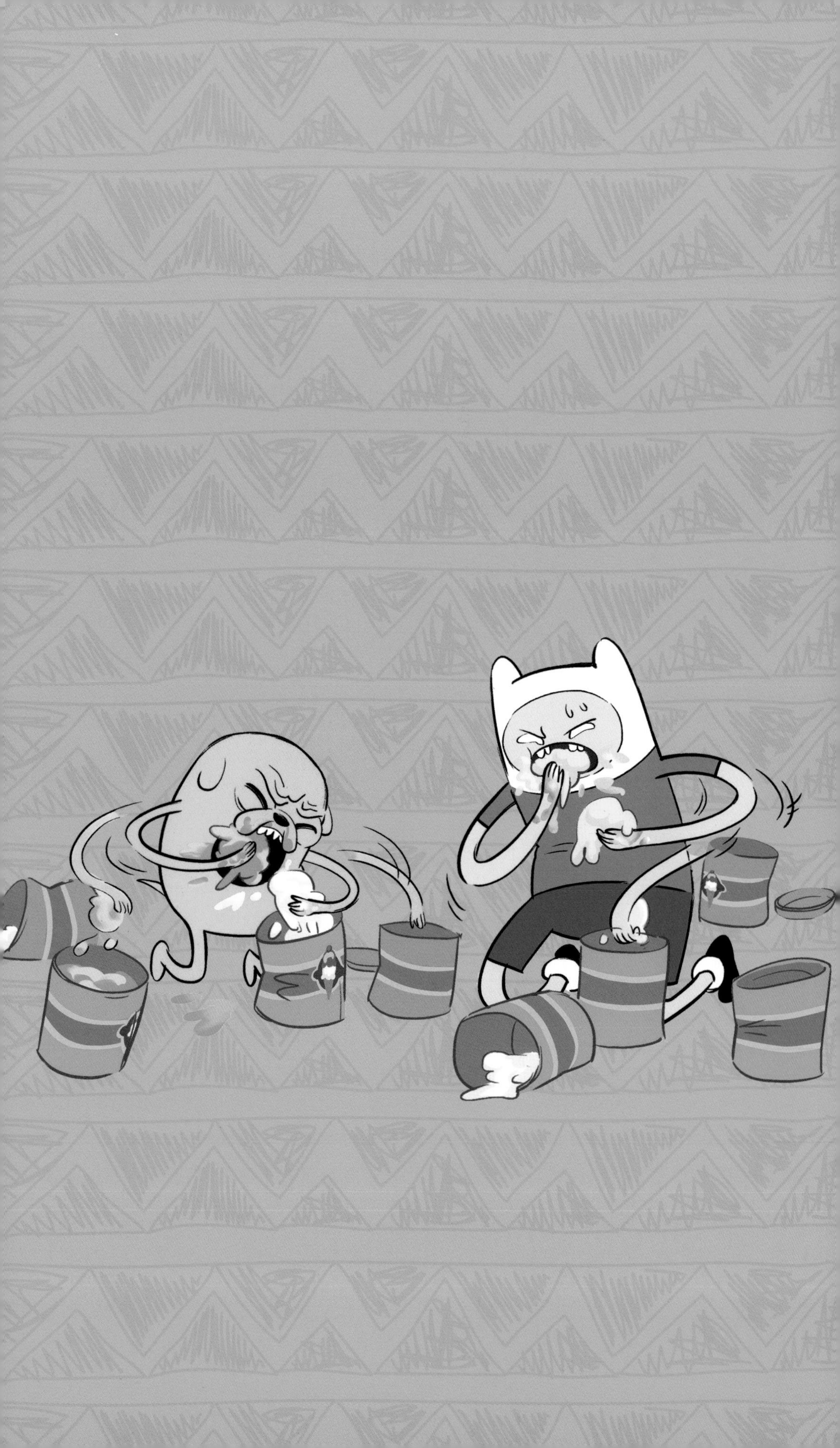

COVER GALLERY

Issue #9 Main Cover

MARIE WU

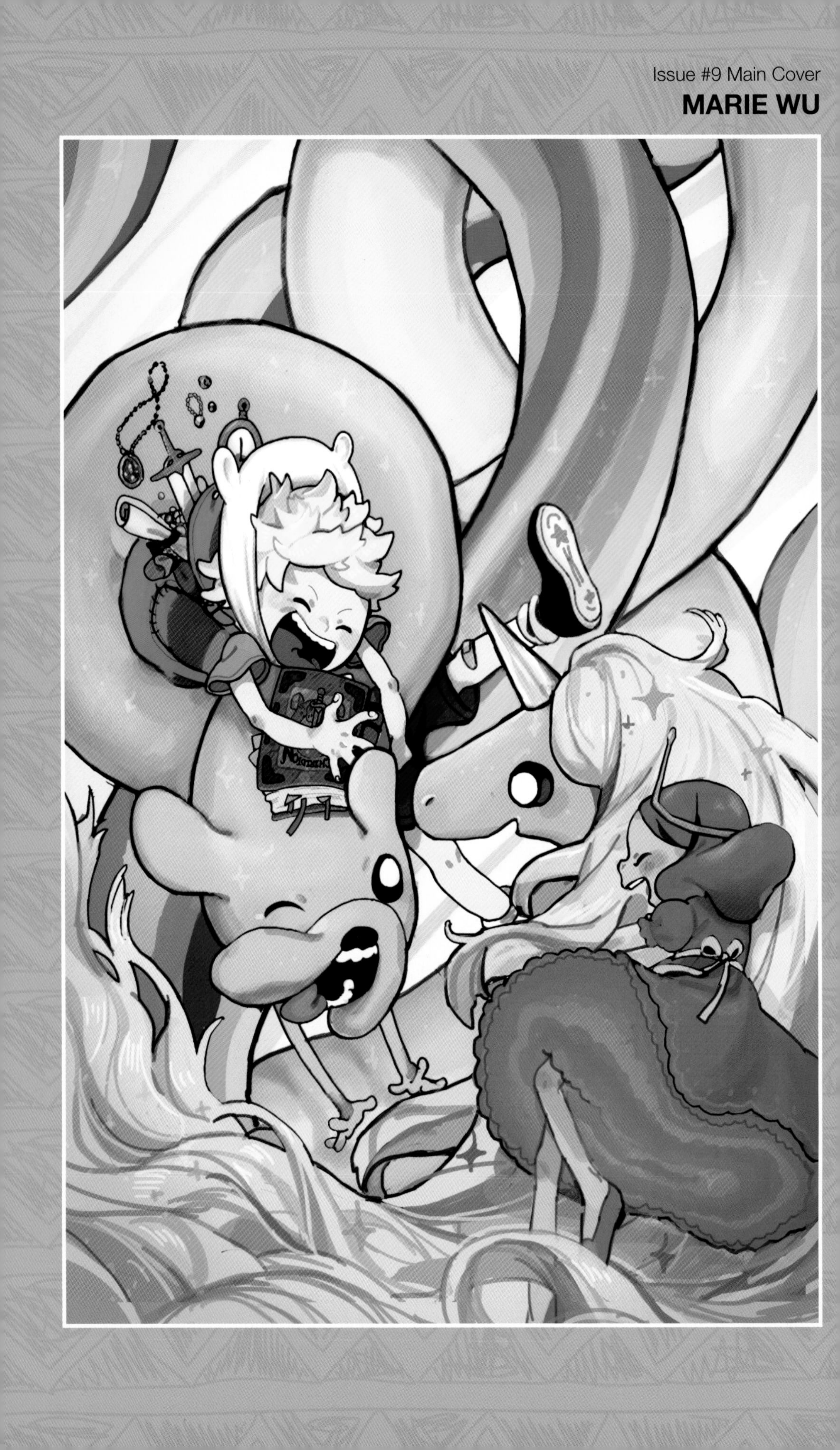

Issue #9 Subscription Cover

ARIEL RIES

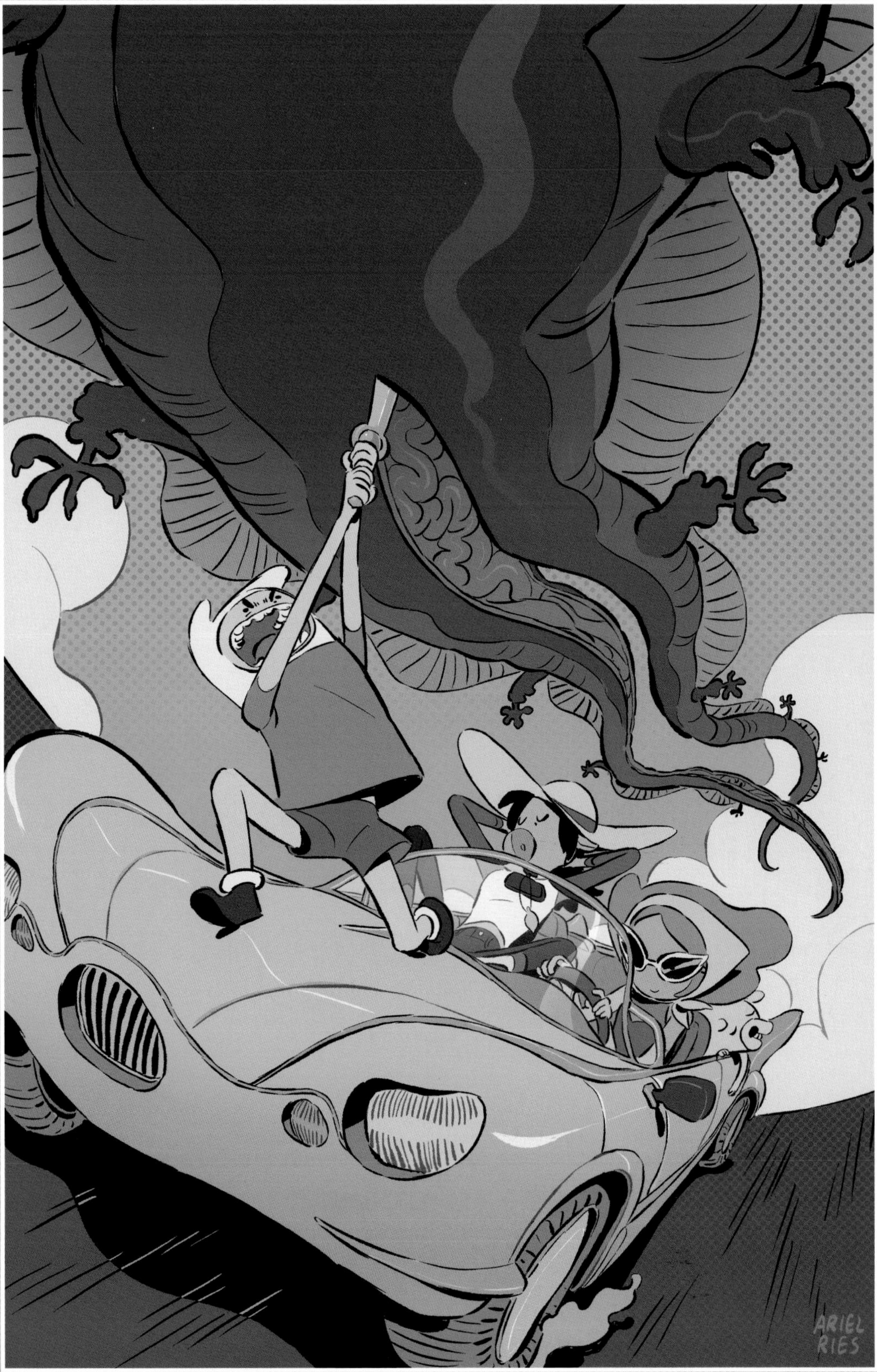
ARIEL
RIES

Issue #9 Variant Cover

FEIFEI RUAN

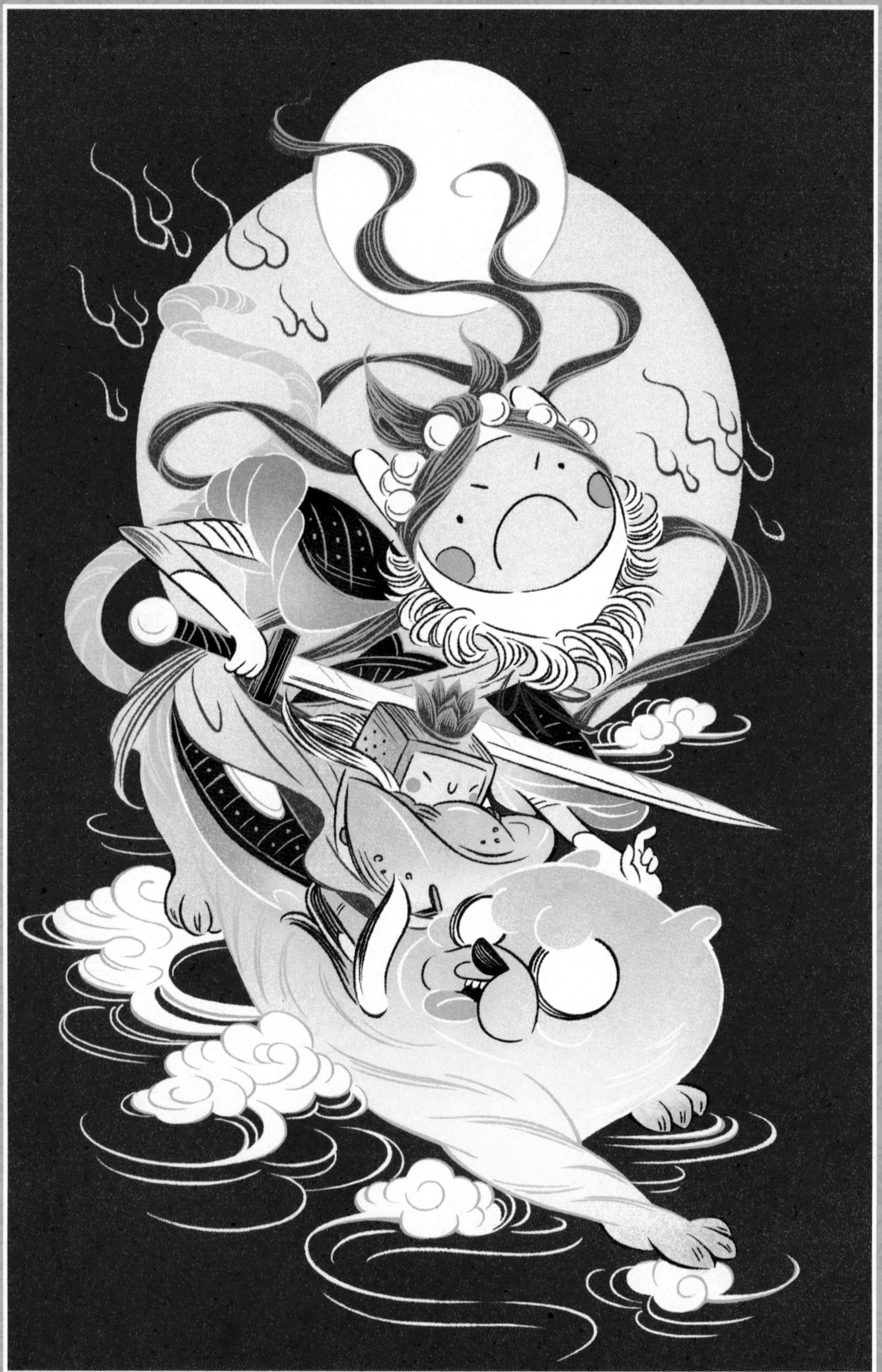

Issue #10 Main Cover

ADAM GORHAM

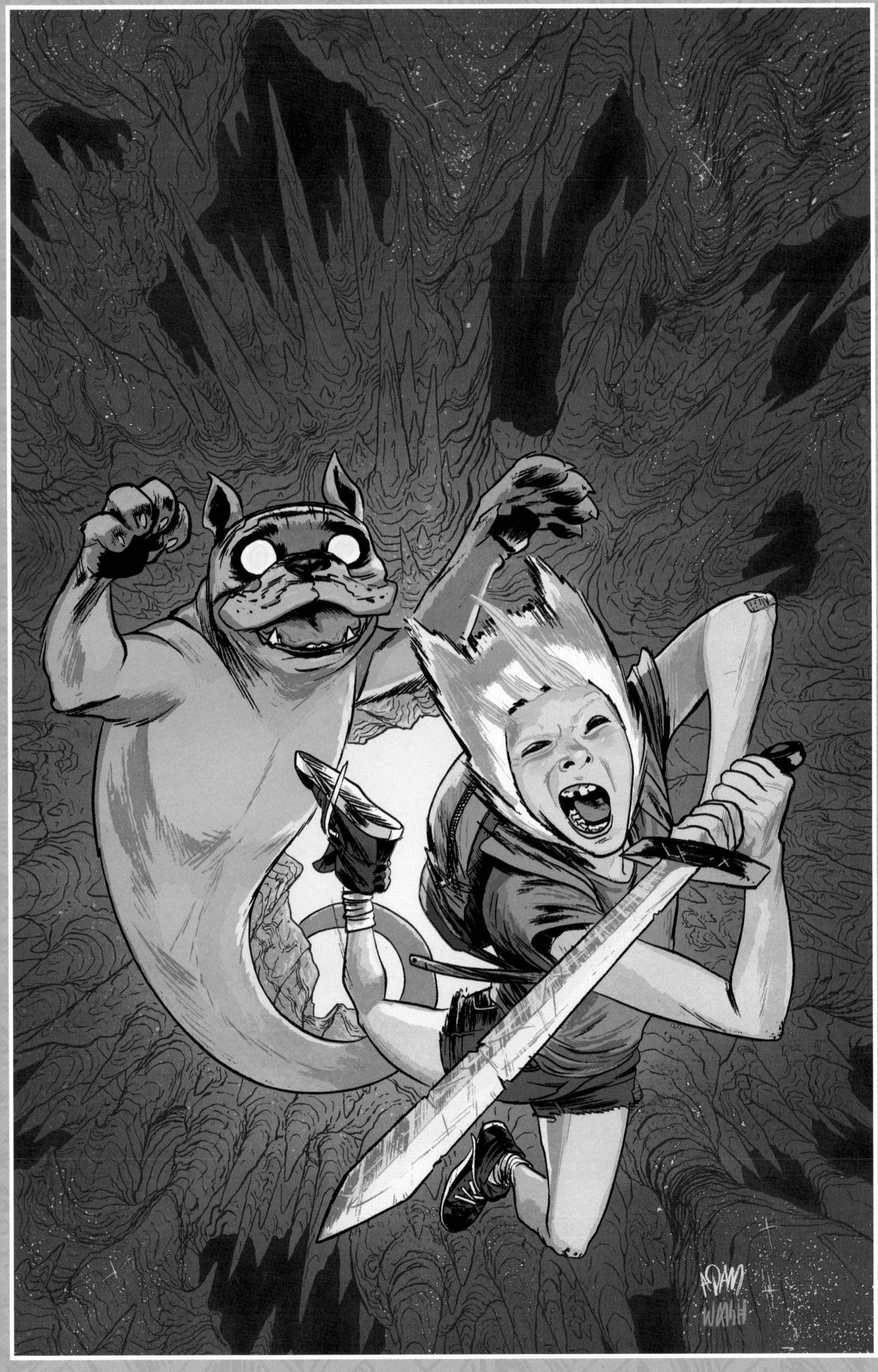

Issue #10 Subscription Cover

KELLYE PERDUE

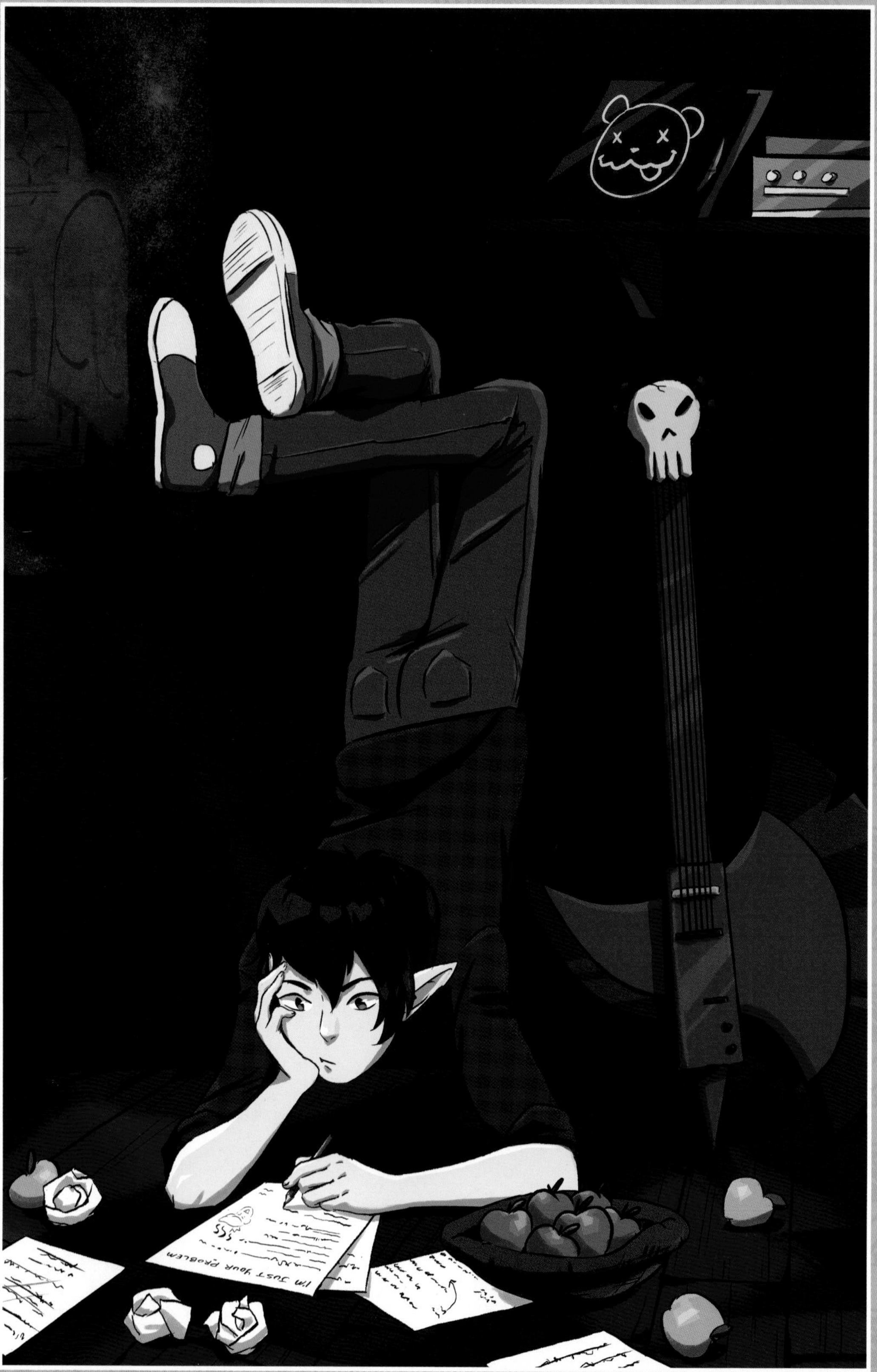
I'M JUST YOUR PROBLEM

Issue #10 Variant Cover

HELEN MASK

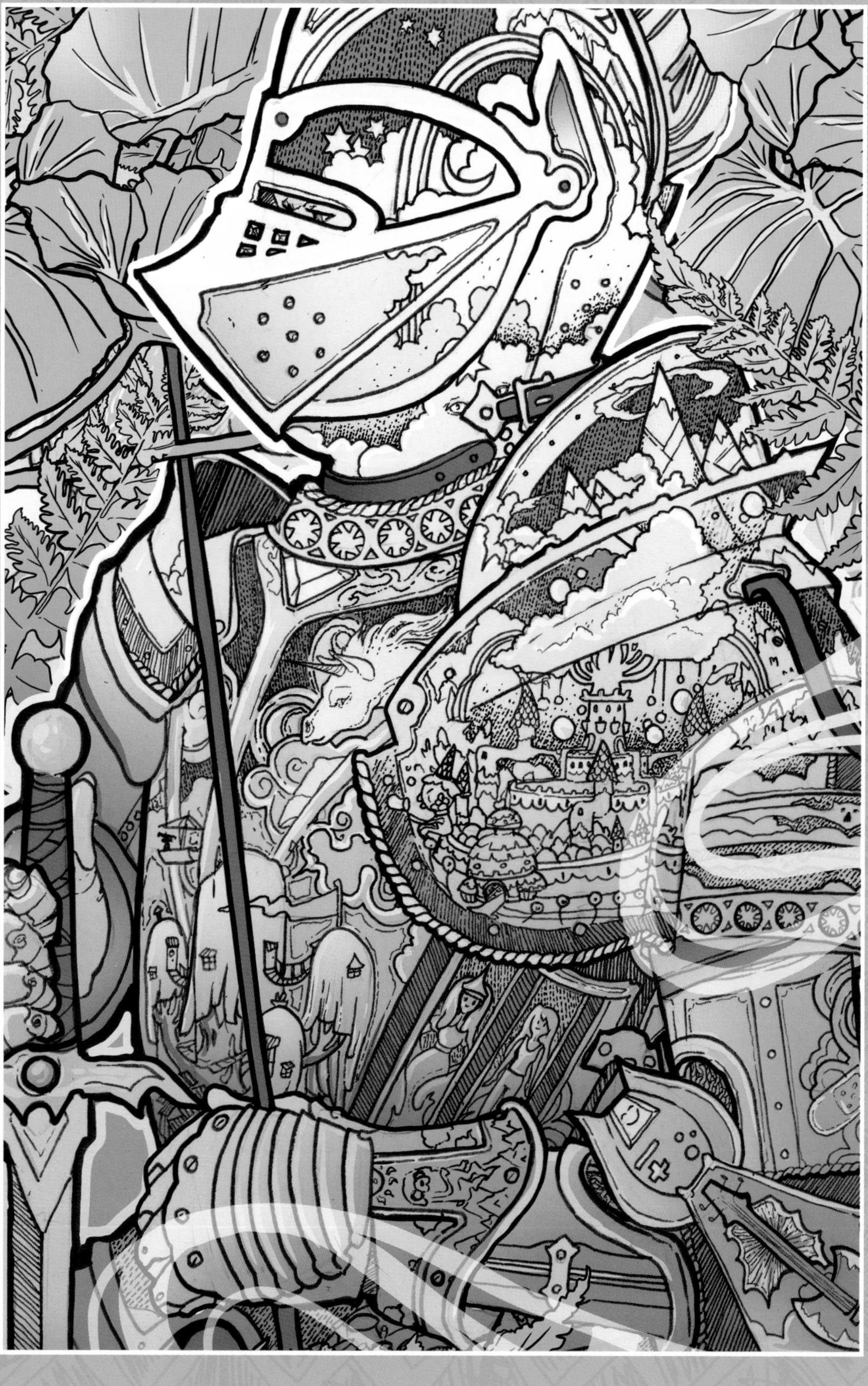

Issue #11 Main Cover
CHASE VAN WEERDUIZEN

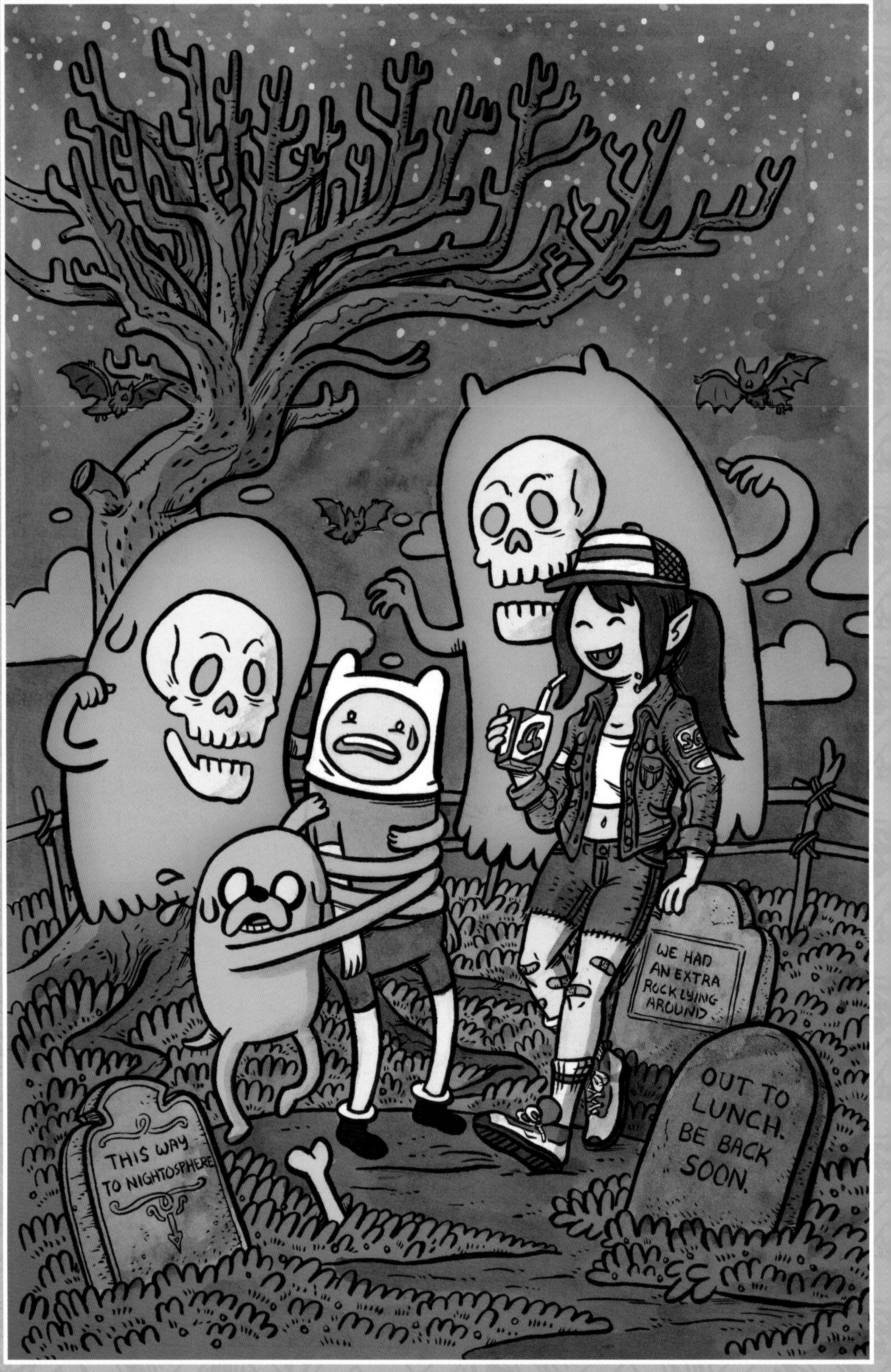
WE HAD AN EXTRA ROCK LYING AROUND
OUT TO LUNCH. BE BACK SOON.
THIS WAY TO NIGHTOSPHERE

Issue #11 Subscription Cover

JEN WANG

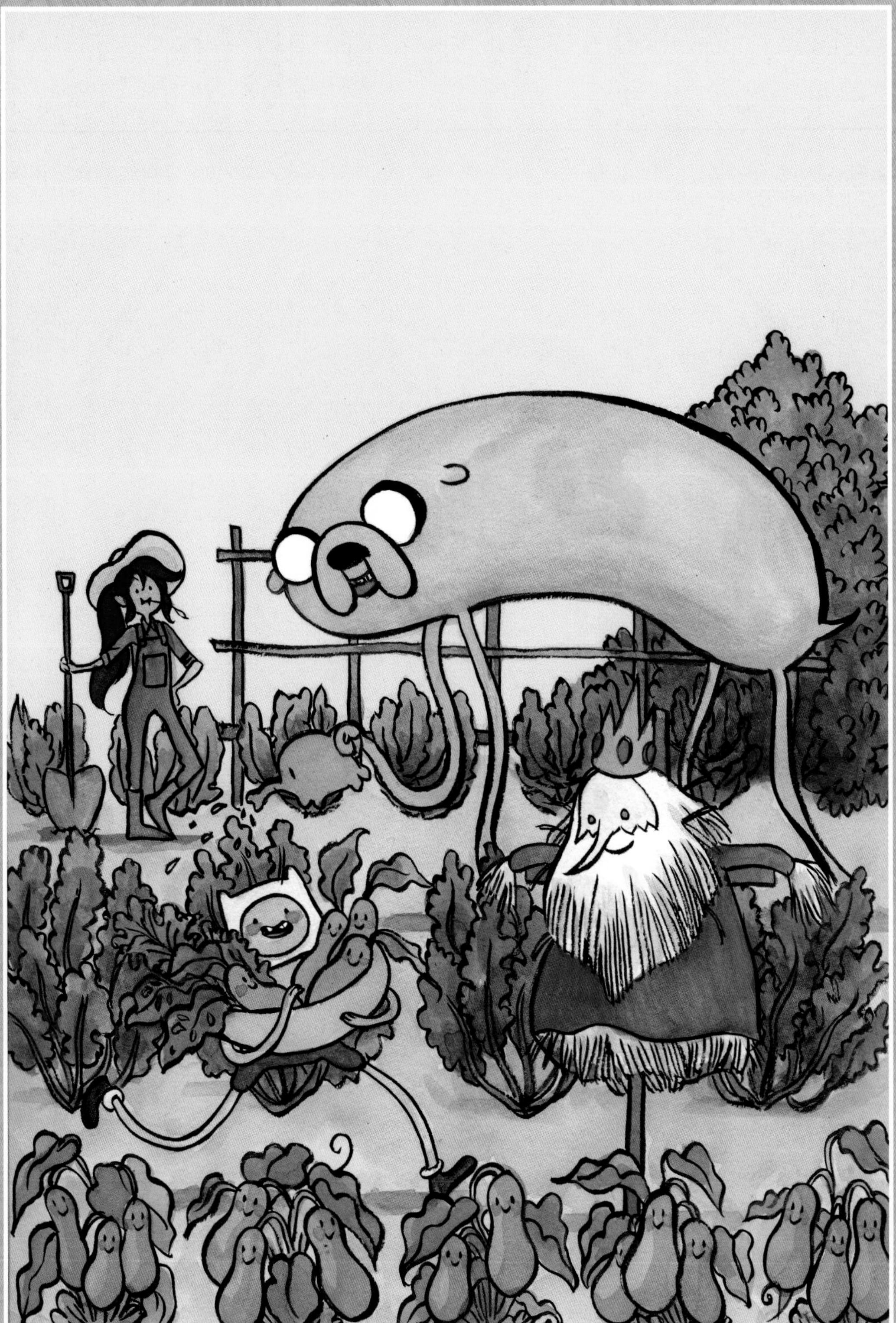

Issue #11 Variant Cover

RENATO FACCINI

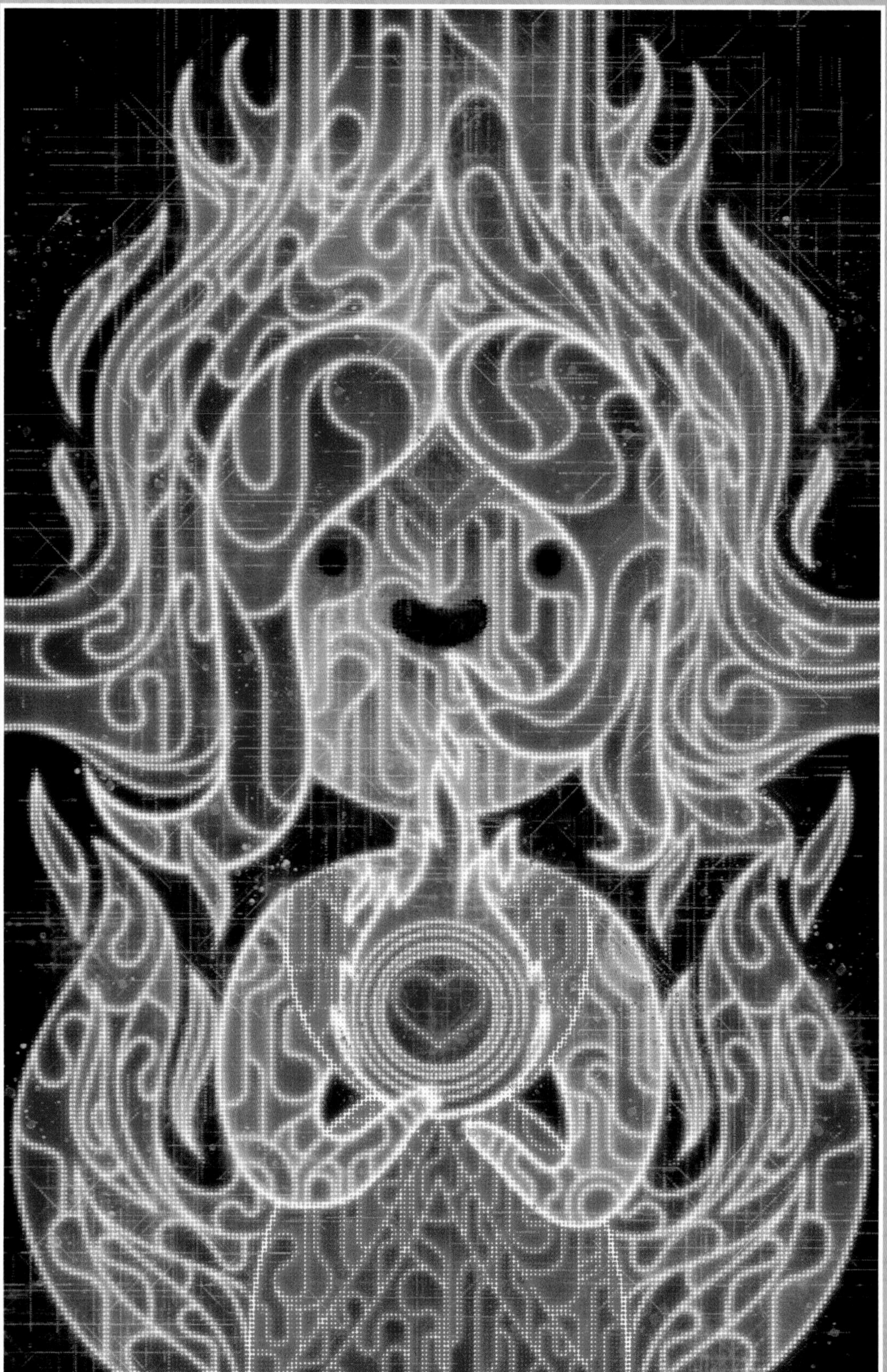

Issue #12 Main Cover

JARRETT WILLIAMS

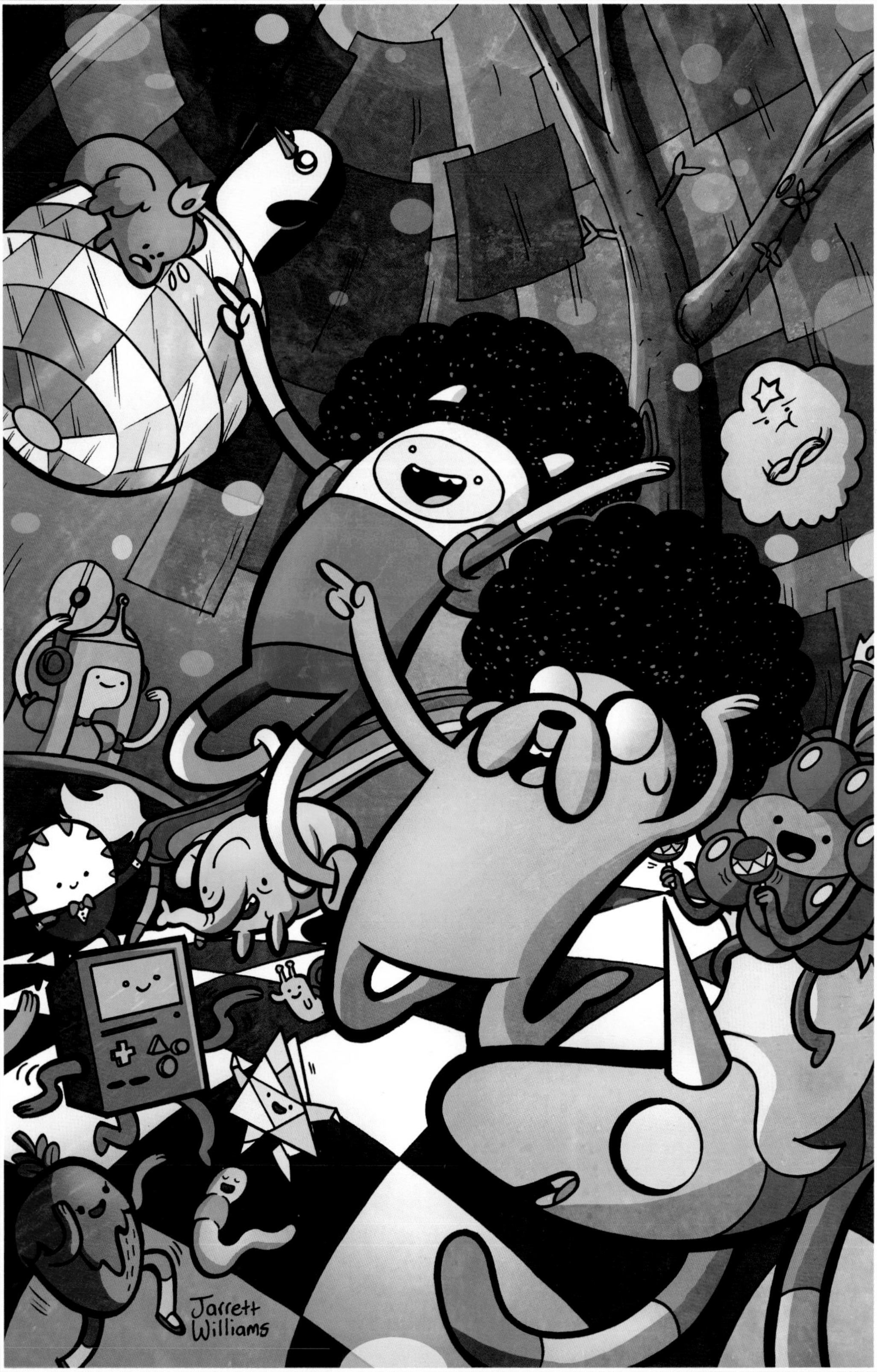
Jarrett
Williams

Issue #12 Subscription Cover

PAMELA LOVAS

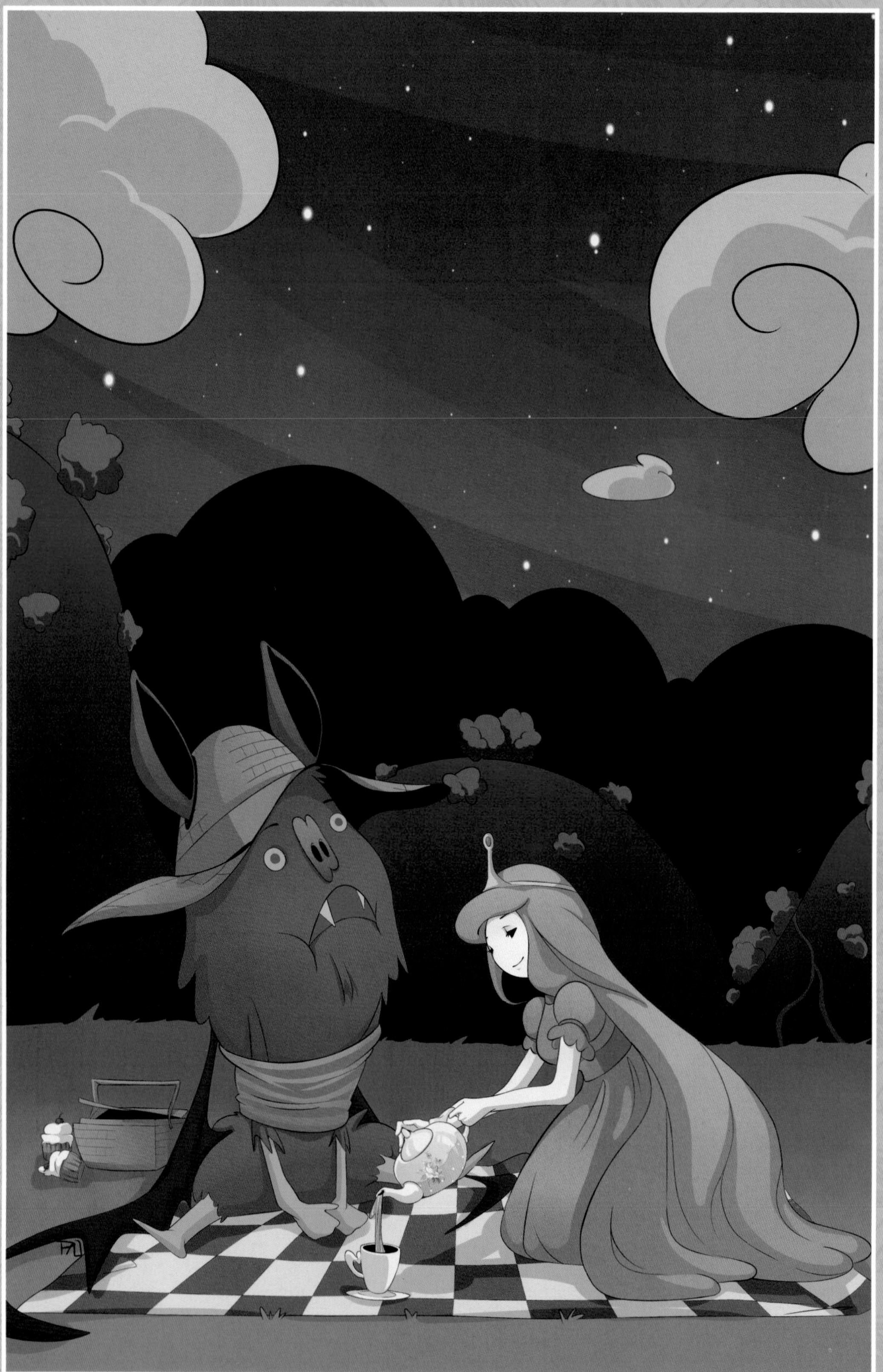

Issue #12 Variant Cover

RENATO FACCINI

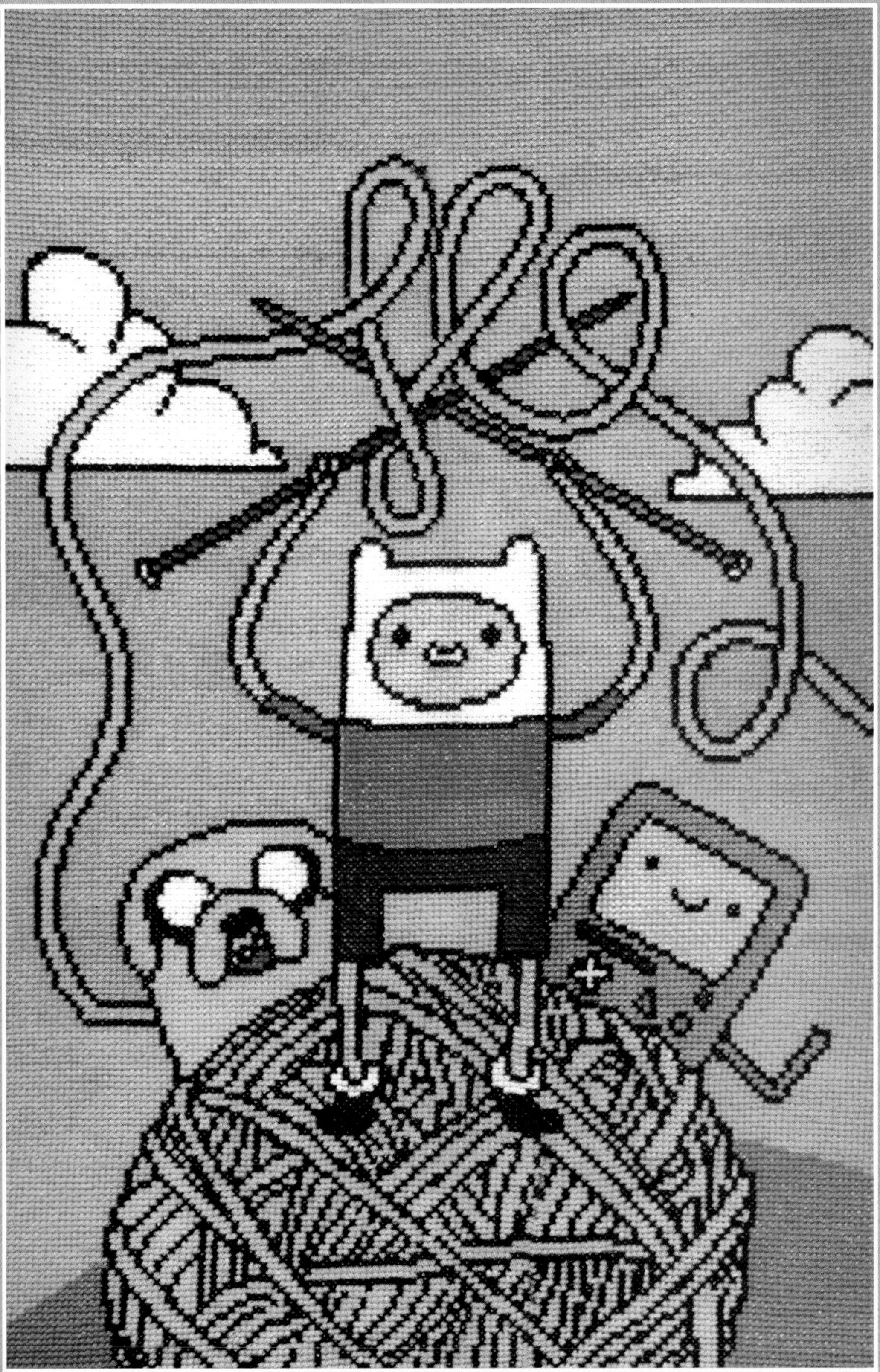

DISCOVER
EXPLOSIVE NEW WORLDS

Adventure Time
Pendleton Ward and Others
Volume 1
ISBN: 978-1-60886-280-1 | $14.99 US
Volume 2
ISBN: 978-1-60886-323-5 | $14.99 US
Adventure Time: Islands
ISBN: 978-1-60886-972-5 | $9.99 US

The Amazing World of Gumball
Ben Bocquelet and Others
Volume 1
ISBN: 978-1-60886-488-1 | $14.99 US
Volume 2
ISBN: 978-1-60886-793-6 | $14.99 US

Brave Chef Brianna
Sam Sykes, Selina Espiritu
ISBN: 978-1-68415-050-2 | $14.99 US

Mega Princess
Kelly Thompson, Brianne Drouhard
ISBN: 978-1-68415-007-6 | $14.99 US

The Not-So Secret Society
Matthew Daley, Arlene Daley,
Wook Jin Clark
ISBN: 978-1-60886-997-8 | $9.99 US

Over the Garden Wall
Patrick McHale, Jim Campbell
and Others
Volume 1
ISBN: 978-1-60886-940-4 | $14.99 US
Volume 2
ISBN: 978-1-68415-006-9 | $14.99 US

Steven Universe
Rebecca Sugar and Others
Volume 1
ISBN: 978-1-60886-706-6 | $14.99 US
Volume 2
ISBN: 978-1-60886-796-7 | $14.99 US

Steven Universe & The Crystal Gems
ISBN: 978-1-60886-921-3 | $14.99 US

Steven Universe: Too Cool for School
ISBN: 978-1-60886-771-4 | $14.99 US

**AVAILABLE AT YOUR LOCAL
COMICS SHOP AND BOOKSTORE**
To find a comics shop in your area, call 1-888-266-4226
WWW.BOOM-STUDIOS.COM

kaboom!